MW00653251

Copyright © 2021 Ron Horsley
All rights reserved
First Edition

Fulton Books, Inc.
Meadville, PA

Published by Fulton Books 2021

ISBN 978-1-64952-963-3 (paperback)
ISBN 978-1-64952-964-0 (digital)

Printed in the United States of America

For Mom, Curtis, Donna, and all those who
continue to inspire us from beyond.

The Last Chinook

On August 9, 2123, eight-year-old Hector rides in his father's Chinook helicopter for the first time. It's a lot more memorable than his toy replica back home, though not for the reasons one might think. Not even close.

For starters, no matter how well-dressed, the cabin reeked something awful. But that's what happens from wearing the same shit for nearly a week. Then there was all that fucking noise. The crying... the praying...and *singing*. Hector could barely hear himself think. Nothing like he had hoped—not one bit. And although this was young Hector's first rodeo, he *knew* this was different.

The Xenos took out most of our satellites pretty quickly; all our "smart shit" got lobotomized. Then they took our skies...then our oceans...our homes...friends...family...and finally, our hope.

Goodbye, Disney.

Adios, Whopper.

Bon voyage, YouTube.

Sayonara, Honolulu.

Paalam, our beloved Statue of Liberty.

Throughout human history, our *us against them* mentality pushed us closer to self-destruction. Then *they* arrived. And our belated *all of us* against *all of them* desperation was way too little and far too late. Although we gave it our best shot, our bell was rung in the opening round.

Common wisdom at the time would have you believe our demise began five years ago. But the truth? These fuckers set up shop long before. Hell, how do you think we got all that smart shit in the first place? Ingenuity?

It was said that once upon a time, our global elitist pimps struck a deal with these devils. A deal that advanced our species while making our Benedict benefactors disgustingly wealthy. But in their never-ending thirst for power and profits, they totally ignored the fine print...or just didn't care.

Meanwhile, we traveled faster. Lived longer. Built enormous structures in a matter of weeks. All the while, we consumed. And consumed. And consumed some more. And once bloated on collective hubris, we neglected the stars—to our collective detriment. For every Faustian bargain our elites and politicians make, the rest of us get stuck with the shit end of the stick. And these...*things* brought one big, fucking stick!

Did our deadbeat "leaders" rip up the contract?
Did our intergalactic loan sharks change the terms?
Was something lost in translation?
Doesn't fucking matter anymore. Time to collect—with interest.

Poetically, it was said that not even the very traitors who brokered this one-sided deal could talk their way out of this repayment plan. Our corporate overlords had the impression that they were special. Above us, even. But in the end, one could argue they were only human. Like us. Even.

They say first step's denial. Ain't no fuckin' denyin' this!
Then, we watched with shock and awe, our own annihilation.
Inevitably, it was every man, woman, and child for themselves.

Through an impressive display of sheer will to survive, a united humanity desperately fought back. Our global might, or what was left of it, threw everything at them—*even our kitchen sinks.* But in the end, it just wasn't enough to rewrite a foregone conclusion.

So what the hell happened to our fucking nukes?

Unfortunately, for some damn reason, they refused to join the fight; our cities fell like dominoes.

Their grand entrance was the checkmate. They knew us better than we knew ourselves. That's because some of us—the ones we now call *zeezees*—had no clue what they were doing to their own kind. And the only cure for these poor souls was a bullet to the brain. *No* exceptions.

Turns out, humans *do* live among the stars; they fare no better, it's said.

Hector, only a shade lighter than his father, peers outside with a pair of *digital binoculars* but has difficulty seeing through the hazy smoke around him. As the smoke clears, he sees a Viper helicopter escort. Hector smiles and waves, but the pilot ignores him, perhaps thinking of his own family out there—somewhere—while the General's son waves at him like a privileged piece of shit.

Hector then looks down and sees an endless caravan of injured, exhausted, and desperate refugees and animals (which were probably all eaten by journey's end), fleeing in the same direction: northeast. Some even pray there's an ark waiting for them at the finish line. Yeah, good luck with that.

Hector follows the trail through his binoculars and spots their destination far in the distance: a group of massive buildings stuffed inside a bowl made of mountains in the middle of the desert while a dark cloud hangs over it.

Hector turns to his mother, Karla, her eyes nearly bloodshot. Karla rubs off the caked trails of tears painted on her Grecian facade. She kisses Hector just as two-star General Hector Elias Contreras V appears and hugs them both. Uniform in tatters, Gen. Contreras— awfully young for such a high rank—kisses both his wife and only son. To this point, Hector's dark-skinned father has never shed a tear. And he didn't this time. Somehow it made Hector feel safe as he turns back to the window.

The massive structures in the distance grow as his father's Chinook approaches. Hector soon realizes that the dark cloud consists of hundreds of helicopters and drones frantically buzzing around. Below, refugees stream into the great desert city.

As the Chinook approaches its landing spot, it hovers over an old commercial retail center designed as a small town now bursting at its seams.

"I found my wedding dress there..." Karla trails off as she partially covers her mouth in shock. On opposite sides of the guard-gated entrance sits a large marquee:
TOWN SQUARE

"Now it's a quarantine zone for those with the connections to stay off the Strip," Gen. Contreras explains. "Nothing you need to worry about."

Gen. Contreras looks across the cabin. Captain Emanuel "Manny" Campos, whose Philippine Marine uniform is just as bloody and worn, waves him over. Gen. Contreras navigates fellow passengers to reach Manny.

"We lost Tokyo," Manny whispers.

"Fuck," Gen. Contreras quietly rages. "Beijing?"

"Not good. Communications are breaking down," Manny says. "And only half the Aussies and Kiwis made it to Madagascar."

"What about the Indians and Pak—"

"They're taking a final stand...*together*," Manny interjects.

Gen. Contreras nods.

"As will we," Gen. Contreras replies.

Manny nods toward Karla and Hector.

Karla silently mouths, *"So sorry,"* to Manny, who nods back in acknowledgment.

"Everything's set for your arrival, sir," Manny says.

"You're the man," Gen. Contreras replies. "Thank you."

"Just following orders, sir."

Gen. Contreras walks back over to Karla and Hector, then kisses Karla. He turns his attention to Hector and leans over his son to look out the window. Gen. Contreras points to the McCarran-Reid International Airport, one of a handful of military outposts accommodating the remnants of Earth's armies.

Karla hugs both of them. Before Gen. Contreras gets a word out...

"Viva Las Vegas," Karla deadpans in a valiant attempt at some levity.

Gen. Contreras turns to his loving wife with a slight grin; she reciprocates.

End of the Line

Below the descending Chinook, refugees swarm the old Town Square shopping center just south of the Strip. Giving birth in a parking lot designated for medical services, Maggie Metzler agonizes while looking up at the Chinook gracefully hovering above her. Fighting through her pain, the thirtysomething desperately focuses on the helicopter's *P413* serial number on its undercarriage. Her younger brother Byron Timmons, a former Marine turned successful businessman, remains faithfully by her side, coaching her as best he can. Fortunately for them, Byron's military and political contacts paid off in the form of two credentials in his pocket, which allows them expedited passage into the city.

"Not…what I had in mind…for my first Vegas trip," Maggie deadpans in between contractions.

"Once you pop little Eugene out, we're on the next shuttle to the M," Byron replies as he gently taps his right hip pocket to confirm both credentials are secure.

"I wish they all could've met him," Maggie says.

"He'll make them proud," Byron replies. "He'll make us all proud."

Maggie's eyes zero in on Byron's breast pocket. Byron looks down, sticks his hand in the pocket, and pulls out a *green Bic pen*.

"Byron, if anything…" Maggie trails off.

"Nothin's gonna happen, Mags," Byron interjects.

"Promise me!" Maggie screams.

Maggie's contractions increase as she vice-grips Bryon's hand.

"I promise! Now deep breaths, please."

A teenaged African American girl stops to check Maggie's vitals.

"Shit, it's coming," Zerina says.

"You a doc?" Byron asks.

"AP med," Zerina answers. "Liberty High."

"Uh…" Byron replies with a mixture of uncertainty and concern.

"As you can see, we're a little shorthanded," the girl responds while checking Maggie.

He looks around at all the chaos overwhelming the volunteers. Numerous expectant mothers—most unattended—give birth alone or unassisted.

"I'll take whatever I can fuckin' get!" Maggie screams in pain.

"What's your name, ma'am?" Zerina asks.

"Maggie!"

"Hi, Maggie. I'm Zerina."

"I'm her brother Byron. We were leaving Riverside when we heard about Hawaii."

"At least you've got each other," Zerina replies, preparing to leave. "Good luck."

"Wait! Where you going?" Byron barks.

"Nothing else I can do for her, sir," Zerina shouts as she walks away. "Push, push, push! Pray, pray, pray!"

And like that, young Zerina disappears into the sea of helpless patients while Maggie screams.

"Push, push, push," Byron says, still holding her hand.

"Don't you fuckin'…" Maggie angrily counters, gripping his hand tighter again.

"Okay, okay, okay," Byron painfully whispers.

Maggie gives birth to a healthy baby boy.

Byron caresses the newborn; the three of them cry. Byron gently places the newborn in an exhausted Maggie's arms. With no cutting tool, Byron chews at the umbilical cord until it snaps apart. He dry heaves as the baby's blood drips from his mouth.

"Welcome to Sin City, little guy," Byron says to the newborn. "You definitely look better than you taste!"

"Eu…gene…" Maggie exhales. Tears stream down her cheeks as she memorizes her crying newborn's features. Then her eyes close.

Byron glances over at her.

"Mags?" Bryon asks. "Come on, Mags. Please don't... Mags... pretty fuckin', please?"

Maggie goes limp. Byron catches crying Eugene before the baby hits the ground. He looks around as restlessness simmers when a crying National Guardsman named John Mariko runs in Byron's direction.

"Hey, wait!" Bryon screams, pulling out his credentials with one hand while holding baby Eugene with the other.

NG Mariko stops.

"We gotta bounce, sir," NG Mariko replies. "They got Moscow!"

"What?" Byron asks.

"They're wipin' us off the fuckin' map, bro! EU's backpedalin' from Berlin," NG Mariko says. "We're fucked."

"Wait, my sister—"

"Where the fuck is she?"

Byron points to Maggie's corpse.

"Sorry, bro—for real," NG Mariko begins with sincerity, "but you and the little one gonna have to shit...or get blown off this fuckin' pot. Your call."

Fights break out among the crowd while desperate National Guardsmen and armed volunteers fire indiscriminately into the air. Byron places the two credentials around his neck and follows NG Mariko.

As bullets whiz past them, NG Mariko, Byron, and crying baby Eugene hop inside an armored transport heading for the *M*. As they exit Town Square, Byron takes stock of the somber expressions around him while the two credentials dangle from his neck; the green Bic pen peeks just above his breast pocket.

City of Sin

The Chinook lands on the tarmac. The pilot and crew quickly exit, replaced by equally weary replacements. Inside, Gen. Contreras and Manny instruct the weary replacement crew to re-prep the Chinook and tend to the civilian passengers.

Hector aims his digital binoculars outside again. He zooms in on a line of bald-headed captives a few yards away. Hector focuses on American and Mexican soldiers painfully extracting tiny objects from their captives' necks where one would find implants commonly placed these days. The objects are then tossed in containers held by Canadian soldiers. Hector's eyes widen as the captives' fates unfold through the Chinook window's reflection.

"Mom…" Hector trembles out.

Karla leans over, catching her son's fear. She grabs his digital binoculars and scans the area. Horrified by the gunshots, she hugs Hector.

"It's okay, *mijo*," Karla replies in a soothing tone. "Those men were helping the monsters."

"Why?" Hector mumbles as he peeks out at the massacre.

Karla rocks Hector.

"Éxi," Gen. Contreras whispers sharply to Hector.

The boy quietly sniffles under his mother's protection. Gen. Contreras grabs the digital binoculars and heads over to Manny for an update. Gen. Contreras then rests the digital binoculars on a box. Manny pulls out and unrolls a wafer-thin digital tablet showing a map of the battlefield.

"Cajon Pass is holding…barely," Manny says.

"Still no word from the Pentagon?"

Pretending not to notice Hector steal back his digital binoculars like a ninja, Manny continues.

"We're down to four workin' sats," Manny answers.

Gen. Contreras looks out a window to see a Japanese officer waiting for him. Gen. Contreras turns to his wife and child.

"Bird up in five," Gen. Contreras commands.

Manny salutes. "Sir."

Gen. Contreras walks over to Karla and Hector. He stares at his devoted partner; she nods—unconvincingly—in agreement. But that's the deal:

They embrace.

She sheds a few tears, quickly wiping them off.

He whispers, "I'll be home soon," in a confident tone.

"Be safe," she whispers back as she watches him go, perhaps for the last time.

Gen. Contreras turns and kneels beside his son. He pulls out a *Distinguished Service Medal* from his chest pocket and shows it to Hector who spots a tiny, faded red stain on it.

"This was your great, great, great, great-grandpa's—" Gen. Contreras begins.

"Distinguished Service Medal," Hector interrupts.

"You remember," Gen. Contreras proudly replies.

"Was he shot?" Hector asks, pointing to the red stain.

"Shaving accident, I'm told," Gen. Contreras replies. "He gave this to his son, who gave it to his son, who gave it to his son, who gave it to Grandpa, who then gave it to me. It gives all the men in our family special powers. Powers that can protect us—and those around us that need our help. Time for you to have it. And soon, you'll have powers too."

"Oxy!" Hector says. "Powers like yours?"

"Maybe. It decides what powers you get. And they won't come right away. But…the longer you keep this hidden and safe, the more powerful you will become. Understand?"

"Yes, sir," Hector replies, nodding slowly.

Gen. Contreras securely places the medal in Hector's shirt pocket and buttons it closed. He embraces his wife and son one last time then summons Manny over.

"Captain Campos will keep you both safe till I get back," Gen. Contreras says to Karla and Hector before rushing off the rumbling Chinook.

Manny salutes Hector. Hector half-heartedly reciprocates before turning his attention back outside. He tracks his father's movements outside using the reclaimed digital binoculars. He sees his father salute a high-ranking Japanese officer waiting for him. The Japanese officer salutes back before bringing Gen. Contreras up to speed.

The remaining passengers board the Chinook as it prepares for takeoff. Securing Karla's permission, Manny sits next to Hector, whose eyes are drawn to the flag on Manny's tattered uniform.

"Ever been to the Philippines, Éxi?" Manny asks.

Hector shakes his head and replies, "No, sir."

Karla cracks a concerned grin. Despite the shit show going on, Manny's smile provides a flimsy sense of comfort.

The Chinook rises, again exposing the *P413* on its underbelly. Manny looks around at all the skyscrapers eclipsing the row of old gambling conglomerates-turned-residences now cowering among the larger megastructures sprouting up around them.

"Hec says you have relatives here?" Karla asks.

"A cousin in Summerlin," Manny brags. "Growing up, my uncle would brag about all mountains and blue skies in every direction when he first moved here as a boy."

"The good old days," Karla rhetorically laments.

The last thing Hector saw as they hovered over the base were more dead captives being loaded onto vehicles not far from where his father and the Japanese officer once stood.

THE GREATER UNION

~an Inhumane saga~

Ron Horsley

02.16.2138

Phoenix Bloc, one of the Zona Sector's two megacolonies, prepares to crack under the extreme pressure of a yearlong siege. Having breached Phoenix's outer defenses, the fledgling Sin Vegas Union government engages a resilient *Founding Fathers* Separatist Movement for control. Although the FF greatly outnumbers the SVU forces currently on the ground, their mostly conventional weaponry prove no match for the Union's superior alien-hybrid tech.

Deep within city limits, Sgt. Crayton Stak and Sgt. Mikhail Gorvich study digital battle plans in their warbox, rectangular metal trailer with small windows. Attached to an armored transport, the warbox serves as a mobile command center. Inside, the two officers survey a virtual battlefield with interior walls that also double as digital displays.

"Reinforcements are comin'," Sgt. Gorvich says.

"All right," Crayton replies.

"In twenty-four hours." Sgt. Gorvich finishes.

"Twenty-fuckin'-four?"

"LA's re-pacification takin' longer den planned, bro."

"So, daddy's gotta bail out his baby boy again."

"Dat baby boy took out a fuckin' Xeno. Lost an arm doin' it."

"Were you dere?"

"No, but it's—"

"For all we know, daddy made dat kill and gave his boy de fuckin' cred!"

More distant explosions create fireballs that illuminate the cloudy sky, exposing hollowed-out buildings along with a few enemy positions.

"Let's hold de line and let dese fuckin' traitors choke on deir dyin' cause."

More explosions shake the ground around them.

"Choke?" Crayton replies. "Sounds like laughin' to me."

Private Yooms, a scrawny, teenaged Caucasian covered in mud and blood, enters.

"Sir, our flanks are bendin'," Private Yooms shouts.

"We can't push too—" Sgt. Gorvich says as another explosion hits close to the warbox, ripping it in half.

On his back, Crayton turns to see Sgt. Gorvich staring at him.

"Mick?" Crayton asks. "Mickey?"

Crayton gently taps Sgt. Gorvich's face and watches as the head rolls away from the ashes of a vaporized body. Crayton spots Sgt. Gorvich's rank pin on the ground. He grabs it and jumps up as laser bullets whiz past him. He runs over to an unconscious Private Yooms and shakes him awake.

"Rise and shine, Private!"

Private Yooms wakes. Crayton helps him up.

"Sir?" Private Yooms says.

"Welcome back to De Unrest," Crayton replies. "Grab a gun!"

"Yes, sir!"

Crayton and Private Yooms grab a few men and run to the front lines where Corporal Janice Samsonite holds the fragile line against a wave of Founding Fathers. Crayton taps Cpl. Samsonite on the shoulder.

"Sir, we could really use some backup," Samsonite says.

"Cavalry's coming. Tomorrow."

"Fuck me!"

"If we make it anudder day. For now, let's push dese fuckers back, Sergeant," Crayton barks as he places Gorvich's rank pin in the newly promoted Samsonite's hand.

Samsonite opens her palm to see the rank pin covered with specks of blood then replies, "Sin Vegas strong, sir!"

Crayton nods then leaves with Private Yooms and a group of Union soldiers.

Samsonite licks off the blood and affixes it to her black uniform, smiling as explosions shake the ground around her. She watches Crayton, Private Yooms, and their band of soldiers repel a wave of Founding Fathers charging at them.

"Fuckin' Cray-Cray." Samsonite says. "Forward!"

Samsonite and her men charge behind Crayton and Private Yooms into battle.

05.23.2157

Nearly two decades after the Founding Fathers' defeat, the Sin Vegas Union finds itself engaged in a *Second Unrest*. As urban warfare ravages the New Diego Bloc, a much stronger Union government now grapples with a new separatist group calling themselves the *Sons of US*. Although the Sons have advanced weapons at their disposal, they're still no match for the Union's upgraded alien-hybrid tech…and conviction.

Competing attack drones fire at the ground and at each other as they vie for air superiority. Colorful—and deadly—ammunitions pepper the landscape as if it were another alien invasion.

Wearing special ponchos that offer both limited protection and camouflage from drones and infrared trackers, Union Bloc Officer Lachlan New Zealand and his teenage nephew Nixon Jolt check to make sure the coast is clear. Lachlan silently summons his wife Mila and teenage daughter Gwenda, both wearing special ponchos, from the shadows.

"Two more blocks," Lachlan whispers.

"I gotta pee," Gwenda quietly replies.

"It's okay, honey. Just let it go," Mila replies with as comforting hand on her daughter's quivering shoulder.

A visibly shaken Gwenda nods. She relieves herself as the brown-skinned family navigates the carnage to avoid the sporadic gun battles echoing around them. Two blocks from their objective, the firefights intensify. Suddenly, they come under heavy fire. Laser bullets skid off their ponchos as they take cover. Lachlan grabs Nix.

"Take Gweny," Lachlan says. "We'll cover."

"Unk, I can cover you guys," Nix tries to counter.

"Dat's an order, Jolt!" Lachlan yells.

Nix gives his uncle a sharp nod. Mila turns to Gwenda and kisses her on the forehead.

"We're right behind you," Mila says to Gwenda and Nix.

"Mom!"

"Go, honey! Or we all die here, yeah?" Mila screams.

Lachlan turns and snaps, "Fuckin' go, baby doll!"

Nix grabs Gwenda when they're suddenly surrounded by an armed group of Sons militiamen. A Son soldier presses an implant on his neck, activating a vocal amplifier.

"Put your weapons d—" the Son soldier says as a laser bullet from an unknown sniper rips through his vocal cords.

Lachlan and Mila fire on the advancing Sons. However, there are soon too many for their laser bullets…or an escape. The Sons charge at them; Lachlan and Mila use their superior fighting skills to take a handful of them out.

Gwenda turns to catch her parents tag-teaming against dozens of Son soldiers. Mila's lethal fighting skills mesmerize Gwenda. Nix aims at the Sons surrounding Lachlan and Mila. However, he can't bring himself to pull the trigger. Instead, like a good little soldier, he pulls Gwenda out of her trance.

"Gweny, c'mon," Nix snaps.

Gwenda and Nix sprint toward their objective while Lachlan and Mila take on their attackers. The power couple put on an impressive display of combat tactics. However, they're trapped and exhausted. Out of viable escape options, Mila whips out a *saucer*. Lachlan and Mila hold hands prior to the grenade's detonation, which liquefies all living tissue within a three-foot radius.

Two blocks from Lachlan and Mila's last stand, Gwenda and Nix arrive at a charred building and enter what used to be a lobby; they rest. Nix turns to see Gwenda sobbing.

"Gweny, dey comin'. Don't worry."

"Den we wait," Gwenda replies.

"Dey can't lead de Sons here. Dey come when we safe, yeah?" Nix says. "So we gotta move now."

Gwenda nods. Suddenly, Gwenda sees a silhouette behind Nix. She pushes Nix out of the way just as a laser bullet rips through her left arm. She falls. Nix turns and fires on the two Sons, killing them instantly. Nix crawls over to Gwenda and checks her pulse. Gwenda sits up, clutching her bleeding arm.

"My arm…" Gwenda grimaces.

"Hang tough, Gweny."

Nix digs into Gwenda's poncho and pulls out a combat grade *Nanorem* patch that he places on her wound. He then walks Gwenda into what used to be someone's office. He lays Gwenda down on top of a desk and moves aside rubble. Nix feels around the dirt until he finds a small numerical panel.

Explosions and gunfire draw closer.

Nix quickly types in a code, and a hatch beside the panel opens. He grabs Gwenda, and they both enter, closing the hatch that locks just as pursuing footsteps trample through the condemned building.

Underground, Nix presses his neck implant, triggering his night vision. He carries Gwenda a few feet through an underground tunnel when bright lights turn on, automatically deactivating his night vision to avoid blindness. Nix regains focus to see the barrel of a gun held by an Asian Union soldier.

"Friendly," Nix forcefully whispers to avoid alerting anyone aboveground.

"Identify!"

"Bloc Deputy Nixon Jolt. NDR34509596. Nephew of Officer Lachlan New Zealand. My cuz took it in de arm. She needs a med."

The soldier directs them to an e-tablet on the wall. Nix helps Gwenda over to it. Nix places his palm on the e-tablet. It turns green.

The Union soldier lowers his weapon and approaches. It's Li Macau, a tall twenty-year-old with a thin frame. He spots Gwenda passing out and rushes to assist Nix by helping him carry her to the underground outpost entrance.

"Where your unk, eh?" Chino asks as he whiffs Gwenda's unpleasant scent.

Nix slowly shakes his head.

"He and auntie took out over twenty of doze fuckers."

"No shit?" Chino replies. "Private Li Macau, by de way."

"Tanks for not deletin' me, Macau."

"Call me Chino, eh?" Chino replies.

Tricks Are for Cray-Cray

Sixty-six years after man's fall, a once lively international space station now harboring a crew of skeletons orbits helplessly around an Earth blanketed with strange gas clouds. The hazy clouds severely limit the sun and moon's visibility while removing any trace of neighboring planets or stars from the naked eye.

Many miles below the floating metal carcass, a heavily armed and extremely dangerous *Lorian* poacher, encased within a protective, four-armed *mechsuit*, adjusts its helmet visor under a new moon and scans west. This monstrosity, a member of the invading species humans commonly refer to as *Xenos*, analyzes the *demarcation line* that serves as a warning to both unauthorized Lorians and inquisitive humans. Searching for a weakness, the alien's visor pans along the seemingly endless north-south wall of strange fog and polluted air about a mile thick. Dispersed within the demarcation line, towers armed with sensors emit the strange fog into an almost perfect wall that fades below the stratosphere. Beyond the transparent wall lies a scrap yard of rusted Lorian and Terran mecha from a past conflict.

A Lorian symbol pops up on the visor display. Seconds later, the poacher's visor scan identifies a tower with the same symbol. The alien boards its nearby *hovershuttle*, types a code into the main console, and transmits the code to the tower. The console turns green as the tower deactivates its sensors. The Lorian then sets the coordinates and silently takes off toward the tower, tossing over a rusty, battered sign:

MARBLE CANYON

With the demarcation line now miles behind it, the Lorian poacher zooms in on a faint light source approximately thirty miles to the west. Lorian symbols on the interior of the visor screen identify the light source as heavily armed Terran fortifications. The visor screen switches to a satellite view of the mountains surrounding the militarized border protecting a heavily populated Terran megacolony a few dozen miles southwest of it. The screen zooms out further, revealing this megacolony as the beating heart of an advanced, over-populated civilization of humans spanning from the former cities of Las Vegas, Tucson, San Diego, all the way up to what was once known as San Francisco.

It was only a century ago that this amount of real estate offered plenty of space for humans to roam somewhat freely. Today, as inter-galactic intruders have made Earth their home away from home, the planet's current reality marches toward an unhappily ever after.

The Terrans' fortified mountains ahead accommodate hundreds of thousands of organic and cybernetic soldiers manning heavy artil-lery and attack drones sworn to defend their capitol to the death.

The poacher presses a button, which opens a small hole in the back of its mechsuit. A drone emerges, expands, and hovers above, waiting for instructions. The Lorian's visor display shows fifty humanoid signals packed into small, lightly armored vehicles speeding north, parallel to the demarcation line. Sensing a prime hunting opportunity, the Lorian poacher triangulates interception coordinates, which it syncs with its drone. The drone vanishes into the darkness en route to the armored vehicles.

Turning its attention back to the mountains, the poacher's visor scan detects something that triggers an electronic warning. It attempts to open up a communication frequency; however, an error message appears on-screen. It tries again in vain. Unable to send or receive messages, it decides to run a system diagnostics check. More error messages pop up. The Lorian manages to trace a faint dot blink-ing only a few yards away, but it's unable to lock on to it. Suddenly, more warnings blare as multiple dots blink in random places—and close in on the poacher. The giant alien prepares to retreat when, out of nowhere, a projectile hits it. The impact disables a few of the mechsuit's countermeasures; the flashing dots vanish.

A second projectile hits the giant creature again, stunning it. Panicked, the Lorian poacher fires projectiles from its mechsuit in random directions. It frantically switches frequencies in an attempt to trace the sources of these attacks. Suddenly, it finds itself surrounded by small attack vehicles filled with smaller, heavily armed soldiers wearing pitch-black uniforms. The Lorian tries again in vain to send a distress signal but only sees an error symbol. It tries to flee, but the mechsuit slows it down enough for its smaller adversaries to catch up. Firing a laser burst, the Lorian kills dozens of soldiers in a single blow. Finally, the Lorian is able to recall its own drone. Its visor confirms the drone peeling off from its original target and returning at top speed. The artillery bombardment weakens its mechsuit to nearly a quarter of its full strength.

Holding a strange object, a human soldier with cybernetic legs leaps toward the back of the giant. However, the Lorian swats the man away as if he were a bug. The bloody, mangled soldier lands in some bushes a few yards away; his metal legs clank to the ground a few feet from his body.

"We need it alive," Colonel Crayton Stak's voice screams over an encrypted comchat.

The soldiers continue their coordinated attack with special concussion grenades that jar the giant without doing any fatal damage aside from chipping away at its protective shell.

The Lorian poacher fires every operational weapon at its disposal, killing dozens more men.

More soldiers join the attack, converging on the alien like a pack of rabid dogs. Soldiers jump onto the Lorian's laser canon. A few manage to attach metal objects to it; none of them survive the poacher's wrath.

The Lorian poacher grabs one poor soldier's head and crushes it like a grape, hurling the carcass at some of his comrades. Detonations from the metal objects disable the Lorian's laser cannon.

The explosions unintentionally allow the Lorian poacher to activate some previously malfunctioning weapons. It fires a series of spikes that slice through metal and bone, killing or disabling men and machine. The Lorian poacher escapes from its siege—still unable to call for help. It makes its way to a nearby canyon for refuge. The poacher spots its large hovershuttle a few yards away—surrounded by a swarm of enemy soldiers.

The drone speeds toward the attack, firing at will; unable to lock on to anyone or anything, it misses nearly all its targets. All its weapons are now spent.

The Lorian poacher tries to redirect the speeding drone. Its visor screen finally reveals that the soldiers' dark uniforms are embedded with Lorian tech—causing the interference. Making matters worse, the drone continues to speed directly toward the poacher, refusing to deviate course. The Lorian's visor warns of potential impact with the drone. Alarms scream inside the mechsuit's helmet. Forced to unleash the mechsuit's remaining countermeasures on its former ally, the Lorian poacher swears in its native tongue. The drone evades the barrage and stares down its former master.

"Silly Xeno," Crayton scolds over his comchat.

The drone slams into the poacher's mechsuit, knocking the giant armored beast to the ground.

Moments later, men swarm the incapacitated alien. Crayton removes his mask, revealing an olive-skinned face with enough scars to think he must have run through an entire blade forest.

"Tricks ah fo Cray-Cray," the fifty-something Pacific Islander with a gray crew cut finishes.

Using his cybernetic eyes, Crayton analyzes the giant's disabled mechsuit. He pulls out a large weapon infused with Lorian tech from one of the armored vehicles and aims it at the Lorian poacher.

Yellow fluid drips from inside the mechsuit.

The immobilized, groggy Lorian poacher wakes just in time to see Crayton aiming a large weapon at it.

Crayton and a group of his men each carrying the same type of weapon fire on the beast. A series of sharp projectiles attached to glowing cables stick to the creature's mechsuit. A burst of energy pulsates through the giant beast, causing it to belt out a deep, frightening cry. Sparks shoot from the mechsuit as sections of metal detach from its host and litter the ground.

Totally exposed, the weakened Lorian poacher watches helplessly as Lieutenant Wishbone Jonas, a twenty-four-year-old Black male and Crayton's second in command—pulls out a laser stun cannon. The Lorian's cries grow faint, as if begging for mercy.

"Shitty dreams, assnuts," Wishbone says.

Wishbone's toned muscles flex as he fires the laser stun cannon at the Lorian poacher, knocking it out. The victorious soldiers notice its chest slowly moving. Wishbone kicks the poacher, but it doesn't flinch. The surrounding soldiers—except for Crayton—take a cautious step back.

"Union strong!" Wishbone shouts.

"Union strong!" Everyone cheers repeatedly.

"Don't worry, bro. You got de hi-rolla suite!" Crayton says to the unconscious alien.

Crayton turns to Wishbone and nods.

"All right, boys! Make sure our guest comfy, yeah?" Wishbone orders.

A large transport vehicle with the Sin Vegas Union government seal emblazoned on both sides arrives. Below the logo, the following:

MESQUITE OUTER GARRISON

The rear opens and a conveyor ramp slides out. Union soldiers load their alien trophy onto the ramp, allowing the large transport to swallow the sleeping beast whole. They load the mechsuit parts and whatever tech they can quickly scavenge from the hovershuttle and roll out.

Sugar Bunker

Crayton's military convoy speeds north through the open desert. Circumventing its mountain sanctuary, it turns off road due west. A few miles further, it slows at the base of another mountain range with their enormous prize in tow.

Sitting in the lead vehicle's cab, Wishbone uses his retinal scan to pinpoint a small hole drilled into the mountain base. He pulls out a special laser data pointer, aiming it into the small hole. Suddenly, a large gate opens up at the mountain base to reveal a paved, lit tunnel. The convoy enters the mountain base, which closes behind them.

"Near de end zone, boys," Crayton cheers via comchat.

"Slamdown," Wishbone confidently replies.

"How many times?" Crayon corrects via comchat. "It's touchdown!"

"Dey slam de ball on de ground, yeah?" Wishbone replies.

"Dey not my rules," Crayton says.

"I still tink Powerball much tougher," Wishbone grouses over his comchat.

"My old man footballer kick any Powerballer ass!"

"I wear body armor. I kick ass too," Wishbone says.

"Fair one," Crayton concedes.

"Only ting good I see 'bout food-ball are de aftah showw-ahs," Wishbone says. "Fuckin' *san-eez* itch my balls!"

"You know, in de *Old Nation*, we used to shoot each udder wit' water to keep cool."

"You old farts fuck it up for de rest of us, yeah?" Wishbone asks.

"Us old farts give you life," Crayton replies. "Maybe you call me Poppa."

For those wondering why the funny accents, you can thank the Lorians for facilitating the laziness of native tongues among those born AMF, or After Man Fall. It also makes it easier for leadership to control the masses. But to be fair, there are those born BMF that have also embraced this new world wholeheartedly.

Crayton's convoy exits the tunnel into a cavernous underground bay within the old *Sugar Bunker*, a former weapons research and storage facility in the middle of nowhere. The place buzzes with activity until everyone notices Crayton's convoy enter. Then, complete silence. As if on cue, the welcoming base soldiers—most of which have some cybernetic trait—open a path for Crayton's convoy to continue until they enter a quarantine annex. As the other trucks park, the transport holding the Lorian poacher continues into a separate, specialized biohazard zone.

Crayton and Wishbone exit their respective vehicles. Their black *Defense Club* military attire, or *skins*, include a dark shield insignia that matches the more colorful ones adorned by Sugar Bunker officers and personnel. They walk over to a thirtysomething cybersoldier named Captain Gerland Theroux waiting to greet them with a friendly smile.

"Look what de fuckin' *rachas* dragged in," Capt. Theroux says.

"Cap," Wishbone replies.

"Gur-lee," Crayton replies.

"Tanks for de house gift," Capt. Theroux says. "General's waitin'."

Capt. Theroux escorts them through the base to Between (or *Tween*) Defense General Hiroshima Tegashito's office. They enter and salute the Union's two-star general and chief intelligence officer, who reciprocates. Capt. Theroux leaves, closing the office door behind them. Wishbone spots a digital rendering of an agitated elderly Japanese woman in military uniform sitting on her porch and holding an AR-15. A half-empty bottle of Japanese whiskey sits beside her left foot. Image date: 09.19.2119.

Behind Gen. Tegashito's wiry frame, the entire wall is a digital display that depicts the former North American landscape before man's fall. However, the display reflects the morphing territorial boundaries over the past forty years. Once a beacon of hope, America has been extinguished. The Old Nation, along with its former ideals and aspirations, have been replaced with five autonomous megacolonies feeding around the edges of a once-vibrant continent like a sluggish parasite:

> VERMAINIA (the Vermainians) covers the former New England territories as well as the southeastern region of Canada.

> CAN-CHI NATIONS (the Can-Cheez) control the northern Midwest region of the Old Nation and the central Canadian territories, ruled by the tribal descendants of the original natives.

> SOUTHERN CROSS EMPIRE (the SoCrows) rules what remains of the Southeast region due to war, climate change, and environmental neglect. White supremacists govern these lands while its relatively few nonwhite inhabitants once more survive as a subservient class.

> NORTHWEST PACIFIC FEDERATION (the NorPacs) covers America's Northwest as well as the Southwestern Canadian territories.

> SIN VEGAS UNION (the Union), which the men in this room faithfully serve, occupies most of a Southwest region covering Southern Nevada, western Arizona, and California from San Diego up to San Francisco.

> The display also shows two large craters signifying inhabitable areas: one covers nearly three quarters of what was once Colorado while the

other covers land stretching from New York City
to Virginia Beach.

The wall display also reveals locations of Lorian-controlled
zones, including three large Lorian mega-metropolises covering:

1. Parts of Kansas, Colorado, New Mexico, Texas, and
   Oklahoma
2. Parts of Indiana, Kentucky, Illinois, and Missouri
3. Parts of Minnesota, South Dakota, Nebraska, and Iowa

Together, these three Lorian mega-cities are
referred to as the TRIFECT.

MEXILAND (the Mek-zeez) has no known uni-
fied government. Rather, it's inhabited by various
human factions, cannibals and *strays*, Xeno-bred
humanoids discarded on Earth like abandoned
pets.

Smaller pockets of known Lorian and human communities or
sightings are also identified on the display.

"Colonel. Lieutenant," Gen. Tegashito gleefully praises. "The
Union is in your debt."

"Oh, we just humble civil servants, sir," Crayton replies.
"Perhaps, a promotion as fair payment?"

The son of a former Japanese officer who served under Gen.
Contreras, Gen. Tegashito, chuckles. "You got jokes, kid. Give you
that."

He remotely opens a wall, exposing a window overlooking the
quarantine annex. Crayton watches as teams of men carry off pieces
of the Lorian poacher's mechsuit.

"Dose not goin' to Nellis, sir?" Crayton asks.

"Not your problem, Captain," Gen. Tegashito replies and turns
to Crayton.

"Yes, sir," Crayton acknowledges with a nod.

"I'm sure you and your men are anxious to spend your two-week leave in the Red Rock Zone," Gen. Tegashito says as he types in the authorization.

"Red Rock?" Crayton replies with a smile. "Yes, sir."

"With three *water creds*."

"Tree...*each?*" Wishbone gleefully asks.

"Transferable, of course," Gen. Tegashito responds with a nod. "Any more questions?"

Taking the hint, the two men smile, salute, and exit the office. A few feet down the hall, Wishbone turns to Crayton.

"Did he say...*she?*" Wishbone asks.

"Wishin' for a date?"

"No, sir," Wishbone replies. "But what if she has a partner?"

"Who don't love reunions?"

"And if it becomes an orgy?"

Crayton stops Wishbone. "Den we fuck dem all, ship 'em to Needles, take deir tech, make betta kills, den repeat! Yeah?"

Wishbone gulps and nods in agreement. "Yes, sir."

"Let's get to Red Rock so doze water creds can wash off dat fuckin' fear stench," Crayton quietly growls.

Sweat already dripping down his face, Wishbone salutes then sprints ahead to the parked convoy to deliver the good news. Crayton smiles as his men's cheers echo through the halls.

The Daughter of Wolf Creek

An hour after the departure of Crayton's caravan, a heavily armored, laserdrill-tipped *Tunnel Two*, the Union's executive tubecar, enters the Sugar Bunker's private underground station for high-level *reps*. Sporting the Sin Vegas Union seal on both sides of each car, Tunnel Two stops and opens its doors. Donning tactical red *Development Club* skins, the Union government's Protection Guards, called *PGs* (or *Pigs* for short), exit Tunnel Two and form a protective ring.

Inside the main car, *Sector One Board Director* Jaxine Coltraine, an athletic, English brunette in her early fifties, and her twenty-two-year-old, olive-skinned assistant Dyson Tolbi each work on their e-tabs, remotely trading docs with each other for Jaxine's review and approval by fingerprint signature, or *finsig*. Jaxine takes a sip of wine. Both wear professional red skins.

"Dye, my fingers are gonna fall off," Jaxine barks, "and I plan on using them later."

"Yes, ma'am," Dyson responds as he stops transmitting.

The nearest window display activates. Jaxine and Dyson can see Gen. Tegashito, Capt. Theroux, Sugar Bunker personnel and Jaxine's PGs waiting for them on the platform. The window display illuminates a transparent green, assuring them of a secure environment. Moments later, Jaxine and Dyson exit the car to greet Gen. Tegashito who's shorter than both of them.

"Ms. Director," Gen. Tegashito says as he smiles and salutes.

"General." Jaxine smiles back.

Brushing aside his thinning hair, Gen. Tegashito prepares to escort Jax's entourage to a waiting tunnel shuttle. "I hope he understands we're goin' as fast as humanly—"

"If you don't mind, I'd prefer a little fresh air," Jaxine says. "I practically live in that bloody tube."

"As you wish," Gen. Tegashito answers. "Gurlee!"

"Chariots on standby, sir," Capt. Theroux replies.

Capt. Theroux redirects the group. Gen. Tegashito checks out Jaxine's toned ass as she passes in front of him.

"Take in as much as you can," Gen. Tegashito mumbles to himself.

Gen. Tegashito and Capt. Theroux lead Jaxine, Dyson, cybernetic PGs Yo-Yo Hemingway, Gitmo Peters, and respective robotic PG partners Jericho-19 and Tom-Tom to a lift. Once everyone's safely inside, the lift rises. At the top, a guarded gate leads them to waiting golf cart transports called mini-commuters, or *minis* for short. Gen. Tegashito boards the driver's side of the lead mini. Jaxine rides shotgun while PGs Hemingway and Jericho-19 sit behind them. In the second mini, Capt. Theroux drives while Dyson sits beside him and PGs Peters and Tom-Tom sit behind them.

As the two minis cruise aboveground, Jaxine looks toward the main gate where Tween Defense Club soldiers grant restricted access to authorized personnel. She spots a janitor wearing his standard green *Production Club* work skins, a loose-fitting jumpsuit with a fist insignia over his heart.

A few yards from the janitor, a secretary wearing a form-fitting yellow-themed *Administrative Club* work skins, a singular outfit an "A" insignia enters another building. Jaxine briefly studies her own red-themed, elastic shirt and pants, gently running her pale fingers with black nail polish across the *D* insignia.

"You think I'd look good in yellow?" Jaxine asks.

"I think yellow would look great on you," the Asian officer replies with a double entendre and devilish grin.

"That was too easy," Jaxine concedes.

"Yes, ma'am," Gen. Tegashito confirms.

A pair of aerial drones cruise overhead, periodically scanning the faces of random Sugar Bunker personnel to confirm they are authorized Union Representatives, referred to as *reps*, or legalized citizens.

On the ground, personnel entering the Sugar Bunker show their inside left wrist, revealing *R* tattoos with RFID chips or stamped QR codes (for elderly reps born prior to the *Second Unrest*) that confirm citizenship, club, rank, and occupation.

In the second mini, Dyson looks up as a once proud sun struggles to pierce the polluted clouds that frequently hold the skies hostage. He spots clusters of two-story barracks in the distance.

"You a verge, sir?" Capt. Theroux asks Dyson.

Dyson turns to Capt. Theroux, his attention to the captain's laser scars peeking out from his sleeves and collar.

"Pard?" Dyson replies.

"Ever seen one up close?"

"No. I mean, I seen sims. Imagine they're very…scary up close, huh?"

"Hell yeah," Capt. Theroux says. "But if you delete one, deir shit tastes fuckin' *deli*!"

Dyson winces at the thought then replies, "So I've heard."

Looking up at the sky, Jaxine inhales deeply. Gen. Tegashito catches her in a moment of bliss.

"I do love it here," Gen. Tegashito says. "Air filters, sanipads, and janitors only do so much with twenty million bodies crammed in a metal bowl."

"That just made me recall my last bowl of real cereal," Jaxine replies.

"Got milk?" Gen. Tegashito jokes as he glances at Jax's breasts.

Jaxine catches him and flashes a stern look. Embarrassed, Gen. Tegashito turns mute. PGs Hemingway and Jericho-19 glance at each other, pretending to ignore the flirty convo up front. Jaxine bursts into laughter to acknowledge she's merely teasing the general. Gen. Tegashito laughs, followed by PGs Hemingway and Jericho-19.

The minis roll into the main building on the opposite end of the base. They drive around back and park on a freight lift. Gen. Tegashito's retinal and voice scans activate the lift doors. The lift descends. Fifteen stories belowground, the lift doors open.

The minis exit and cruise down a tunnel. They pass through two tunnel checkpoints that lead into an enormous warehouse packed with liquid-filled tubes containing fetuses. The minis cruise between two rows of the tubes as lab techs carefully inspect each one. Although the fetuses are in various stages of life, they all have minuscule blinking devices embedded in their transparent brain stems. A panel on each one displays a solid red light on 90 percent of the tubes. The remaining 10 percent show solid yellow lights, an indication of minimal progress. Jaxine lowers then shakes her head in disappointment.

"We're making progress," Gen. Tegashito promises.

"I'm not the one you have to convince," Jaxine retorts.

The minis park in their designated spots, and everyone exits. While the others enter a private guest lounge adjacent to Gen. Tegashito's office, Jaxine and Gen. Tegashito continue down the hall to the control room. PG Jericho-19 turns to PG Tom-Tom.

"Ten *socreds* they fuck," PG Jericho-19 says.

"Offer declined," PG Tom-Tom replies.

"Puss," PG Hemingway counters. "She ain't fuckin' him."

"I'll take that action," PG Peters chimes in.

Using their retinal displays, PGs Hemingway and Peters agree to bet some of their social credits, the Union's currency, against PG Jericho-19 while a nearby wall displays run ads for:

Powerball, a brutal basketball-like sport similar to what the Aztecs and Mayans played to the death, followed by…

An ad for Nanorem, the Union-sponsored healing treatment featuring nanotech that comes in various patches, sprays, ointments, and gels, then…

There's a news report of domestic terror attacks in both New Diego and Phoenix Blocs attributed to a domestic terrorist group led by a shadowy figure known only as "The Man," followed by…

Inner (or Inny) Defense General Quint Monahan, the Union's law enforcement chief, reminding citizens that all nonreps are strictly forbidden from entering Sectors One, Two, and all military installations—though exemptions exist. And finally, an ad that extols the benefits of working long hours "For The Greater Union."

Inside the control room, Jaxine sits on the couch when she notices Gen. Tegashito nonchalantly pick up a small remote control and walks over to a wall.

"Holding out on me again?" Jaxine asks.

Gen. Tegashito uses his retinal scan to open a secret vault inside the wall. He places the remote inside the vault and secures it. Gen. Tegashito turns to the wet bar beside the vault. He grabs two frosty cups and an old bottle of spiced rum from a *chillbox* below the bar.

"Getting harder to find the good stuff," Gen. Tegashito answers.

He places the two small cups in front of her then hands her the bottle to examine. She unscrews the cap.

"The things we take for bloody granted," Jaxine replies, taking a whiff of liquor. "Mmmmmm. I could bathe in this."

"Shall I pour?" Gen. Tegashito replies, holding the bottle in midpour.

Smiling, Jaxine points at the cups; Gen. Tegashito pours into them. They toast, sip, and savor; Gen. Tegashito's eyes fixate on a well-aware Jaxine.

"Shima," Jaxine responds, holding up the small gold band affixed to her left hand.

"A faulty construct from a world long dead," Gen. Tegashito retorts.

"Old habits die hard."

Gen. Tegashito walks back behind his desk and types into his console.

"Then it's time to show you the big boy," Gen. Tegashito replies.

Suddenly, another wall slides open, exposing the window overlooking the biohazard zone. Still sitting, Jaxine looks through the window. Her eyes widen. She rises.

"Fuck me!" Jaxine barely manages to get out in one breath, maintaining her hypnotic gaze straight ahead.

"Or in this case...*girl!*" Gen. Tegashito adds.

Jaxine slowly rises from her seat, oblivious to Gen. Tegashito as he refills her glass. She walks over to the window then wipes away the steam from her foggy breath on the glass.

"Bigger than the last one," Jaxine replies. "Losses?"

"Fifty dead. One hundred fifty-two wounded. Thirty-three critical," Gen. Tegashito answers.

Jaxine scoffs as she downs her glass of rum then asks, "The commanding officer?"

"Gave him and what's left of his men some R & R in Red Rock. Along with three transferable water creds each."

"Three?"

"See that thing down there? I would've given four if he asked," Gen. Tegashito proudly replies.

"He would've taken two if I did," Jaxine counters. "So how much longer we talking?"

"Hard to say."

"Damn it, Shima."

"Jax, my guys are workin' around the clock—under the radar. We push harder, and the wrong people start askin' questions. Feel me?"

Gen. Tegashito wipes a few sweat droplets from his forehead, pours himself another shot, and quickly downs it. Jaxine places her shot cup on the table and seductively walks over to a fidgeting Gen. Tegashito and caresses his crotch.

"I feel you," Jaxine replies.

Gen. Tegashito exhales as he leans in for a kiss. However, Jaxine pulls away.

"Now who's holding out on who again?" Gen. Tegashito asks.

"Finish for me, and I promise to finish for you."

Jaxine exits, leaving the blue-balled general still holding his empty shot cup.

Sev's Renewal

Back in the capitol sector of Sin Vegas, guests pack the Boulder City Defense Club's Great Room, one of the few venues in Union territory with enough space to accommodate large groups. Along with air and water, space and privacy have become increasingly valuable commodities. And although all citizens have *access rights* to vital resources, citizenship, club, and rank dictate the amount of access one is allotted or earned.

Sporting a scruffy beard and cybernetic right arm, Hector, now nearly six decades removed from the frightened little eight-year-old in the Chinook, proudly looks toward the podium.

Hector's forty-two-year-old son, Defense Club Major Sev Contreras, and Sev's beautiful *lease-mate* Hilga, wearing a yellowish jumpsuit, stand opposite each other with their right index finger on a transparent pad cradled in a pearl-hued podium. The pad scans their finsigs while a cybernetic officiant looks Hilga in the eye, taking a retinal and audio scan to verify her identity.

"I renew," a teary Hilga replies.

The *oh-fee* then turns to Sev.

"I renew," Sev replies.

The transparent pad turns green.

"I now pronounce this contract extended," the oh-fee proclaims. "You may now seal the deal!"

Sev and Hilga passionately kiss. The guests applaud and fist-bump, a more common replacement to the traditional—though increasingly rare—handshake. Sev and Hilga's nine-year-old son, Ocho, whose athletically gifted frame has no discernible tech implants or enhancements, nods off on his grandfather's cybernetic arm.

Hector and Ocho both wear formal black skins as Defense Club members. Hector turns and smirks at a teary-eyed Toi, his *roomie* for nearly a decade, who wears a yellow-themed dress, which accentuates her toned, dark skin and identifies her as part of the Administrative Club.

Whereas a lease-mate would be considered an equivalent to a spouse, a roomie would more closely resemble a live-in significant other-slash-housekeeper. Although lots of roomies are included with Union domiciles, reps often keep their own roomies wherever they live. In turn, the "unwanted" roomies are either retained at an additional cost or must relocate to the new roomie's previous home. Those lucky enough to become lease-mates are automatically granted full citizenship.

Sev and Hilga turn to embrace their *personal advocates*: Capt. Chino Macau, Sev's best friend and tactician, and red-skinned female Rusani Cutwater, Hilga's advocate, who serves the Union as an Administrative Club public educator.

The room suddenly transforms around the jovial audience, becoming a dining and entertainment area. Soft pulsating electro-pop music plays. Revelers wash down an assorted menu of processed insects with flavored cocktails infused with SinWater, the Union's liquor of choice, which Hector prefers neat. Hector replaces his empty glass with two virgin drinks from a robotic waiter and hands them to Toi and Ocho, who guzzle them down. They hand their empty glasses to another robotic waiter passing by with a tray of used glasses.

"Time to put de liddle one to bed," Toi says.

"I'm not tired," Ocho whines.

"Your mom make de rules, yeah?" Toi replies.

"G-Pop?" Ocho pleads to Hector.

Hector turns to Ocho.

"Oach, I've seen a lot of scary shit around your age. And believe me when I say there ain't nuttin' scarier than an angry mother," Hector says as he stares at Ocho. "Feel me?"

"Yes, sir," Ocho says, pouting.

"At least you're smarter than I was at your age," Hector says as he hugs Ocho.

"Still on for Sunday?" Ocho asks.

"Fo-sho," Hector replies.

Another robotic server passes by. Hector grabs another glass of SinWater.

"Don't puss out," Ocho counters.

"I won't. Now get goin'," Hector responds.

"Love you, G-Pop."

"Love you too, Oach."

"Be safe, yeah?" Toi says to Hector.

"Always," Hector replies then sips his drink. "And thank you."

"No, I love Oach," Toi affirms. "But dey need some time alone."

"And so could we," Hector responds.

"So now you in a rush?" Toi sarcastically questions as she kisses Hector on the cheek, then walks away with Ocho. Smiling, Hector watches as Sev and Hilga hug and kiss Toi and Ocho goodbye. Hilga then uses her implant to order two security lease-bots—included with the ceremony package—to escort Toi and Ocho home.

"Badass chops, Pops," Lt. Angelino "Angel" Spazzi, Sev's intelligence specialist, says while stroking his own scruffy blond chin.

Rubbing his beard, Hector turns to Angel and replies, "Thanks. Thinkin' about addin' a few more inches."

A cybernetic female server with a tray of small glasses filled with white liquid walks up to six-foot-nine weapons specialist Sgt. Ivor Vitchenko.

"Mother's milk?" the smiling server asks.

"I only drink milk from de nipple," Vitchenko replies with a smile.

Still smiling, the server winks at Vitchenko then walks away. Vitchenko follows the server with his cybernetic eyes to upload her profile when Chino, carrying two drinks, blocks Vitchenko's line of sight by sticking one of the drinks in his face.

"Careful, bro. Doze models you break, you buy," Chino says. "Union strong."

Vitchenko nods, deletes the server's profile, then grabs the drink from Chino.

"Union strong," the towering Vitchenko belts out in a faded Russian accent.

He and Chino toast, drink, then join Hector and Angel.

Across the room, Hector spots Hilga talking to guests. He searches for Sev, oblivious to his son creeping up from behind.

"Dare's de Old Man of Honor," Sev says as he bear-hugs Hector from behind. "No shave for dis one?"

"Maybe the next renew," Hector counters.

Hector hands Vitchenko his glass then manages to slip out of Sev's playful grasp. The men laugh when Angel, reading an encrypted message on his retinal screen, joins them. Vitchenko hands Hector back his glass.

"Bros," Angel says. "*De D* say Cray-Cray took down a fuckin' Xeno last week!"

"Bullshit," Vitchenko says, crossing his arms with disbelief.

"For real," Angel says.

Angel transmits the same report to Sev's, Chino's, and Vitchenko's retinal displays.

"Fuck," Chino says.

"Cray-Cray?" Hector asks.

"Col. Crayton Stak," Sev replies. "Gen. Tegashito's tweenie psycho bitch."

"We had a few of those back in the day," Hector replies.

"Pity de fucks who land in dat unit, eh," Chino adds. "You lucky to get fiddy-fiddy chance—maybe. Unlike our major here!"

"Den you got fiddy-six," Vitchenko jokes.

"Cray-Cray trows a hundred men into de fire witout baddin' a cyber-eye," Angel says.

"And the Xeno?" Hector asks.

Everyone shrugs.

"Probably chopped up in a lab," Vitchenko offers.

"Boss, tell me you got Xeno shit on de menu," Angel begs.

"Too pricey, bro," Sev answers. "Maybe next time."

"Cray-Cray take tree hundred men to delete de fucker, eh," Chino says.

"I needed double," Hector says as he downs the rest of his drink. "And now I need double again."

Hector signals a waiter to trade his empty glass for two full ones.

"Guess we make progress," Angels says.

"Dat what you call it?" Hector replies while taking a swig of his liquor.

"What you call it, Pops?" Angel asks.

Hector looks around to see everyone awaiting his next words as if he were a prophet. He downs one of his drinks and hands the empty glass to a waiter making the rounds.

"Guess I'd...call it a day," Hector says as he turns to Sev. "Gentlemen."

Sev looks over at Hilga conversing with a table of roomies, the majority of which are female.

"Pop—" Sev replies.

"I'm a big boy," Hector says. "So unless you need a sub, go make your father proud!"

The men cheer as Hector pushes his son in Hilga's direction.

"Pickin' you up Sunday, right?" Sev asks.

"Focus on the mission at hand, Major," Hector says as he playfully salutes. "See you Sunday!"

Hector watches Sev and Hilga exit the Great Room. Angel turns to Hector.

"Tink we get a rematch wit' de Xenos, eh?" Chino asks.

Hector looks around and notices that everyone in the room has some level of cybernetic implants. Very different from what he remembers growing up in the Old Nation.

"I *tink* we still got lots to learn," Hector answers, mocking the men's lazy English now assimilated by the younger generation.

After a final shot of SinWater, Hector pats Chino on his shoulder, nods to Angel and Vitchenko, and then exits with a security lease-bot. The soldiers turn to each other.

"Hard to tink Pops take out a fuckin' Xeno, huh?" Angel asks.

"Not hard to tink," Chino wisecracks with a tap on Angel's shoulder before finishing, "if you smart."

The men laugh when the female cybernetic server returns with her tray of breast milk and says to Vitchenko, "Your order, sir."

She hands a stunned Vitchenko the lone bottle-shaped glass fitted with a plastic nipple cover, then disappears back into the crowd. Chino and Angel stare silently at Vitchenko holding the bottle of breast milk. Vitchenko shrugs.

"What?" Vitchenko rhetorically asks as he casually sucks down the breast milk through the plastic nipple.

Welcome to Sanjose

Nor-Cal Sector Director Metamucil Ferouk greets Outer (or Outy) Defense General Derek Lawson, chief military officer, whose digital V tattoo embedded on his muscular right bicep illuminates through his black skin. Gen. Lawson's equally dark-skinned subordinate, Major Mayweather Hickson, stands beside him in front of the newly constructed *Sanjose* Veterans Arena.

Thousands of workers and janitors continue to put the finishing touches on the massive venue. Some workers install solar panels on flat surfaces. Others coat the more angled parts of the exterior with a thin, transparent material called solar film, or *solfil* for short. Though more expensive, solfil can harness the slightest sunlight into electricity. One of many generous contributions from our alien overlords.

Dir. Ferouk leads Gen. Lawson inside the stadium while Maj. Hickson trails behind with a small box in one hand. Armed Union soldiers guard the facility.

"Welcome to de new San-joh-zee, General," Dir. Ferouk greets in a Pakistani accent, referring to a city those before MF referenced in two words.

Gen. Lawson turns to Maj. Hickson. "May?"

Maj. Hickson looks around.

"Mos def not de shithole I recall as a pup, sir," Maj. Hickson answers.

"Mos def indeed, Major," Dir. Ferouk responds. "Check out de new solfil spread! First batch from Needles!"

Gen. Lawson points to construction taking place outside the stadium and says, "Don't recall seeing those on the plans."

"Ah…de Framers Outpost. A new addition. Private space with retractable roof for special events and high-level dignitaries. Away from de noise…and de nosy."

"Uh-huh," Gen. Lawson replies.

"You see de recent *geostats*? In five qua-tahs, San-Jo-see will suhpass Bayland as biggest Bloc in de Sector!"

"Also helps that San Fr… Bayland's takin' on more water than a So-Crow," Gen. Lawson counters.

"More reason to promote San-joh-zee!" Dir. Ferouk replies. "But deez *Chill-ren* and *Eye-lan-dahs* causin' major probs for me."

Gen. Lawson nods Maj. Hickson over. Maj. Hickson hands Gen. Lawson the small box. Gen. Lawson then shoos Maj. Hickson away. Both arms triumphantly in the air, Dir. Ferouk escorts Gen. Lawson into the building.

"Three hundred fifty thousand," Gen. Lawson laments. "You sure it'll be ready on time?"

"Oooh…yeahhhh!" a booming voice shouts. "Chicka-chick-aaah!"

Clutching his sidearm, Gen. Lawson looks up and jumps back and says, "What the—"

Both men look up to see a giant, lifelike hologram of Dir. Ferouk projected on the stage. The hologram bends forward, face-to-face with Gen. Lawson.

"Fah-rook… I need a dock-tah," the giant Ferouk hologram says, mimicking Darth Vader. "Oxy, huh?"

Gen. Lawson turns to Dir. Ferouk.

"Yeah, if you wanna a fuckin' laser bullet to the brain," Gen. Lawson snaps.

Dir. Ferouk clears his throat, then leads the general into a nearby lift up to a private VIP lounge that overlooks the arena. The lift door opens to a robotic waiter offering each a glass of SinWater. Both Gen. Lawson and Dir. Ferouk accept the offer and toast.

"So what about dis Xeno dat Shima catch?" Dir. Ferouk broaches.

"Can't confirm or deny."

"C'mon, Dee."

"Why don't you ask Jax at de next develop-mental cock and tail party you guys love to host?"

"I got rights to know what goes down in my sec."

The two men sit on a couch. Dir. Ferouk puts his feet on the small table between them.

"Between the NorPac merger, Framers Day and New Year's, we both have enough on our plates to worry about."

"Same Old Nation tinkin' dat got us in dis mess," Dir. Ferouk.

"And what are you thinking, Meta?" Gen. Lawson rhetorically asks.

The robot waiter returns with more beverages and places them on the table. Gen. Lawson places the small box in his possession on the table and slides it over to Dir. Ferouk.

"Dis de Bon-Bon?" Dir. Ferouk asks. "Or de bah-ton?"

Gen. Lawson rises. "See for yourself."

Dir. Ferouk opens the box and takes out a pair of modified *zoomers*, high-powered binoculars augmented with Lorian tech. He rises and puts them on. Gen. Lawson escorts him to an open area exposed to the elements and a hazy sunset. A few Lorian ships dart across the upper atmosphere.

"Wow. De sun for real."

"Press the button on the right side."

"You gonna blind me or sometin'?" Dir. Ferouk asks.

"The fuckin' button, pussy."

Dir. Ferouk presses the button. He observes the tail end of a Lorian ship vanish over the horizon.

"Now what?" Dir. Ferouk asks, still scanning the sky.

"Just watch. It'll replay what you just saw in slow speed."

The zoomers replay the previous thirty seconds. However, it now shows silhouettes of dozens more Lorian ships speeding across the upper atmosphere—and in space—much faster than the ships he can see with his own eyes.

"De fuck…" Dir. Ferouk trails off as he looks back up at the sky. "Dat for real?"

"Yup. So you see, yours is not the only sector about to get more crowded."

Dir. Ferouk slowly hands Gen. Lawson back the zoomers. The general places the zoomers back inside the box.

"I gonna be sick," Dr. Ferouk says.

Gen. Lawson places a hand on Dir. Ferouk's shoulder and sarcastically replies, "Looks like you could use another."

Gen. Lawson signals the robot waiter to bring more drinks.

"Why show me dis?"

"To see de bigg-ah pick-cha," Gen. Lawson answers in a mocking tone.

"Not fuckin' pretty,"

"My mandate—our mandate—is to make Earth great again. No questions. No hesitation," Gen. Lawson says. "Feel me?"

The robot waiter returns with two drinks. Gen. Lawson grabs one and hands it to Dir. Ferouk.

"I can drink to dat," Dir. Ferouk replies as he raises his glass.

Gen. Lawson grabs the other drink and holds it up. The men toast and drink.

"And Meta," Gen. Lawson says. "I want the full plans to dis place."

ТРИ

The Upgrade

"G-Pop!" Ocho calls out in the darkness.

Hector opens his eyes to find himself in a SkyHawk aerial-assault shuttle parked beside the ruins of a commercial building. He looks outside to see Ocho wearing vintage Outer Defense Club battle gear. Hector looks down to discover himself in similar skins. His virtual environment briefly glitches.

"Old school, huh? I thought this was CapFlag."

"It is CapFlag. Dis de new Unrest Combo Pack. I download it dis mornin'."

"Combo Pack?"

"Yeah, First and Second Unrests," Ocho cries out.

"Union strong, buckaroos," a random voice interjects with a country twang.

Hector turns to the cockpit and sees Otto, a virtual autopilot whose likeness resembles a twenty-first century movie actor. Wearing American military pilot gear from the 1960s, Otto rests his feet on the console and closes his eyes.

"Otto?" Hector asks. "You're a military program."

Ocho ticks his head inside the SkyHawk. Otto leans toward them and replies, "It would appear that I have been…domesticated."

"Guess so," Hector deadpans.

"But I have to tell you," Otto says with in a foreboding tone before smiling. "This simulation is brought to you by the Union-wide premier of Ed Sherman's *Li'l Marco's Space Adventures*, streaming Jan fourteenth everywhere!"

"Thanks, but I've read it a million times," Hector replies.

"But, G-Pop," Ocho pleads with puppy dog eyes. "It's de streamin' premier!"

Hector's heart melts; it's like looking back in time. "Fuck it. First time for everythin', right?"

"Now if y'all would stop yappin', it's time to start zappin'," Otto chimes in.

"G-Pop, defend or attack?" Ocho asks Hector.

Hector exits the SkyHawk and looks around at the war-torn metropolis.

"Just when you think VRs can't get any realer," Hector says as he looks around.

Concrete from blown-out buildings crumble to the ground and burst into dust. Virtual rats scurry across the urban war zone. The virtual landscape's so lifelike, it's impossible to tell what's real and what isn't. Even the gentle breeze feels real.

"G-Pop, I got homeschool soon!"

Not wanting to disappoint, Hector takes a few deep breaths and closes his eyes.

"The best defense is a good offense," Hector replies. "Attack."

"'Bout damn time," Otto mumbles before pushing a button on his console.

Hector opens his eyes. Alone and heavily armed, he cocks his gun and spots a flashing black arrow in the sky, pointing down at the location of Ocho's flag through a quarter mile of apocalyptic urban landscape. A virtual timer appears.

"Let the Unrest begin in five, four, three, two..." the Game OS counts down in Hilga's voice. "Union strong!"

Suddenly, virtual soldiers under Hector's command appear, waiting for orders. Hector smiles. Switching to a shared comchat frequency, he and Ocho taunt each other. Hector engages in a brief firefight with a virtual enemy combatant when a laser bullet grazes his cybernetic arm, triggering an electric shock sent to his brain. Hector looks at his bionic arm to see blood dripping from it.

"My bad, G-Pop." Ocho laughs via comchat. "Forgot to lower de pain level!"

Hector's display shows Ocho remotely lowering the pain settings to mild.

"Keep talkin'," Hector playfully barks.

"Hope you recall to bring your san-eez," Ocho taunts.

Ocho directs his armed men to seek and kill Hector's soldiers; however, one by one his men die. Ocho reluctantly orders his last soldier to guard the flag while he hunts down his grandfather. Suddenly, Ocho finds himself pinned down in an ambush.

"Don't worry about me, you little…" Hector taunts through his virtual comchat. "I got plenty of water creds!"

At Ocho's flag, a virtual guard takes a virtual laser bullet to its head and crashes to the virtual ground. Hector appears from the rubble, victoriously waving Ocho's flag.

"Fuck!" Ocho screams.

"Who's the man?" Hector brags as the sun peeks out from the clouds.

A large shadow appears on the ground. He turns into the sunlight, which partially blinds him as a silhouette emerges. Hector regains focus to see an agitated Lorian staring down on him. Panic sets in as Hector experiences flashbacks of *rain and yellow fluid pouring down its body, a ferocious Lorian roaring at a frightened Hector, who pulls out a magnegrenade.*

Hector takes a step back, loses his balance, and falls on his butt. He panics when his guardian aide, an avatar clone of Toi, suddenly appears.

"Hec, chill. Look at me. Deep breaths," GA Toi instructs. "Breathe deep. There you go."

A concerned Ocho kneels beside his grandfather while GA Toi looks on.

"You oxy?" Ocho asks as he helps Hector sit up.

"I'm fine, Oach. Just tired."

"Aside from blood pressure and heart rate, vitals are within normal range," GA Toi says. "Brain scan indicates symptoms associated with traumatic stress syndrome."

"My bad, G-Pop."

"Not your fault. It's Mother Nature."

"Who she?" Ocho innocently asks. "A hack-ah?"

"Just an expression, kid. Time for homeschool. Don't want your pop mad at me. Again."

"You don't tell Pop?" Ocho asks.

Hector hugs Ocho.

"You don't tell. I don't tell."

Perched above in one of the condemned skyscrapers, Guardian Aide Hilga spies on Hector and Ocho hug and virtually disappear.

Moments later, Hector opens his, eyes which automatically deactivates his virtual glasses (since he has no neck implants). Lying in bed, a shirtless Hector wakes, sits up, and places his VR glasses on the table beside him. Battle scars crisscross what remain of his aging organic body parts. Although his thin frame's not as toned as it once was, Hector still looks closer to a man in his late forties than early sixties. Scratching his crotch with his left hand, Hector tramples over Toi's littered clothes past the closet and presses a button on the wall console that opens a door to his bedroom *bathstall*. He enters the bathstall and fully undresses. Now naked, Hector relieves himself down a drain that also analyzes waste. He then presses a button on the stall wall console which dispenses large recyclable sanipads to clean himself. He then tosses them in a hidden bin, which cleans them for reuse.

"Fuck it," Hector says to himself.

Pressing on the bathstall display, Hector activates the shower menu. A showerhead appears from above and dispenses trickling water. Hector quickly rinses himself off while the water cred counter ticks downward—though it's apparent he has more than enough credits to bathe a household of four. During these few moments of bathing, Hector recalls his last, full shower the morning his father sent for him and his mother, before man's fall. A memory forever imprinted in his mind.

Gallons of water freely pour down on him. Young Hector savors every drop when the flow abruptly stops. Puzzled, the young boy looks up at the showerhead.

"Manual ration cap reached," Home AI interrupts. "Shall I increase and continue?"

Hector stares at his reflection.

"No. Activate *U-Stream*," Hector replies.

The mirror switches to the Union Streaming Network, also known as the USN, the U-Stream or more commonly the stream, which traffics all digital media. He flicks through various channels (some things never change) until he stops at an ad for an upcoming Inter-Sector Powerball Match.

Extremely violent, Powerball descends from the extinct Mesoamerican sport. However, rather than human sacrifices taken from the worst teams in each conference at season's end, the poor souls are shot through the demarcation line—with limited supplies—and into No Man's Land, sacrificial lambs for whatever elements or monsters they encounter.

Once dry, Hector operates the touch menu to review his water cred account—among the highest in the Union. Using his bionic arm, he orders, receives and chews a *taste pill* supplied for both oral hygiene and (relatively) fresh breath. Hector spits his foamy saliva into the empty taste pill dispenser, which takes its liquid gift back inside the wall for analysis and disposal. He watches a *Framers Day* promotional ad for the Union-wide event. It also features a few of the remaining Framers that will be attending events in each sector, including Hector.

"It's for a good cause," Hector mumbles at himself. "Keep tellin' yourself that."

Suddenly, the stall light blinks, which prompts a second display showing Toi standing on the other side of the bathstall door.

"Bedroom audio," Hector commands. "You okay?"

"Sev's combat exercise went over. He gonna be late, yeah?" Toi says over the intercom.

"Thanks for the heads-up!"

"And I got a message from your guardian aide requestin' a checkup."

"Just playing a little CapFlag with Oach. That new upgrade was fuckin' insane."

"Bedda safe den sorry, yeah?"

"I'm fine, Tee!"

Hector looks at a muted broadcast of merger talks between Union and NorPac officials. *Media drones* snap images of NorPac

Prime Minister Archon Devore shaking hands with Union President Dr. Terrence Gee, affectionately nicknamed P-Doc. Hector spots a quick shot of Jaxine clapping in the background. Hector manually rewinds the shot and freezes the frame on Jaxine midclap.

"Open," Toi orders.

"Off stream," Hector whispers.

The display shuts off as the bathstall door opens. Toi enters.

"I saw de replay, Hec."

"It's just a game."

"Your life is no game! So you let de scan decide…or Sev," Toi demands. "Choose."

"Okay," Hector relents. "I'll take the fuckin' scan."

"Before you go," Toi counters. "Repeat."

"Before you go," Hector replies. "I kid, I kid. Before I go. Okay?"

Toi's frown transforms into a grin. She walks over and kisses Hector on the cheek.

"Tanks," she says, pinching his cheeks while smiling.

"Tanks kill people," Hector says.

"More when you ignore dem, yeah?" Toi replies, smirking as she shuts the door.

Hector turns back to the black screen. "Reflect."

The screen becomes a mirror again. Hector stares at his reflection and sighs.

Roomie!

Welcome to the Old Summerlin Bloc, a protected zone—or *PZ* (peezee)—where distinguished reps who long for the Old Nation live out their final days with dignity. Unlike most communities these days, Old Summerlin offers its residents prime benefits from *privacy rights* to more personal space. And an even luckier few, like Hector, get to reside in a freestanding smart home neighborhood complete with security cameras, or *sec cams*, strategically placed on certain streetlights.

Across the street from Hector's residence, an automated Needles recycling commuter, or *reck*, sits in front of another smart home. A janitor detaches a large waste module from the outside of the home by the kitchen, glides it over, and attaches it to the reck's flash incinerator. Once finished, she glides it back then reattaches the module to the smart home. A second janitor loads larger waste into the reck. Both janitors then proceed on foot to the next smart home while the unmanned reck, with its trademarked *N* emblazoned on both sides, follows.

Inside Hector's smart home, Toi valiantly fights off two masked intruders who don a *C* logo that identifies them as members of the *Children of Kah-Lee*, the most feared domestic terrorist organization at odds with the Union. Though both attackers are larger, Toi's fighting skills are slightly superior than either. Toi knocks one of the men out with a side kick to the face, then turns to the *wellness room*; a red cross blinks to signal usage. Suddenly, the second terrorist grabs her left arm, pulling her toward him. Toi grabs a piece of broken recycled plastic from her broken couch and shoves it through the intruder's eyeball. Just as the second intruder regains consciousness, a bell rings.

Sitting upright on her *undamaged couch* and wearing a fitted, yellowish athletic skin, Toi's retinal display ends her virtual self-defense simulation to signal a missed incoming transmission:

ID: 1-39302940566030505-Q
Citizen: Retanga, Sabrine
Club/Occ: Admin/Roomie
Designation: Nonrep
Sector/Bloc: 2/Barstow

Small clean bots tidy up around Toi. She looks over at one of the small bug boxes with its tiny flashing light in the corner. She walks over, presses a small button on it, then takes the box to the kitchen. She presses a button on the protein storage unit, or *pizzu*, to release an empty bug box. She replaces it with the full container and closes it. She then goes back to the corner and places the empty bug box where the full one once was. She presses the small button on the empty bug box to begin collecting more vermin; the bug box's tiny light remains solid until it is full. Toi presses the implant behind her right ear to activate her *LiveLink*.

"Contact last caller," Toi instructs the device. "Private mode."

"LiveLink Private Mode Initiated," Home AI confirms.

A living room wall transforms to reveal the mirror image of another living room. Sitting on her couch, Toi sees her friend Sabrine Ratanga, a slim woman of Nigerian descent, sitting on her own couch, which appears as an extension of Toi's couch. Sabrine wears yellowish casual skins. During Private Mode, audio filters through their implants directly into their ear canals.

"*Nudda day*, roomie," Sabrine greets Toi.

"Nudda day, roomie," Toi replies.

Sabrine notices Toi's workout skins.

"Lookin' good, sexy."

"Not like you, sexy," Toi responds. "I can take on two now."

"Shame your idea of a treesome is not like mine," Sabrine deadpans.

"Keno and Danori workin' OT, yeah?" Toi asks, changing the subject.

"Fo de Greater Union," Sabrine sarcastically parrots with an eye roll.

"Anywho, I got you de tree Sec-Passes for FD! Plus, one room, two nights and two water creds each! Nontrans."

"Bitch, I love you!" Sabrine shouts in excitement.

"Sorry. I really tried to get you guys in de penthouse."

"Girl, you give enough," Sabrine replies. "Hey, I met someone on U-Match."

"Nudda one? Tween de match and your *co-tens*, how you get work done?"

"Girl, you know I can multitask!"

The women laugh.

"Ain't dat de chroot. So identify!"

"Chadman. An educator—"

"Specs," Toi playfully requests.

"All right…"

Sabrine presses a virtual button on the wall between them. Chadman's profile pops up on Toi's wall: a middle-aged, clean-shaven male with short, spiked black hair with frosted tips spins three hundred sixty degrees beside a brief bio.

"Not bad, Sah-bee," Toi responds.

"We only cloud date. He's a Sec-Five, Nonrep. Can't go nowhere."

"De cloud can take you anywhere," Toi counters.

"Den you free to join, yeah?"

"I got no interest in your cloud orgies."

"You don't miss some of de ol' times?"

"Just wit' you."

"Men-Tee," Sabrine replies. "When de last time you cum?"

"Very satisfied, tanks."

"Den when you gonna seal the deal, huh?"

"Not cool, Sah-bee."

"No diss, Tee. Just sayin' life's too short."

The doorbell rings.

"Front door, identify," Toi orders the Home AI.

The front door turns transparent, revealing a clear image of Sev waiting patiently outside in his black Defense Club formal military skins.

A few yards behind Sev, a couple of random reps wearing green Production Club skins casually stroll by. Sabrine practically drools at the sight of Sev.

"Nudda day, Sah-bee," Toi says.

"Tell Sev I'll su—" Sabrine says as Toi presses her implant to end the transmission. Toi opens the door.

"Sev," Toi greets him with a smile.

"Tee," Sev reciprocates as he enters.

"Pop's finishin' his checkup," she says, shutting the door.

Toi walks over to the kitchen. Sev looks over at the wellness room door as the red cross blinks above it.

"He good?" Sev asks.

"Bedda safe den dead, yeah?"

"Good," Sev replies. "Hil told me her GA shot her a text."

Sev smells something. Using his cybernetic eye, he locks in on an empty plate Toi picks up from the table.

"Old man likes his bacon, yeah?" Toi says. "Too bad for me."

"And me," Sev replies. "But I could use a quick boost."

Sev walks over to the kitchen and presses another button on the pizzu, which releases a protein bar. He retrieves the snack and eats it.

Toi places a dirty plate in the *InstaClean* with the rest of the dirty dishes. She presses a button on the machine to activate it.

"So Hilga got more students, yeah?"

"Seventy-eight per class now."

"Fuck. And Oach?"

"Good. Studying for Defense Exams."

A bell sounds. Toi opens the InstaClean and starts putting away all the sparkling-clean and bone-dry dishes.

"Bring dem next time."

"You and Pop can visit us for alt. Try some of our recycled, capitol air for change."

"You play to de base. But only nudda Unrest will make your pop leave Ol' Summerlin."

Sev looks at the kitchen-clock display.

"Yeah," he says as he walks toward the wellness room. "We runnin' late."

Toi heads for Hector's bedroom.

"Nudda day," Toi says.

"Nudda day."

Inside the wellness room, Hector peacefully rests while encased in his horizontal meditube. The contraption administers painless injections into his body as soothing music bounces around his body. Red lights transform into green followed by a series of beeps.

"Status check complete," the Home AI announces in a soothing voice. "Please review my full analysis."

Hector opens his eyes and yawns as if he had the most peaceful sleep in days. He ignores the meditube's diagnostic list on the display glass inches from his face. Instead, Hector focuses on a digital photo of himself and former Liberty High AP med student Zerina, then in their twenties, smiling during a lost moment; his eyes betray a silent conversation.

"And please reduce your alcohol consumption," the Home AI recommends. "This has become a frequent reminder—"

"End diagnostic," Hector commands. "Open!"

The meditube positions itself vertically, allowing Hector to easily exit. Hector puts on his black Defense Club skin. He walks over to the door and opens it. He smiles at the sight of Sev standing before him.

"Anudder day, Framer."

"Another day, Major."

The two men salute each other and embrace.

"Sorry for my lateness," Sev says.

"No worries. I needed a power nap. And now I need a quick one for the road," Hector whispers.

Sev rolls his eyes as Hector taps his shoulder. The two men head for the kitchen.

"Two SinWaters, straight," Hector commands.

A hidden liquor cabinet opens. Two small cups filled with liquor appear. Hector grabs them.

"These old eyes aren't what they used to be."

Hector hands his son a glass.

"I keep tellin' you to get new ones," Sev states as he taps his own cybernetic eye. "Under twenty mins, good as new!"

"Everyone's so eager to be...enhanced. Eyes that see for blocks. Legs that run for miles. You know...we had voices in our heads long before you had those damn things," Hector counters, pointing to Sev's implant.

"Fists dat punch chroo medal," Sev adds as he points to Hector's cybernetic arm holding a glass of SinWater.

"Hey, if the last one stuck around this wouldn't be here," Hector replies.

"Okay, let's go," Sev says.

Sev's enhanced eye analyzes the SinWater content in his father's glass: approximately 190 proof. They toast.

"To the fallen," Hector says.

"And de livin'," Sev returns.

Both men down their shot. Hector feigns reaching for another shot when Sev playfully pulls his father toward the front door.

Bic and the Stray

Although the harsh sun manages to pierce the weakened atmosphere, it's still not strong enough to penetrate a dense forest unscathed from destruction hundreds of miles away. Bic, an enhanced man in his midfifties, uses his retinal scan to analyze what appears to be smoke emanating from a large metal box a few dozen yards away. His comrade, Invoice Malikian, keeps watch for hostiles.

"Bad feelin', mang," Invoice says.

"You always have bad feelins," Bic asks.

"Xenos very smart," Invoice replies.

"Not smarter den Invoice!" Bic replies as he signals a few men to join them while the rest remain to keep watch.

Bic, Invoice, and a few dozen armed men—one of which has the letter *C* tattooed on his arm—surround the smoking metal box about ten feet long and five feet wide.

His finger on a high-powered trigger, Invoice's cybernetic eyes switch to infrared vision. No sign of hostiles in the vicinity. Inching closer to the box, they encounter a cool mist.

"Careful, yeah," Invoice says.

Bic runs his hand over the box's cool metal surface when a touch screen lights up with Lorian symbols. Invoice has his trigger finger ready for whatever's inside.

A blue dot flashes on the screen.

Bic presses the button. After a series of beeps, the box opens, releasing cool air that refreshes the men. Using their cybernetic eyes, Bic and Invoice see through the cool fog exiting the box. They aim their weapons at whatever's inside. Invoice turns to Bic, who lowers his weapon.

"Gimme a hand," Bic orders Invoice.

Invoice helps Bic pull out an unconscious, rail-thin, bald teen-age humanoid wearing strange clothing. Natural light reflects faint colors from the random tan patches covering the body's exposed skin.

Bic moves the humanoid's hair and sees a ring of small, circular burn marks around his scalp just above the boy's hairline.

The cool fog dissipates, revealing a grayish, crystal-like orb, a small crate with weird-looking food packets and a full, purified water container inside the box.

"Neva seen a real stray dis close before," Invoice says.

They gently lower the humanoid to the ground while the others load the box's contents into one of their vehicles, a retrofitted reck.

"Fresh collah marks," Bic replies. "Just got dumped."

Invoice points to the rings around the boy's head. "Like fuckin' garbage!"

"He goes wit' us."

"Dey got stray colonies in Mexiland, yeah?" Invoice asks.

"Dey got lots of tings in Mexiland," Bic answers. "Quick check."

Bic uses his retinal scan to check the sleeping humanoid's vitals; Invoice uses his retinal scan to check the boy's interior.

"Normal," Bic says.

"No internal tech," Invoice says. "No trackers, eider."

"Strange," Bic responds. "Okay, grab everytin' and go. Boy too!"

"You fuckin cray-cray, mang?" Invoice asks. "Dis pet still a zeezee!"

"Dis a pup!" Bic snaps back.

"Okie-dokie, boss," Invoice concedes. "Let's go, fellas!"

Bic takes out a small injector gun. He sticks it into the boy's arm; the boy passes out.

"Don't worry, liddle one," Bic assures. "You sleep good till your new home!"

Four men carry the humanoid toward their modified reck, ret-rofitted for their covert scavenging operations south of the border. Two more men grab the small crate and water container. Invoice grabs the orb and scans it with his cybernetic eye. Satisfied it poses no immediate threat, he tosses it in the air with one hand.

"You see anytin' like dis?" Invoice asks, dropping the orb.

The impact on the ground triggers the orb, causing a holographic male stray to appear in a fighting stance; the male stray speaks in a weird tongue.

"Hold your fire," Bic orders as he rushes over to grab the orb.

"My bad, boss," Invoice sheepishly apologizes.

Bic shakes the orb until the hologram vanishes, following a few parting words in its native tongue.

Bic cautiously looks around and listens. "Let's get de fuck outta here before someting worse drop on us!"

Bic heads back to their vehicle with the orb. Invoice follows closely while keeping an eye out for danger.

"What de fuck was dat?" Invoice asks.

"I tink de boy's brudda," Bic replies. "Challenging him to fight."

"Fight for what?"

"Survival."

Reh-ee

The Lorian Ree, a Terran-protection advocate, surveys the charred metal and human corpses with her four oculars, or eyeballs, settled into what would be considered a human's chest area, relatively speaking. Lorians technically don't have heads. Protruding from their backs are four grapplers which look like a giant, hairy insect arms with four nasty, blistered "fingers" attached to each one. (Strangely enough, the sweet-smelling, pus-like fluid that sometimes drips from those grapplers has become a coveted ingredient in some of the best SinWater in the Union.) Surprisingly, these things utilize their two legs, feet, and orifices; a mouth between their oculars for eating and breathing; and a hole between their legs for shitting, just like humans do. Only their legs are more muscular, their feet have four toes, and their shit don't stink—literally. In fact, it turns out their shit tastes pretty damn good. They also have much tougher skin than on any other part of a Lorian's softer-tissue skin, one of the few weak spots—if you're lucky (or crazy) enough to catch one without a mechsuit on. And they all look the fucking same! Regardless, all of the above still won't prepare a person who encounters one initially.

Using scanners, Ree spots a camouflaged Lorian spy cam resting on the side of a nearby mountain. She slightly adjusts her lightly armored covering.

"Soon," Ree answers.

A few yards away, her fellow advocate, Hyfor, who has a missing ocular, scans her immediate area for signs of life.

"We approach two Terran centuries in a few cycles," Hyfor responds.

"Noted," Ree counters.

Nooz, a male advocate, fires a nonviolent, sonic disrupter to shoo away the vultures feasting on charred human flesh.

"The aroma induces my appetite, I confess," Nooz chimes in.

"My mate, remember the cause," Hyfor orders.

"My mate, I remember," Nooz replies. "Perhaps someday these Terrans will appreciate our compassion."

"My sisters did not receive compassion during the First Resettlements," Hyfor counters.

"They defend their hives," Nooz replies. "As all species do."

"Genetic fluid identified," Ree states. "Approximately, six moon cycles ago."

Hyfor collects the few tiny remnants of a heavily damaged mechsuit left among the human corpses blanketing the dry surface.

"The hunter was hunted," Hyfor quips.

"Their ability to adapt our tech impresses," Nooz states.

Ree looks up at the hazy sunset. "The next cycle approaches. We must avoid this poacher's fate."

Ree and Hyfor collect their things and head back toward their hovershuttle. Nooz lags several yards behind them when something shiny catches an ocular's attention. Nooz walks over toward it. Using two grapplers, he lifts up two metal legs that could only fit a human. Another of Nooz's oculars then spots the top half of a mortally wounded Union soldier staring up at him from the bushes. Carrying the metal legs, Nooz cautiously approaches the soldier.

"It lives," Nooz calls out.

Nooz inspects the soldier.

"Little one, shall I show you compassion?" Nooz asks.

Although the frightened soldier doesn't understand Nooz, the Lorian's strange, soothing vibrations course through the injured soldier's body.

"Go fuck yourself," the soldier ignorantly replies.

However, a Terran's sounds barely register to Lorians. The wounded soldier closes his eyes and releases a small object from its grip.

"Caution," Hyfor barks.

Ree quickly arms and fires her nonlethal shock-cannon; the concussion forcefully propels Nooz away from the soldier as the grenade detonates.

Nooz floats backward in midair. However, a part of his body is caught just inside the grenade's blast radius. Nooz hits the ground about twenty feet from where he once stood. He lies motionless as yellow fluid trickles out from his injuries.

Ree and Hyfor race over to Nooz. At his side, Ree pulls out a Lorian device that scans vitals, stops the bleeding, and applies an antiseptic.

"Vitals declining. He requires immediate medical attention," Ree states.

They carry Nooz into their hovershuttle and place him on a floating medical pad. Hyfor tends to Nooz while Ree takes the pilot's chair and sets a course back to base camp.

"My mate, survive," Hyfor promises.

Nooz regains partial consciousness.

"Don't…blame… Terrans," Nooz exhales.

"Conserve," Hyfor replies.

Once in motion, Ree activates the autopilot. She heads back to Hyfor and Nooz, arriving as Nooz falls asleep. Ree checks the medical scans.

"Praise Loria," Ree confirms.

"The recording," Hyfor says.

"Another time," she responds.

"I fear our cause will be ignored," Hyfor laments.

"Perhaps. But effect only comes with a cause."

"You repeat your father's words, yet not his actions."

Lights flash on the console. Ree looks out the window as they fly through the demarcation line.

Minutes later, the hovershuttle lands next to three others parked at a remote base camp. The doors open to waiting Lorian medics. Ree and Hyfor exit the craft with Nooz sedated on the floating medical pad. They hand over their badly injured friend to the medics, who escort him into a nearby medical pod.

Ree places one of her four appendages on Hyfor.

"Success to the healers," Ree says.

"My faith wavers, I confess," Hyfor replies.

"My friend, your mate lives."

"My friend, I do not reference Nooz," Hyfor barks.

Hyfor walks toward Nooz's medical pod. Ree looks down as chemical imprints of her recruitment of Hyfor and Ree course through her senses. After the brief hesitation, she slowly shuffles toward the medical pod.

De Hive

Commuters have become the standard mode of private transport for high ranking citizens. Nonreps are restricted to metro commuters, or *micks*, that run on tracks (or trackless off main roads) and can interlock or separate during transit. Whether manned or automated, micks can operate either on elevated tracks or underground tunnels as most ground transports are heavily restricted. Pedestrians and smaller personal transports, nicknamed *peets*, enjoy right-of-ways.

Sitting inside Sev's defense commuter, Hector and Sev review Sev's e-tab of video and images taken in the aftermath of Crayton's ambush of the Lorian poacher while the four-seater DC runs on autopilot. Defense is the only club to have their own specialized commuters.

"Good call on de training exercise cover," Sev says.

"You seemed determined to risk a court martial," Hector replies.

"I know. But dis might be the closest I get to a live Xeno," Sev says.

"Trust me, son. That's as close as you wanna be."

"I wanna be general."

"Stubborn like your grandfather." Hector sighs.

"Must be in de blood," Sev counters.

"They give you any trouble, Major Wiseass?"

"No, sir," Sev answers. "I was extra careful. Why I was late."

Sev points to an image that includes a set of large faint tire tracks.

"Definitely big enough for a Xeno," Hector says.

Hector's beard partially blocks Sev's view.

"When you gonna shave dat?"

Hector caresses his beard then replies, "Why waste a blade?"

"No waste—trust me," Sev counters.

Hector points at the screen and commands, "Stop. See that?"

Sev reviews the image and says, "I see bones."

"I see blood," Hector answers. "See those rocks?"

Moving the screen's images with his fingers, Sev studies one showing charred soldiers scattered across the ground near a pile of rocks. His father points toward the dried gray matter sprinkled on the ground and nearby rocks.

"Thought you say Xenos bleed yellow," Sev replies.

"They do. But turns after a few days. Appears your buddy's the real deal."

Sev turns his attention outward as the serene, spacious Old Summerlin neighborhood is replaced by a densely populated—and louder—city core.

Megascrapers with either solar panels on flat roofs or roofless tips coated with solfil nearly block once-unobstructed mountain views. A group of pigeons dart across the skyline. However, two of them are shot down, likely for someone's consumption below.

"One day, we gonna take back our planet, yeah?" Sev asks.

Hector studies Sev's neck implant then looks outside.

"And do what with it?" Hector rhetorically asks.

Sev hands his father the e-tab and pulls up his DC's holographic display.

"Pop, check this."

The display shows the DC's security page. Briefly concerned, Sev pauses momentarily before backing out to the main menu.

"Something wrong, son?" Hector asks.

"Don't recall accessing dis menu," Sev answers. "Maybe de Hive runnin' a remote system check."

"De price of freedom," Hector sarcastically replies. "Yeah?"

Sev clicks through the menu of options and selects *ThinkLink*. He then presses and holds down his implant, which triggers a flashing green light on the display to acknowledge a successful link.

"ThinkLink established," Sev's DC confirms.

"Now I can think wit' my *dick*!" Sev jokes.

"Great. Another thing we didn't need a machine to do for us—" Hector deadpans.

"Seat massager activated," Sev's DC says.

Hector's seat rumbles, taking him by surprise.

"What the..." Hector responds.

"Detecting elevated heart rate," Sev's DC replies. "Deactivating massager."

The rumbling stops, to Hector's visible disappointment.

"Thanks a lot, Dick," Hector sarcastically says.

"You're welcome, Framer Contreras," Sev's DC replies. "Transmitting entry codes to Hive Command. Entry codes accepted. Hive Zone access granted. Resetting coordinates to Lake Sin Vegas VIP Lot 67."

Hector and Sev look outside. Marvelous mixed-use monstrosities dwarf the iconic buildings located in the Historic Strip District (forever known as the Strip) where the lowest ranking citizens reside.

As traffic thickens, Sev's DC emits encrypted signals that command lesser-priority commuters to stop, slide right, and allow Sev's DC to pass.

Hector points toward the Strip.

"Zoom in there," Hector orders his son.

"What we lookin' at?" Sev asks.

The windshield display zooms in to the Strip, a now heavily congested section of town where hundreds of thousands of citizens live, work, and play both above and belowground.

"Paradise lost," Hector responds.

"I see a collective workin' for a greater purpose," Sev counters.

Hector chuckles, his gaze still focused outward. He scans the thick sea of pedestrians concealing the ground below when a faint horn blares. Instinctively, the pedestrians part like the former Red Sea, creating a path for a convoy of authorized ground transports to move through. The unfortunate few who don't move in time are run over by the convoy. Another horn blares once the convoy passes.

Janitors wearing specialized *hazskins* arrive to clean up the bloody mess and load everything onto HazRecks while the living continue their day without skipping a beat. Patrol drones hover overhead to ensure continued compliance. How the Union can sustain so many people is an absolute marvel.

"Nothin' like near extinction to pull us all together," Hector deadpans.

Sev's DC cruises past a flashing electronic display:

ENTERING HIVE AUTHORIZATION ZONE / AUTHORIZED CITIZENS ONLY

"Entering Hive Authorization Zone," Sev's DC warns. "Zone access confirmed. Estimated arrival time eight minutes, forty-three seconds."

Supervised by the occasional SkyHawk, Sev's DC continues on its path. To their right is a giant holographic display outside:

BOULDER CITY LIMITS—5 MI / REPS ONLY

Then another:

DEFENSE CLUB HQ—2.25 MI / CLUB MEMBERS ONLY

Sev's DC heads to the left where they encounter another sign:

LAKE SIN VEGAS—3.6 MI / REPS & AUTHORIZED NONREPS PERMITTED

Sev notices Hector repeatedly trying to keep the e-tab from slipping onto the floor.

"Pop, toss de e-tab into de box, please?"

Hector presses a button on the console, and a small drawer sticks out. He places the e-tab inside, when a small disc with a tiny red button catches his attention.

"Wow. You know, a long, long time ago we used to play music vids with these," Hector says.

"Put dat back before you get us killed, please. Dat's a mini EMP mag."

"Magnediscs?"

Sev nods. "Hit dat button and dis dick's goin' down."

"Coulda carried a lot more of these at The Pass," Hector laments as he places the mini EMP mag back in the drawer and closes it.

He looks outside and sees the Hive, Sin Vegas Union's enormous, heavily guarded government command center. Defense Club drones swarm around the fortified superstructure, the center of which consists of a large dome-shaped building surrounded by five smaller, but still impressive, dome-shaped buildings. Automated and manned laser cannons stand ready for any approaching threats. Easily the tallest allowable structures in the Union, the Hive spans dozens of kilometers of real estate with multiple levels belowground.

"Welcome home," Sev says.

Hector strokes his beard. He notices a lone Defense Club drone watching him then quickly float away.

Lake Sin Vegas

Sev's DC pulls up to the Hive-Lake Sin Vegas Checkpoint manned by two-armed robotic capitol guardians, or *CGs*, with automatic gun turrets above them. Although Sev's DC has been granted access, it must wait behind a line of similarly ranked DCs ahead of it.

"The lines, on my face ate away my smile. Could it be that I, fell apart? It shows," Hector sings as he studies his reflection in the window glass. It shows. It shows. Could it be that—"

"You...were!" Sev sings along with a grin. "You...were!"

"You were a pup when your mom and I were at the Boulder City checkpoint, and I had to take a piss. You wouldn't stop crying, and I couldn't leave the mick. People everywhere. Got so bad I had to dump your formula out and pee in your bottle."

"Don't recall dat," Sev replies.

"You were cryin' for your bottle, so I pretended to give it to you. But your mom thought I was for real, and she slaps the bottle—I didn't seal it right. Your mom can't stop laughing. You? Laughing so hard your face was red like the sun. And I end up the one pissed. So finally, we pull up to an organic Cee-Gee. He takes one sniff...waves us right through."

Father and son laugh.

"Oach was like her, yeah?" Sev rhetorically laments. "Really wish I could recall."

"She was a good woman. Selfless."

"Like Toi, yeah?" Sev rhetorically counters. "It's been a dec now, Pop."

"Nine years and four months," Hector replies. "But who's countin'?"

"Who you tink?" Sev rhetorically asks.

73

"She's fine. We're fine," Hector says.

Hector looks over at a public-access gate a few yards away where a group of connected, Union-owned public commuters, or *picks*, form one long train filled with lower-ranking citizens. Suddenly alarms blare as one of the picks in the train lights up inside. Armed CGs enter, pull out a woman, and take her to a designated *killspot*. One of the CGs rips out a Lorian implant hidden in the woman's back then executes her; everyone cheers. Unfazed, the CGs return to their post. Janitors wearing specialized *hazskins* rush to the scene, clean up, and load the corpse into a HazReck.

"Fuckin' zeezees," Sev says.

"Xenos gettin' smarter," Hector responds.

"So are we," Sev counters.

Hector turns to Sev and says, "I knew you were gonna say that."

About halfway to the main gate they pass under a gigantic SecScan, as all commuters must undergo. After clearing Sev's DC, the SecScan employs facial recognition.

Lights flash. A maglift arrives, hovers over Sev's DC, and activates a magnet to attach. The maglift carries Sev's DC from the checkpoint to the valet lot a few yards away. Starstruck gate guards salute Sev's floating craft as it heads to Lake Sin Vegas valet lot 67.

Sev turns to Hector.

"You miss dis shit!" Sev says.

"Maybe a little," Hector concedes, looking out again to see citizens and Hive personnel holding welcome signs with his name. They hover over a military welcome befitting a Union hero. Clearly embarrassed, Hector half-heartedly salutes the crowd, which goes ballistic in return.

The maglift lowers Sev's DC onto a private Valet parking slot. Sev helps Hector out of the DC. They walk a few feet when a recharging bot tends to Sev's DC.

"Two hours, Arby," Sev orders.

"Yes, Major," the recharging bot acknowledges.

Gen. Derek Lawson and Maj. Hickson greet Hector and Sev. The four men salute each other.

"General uh... *Framer* Contreras, an absolute honor," Gen. Lawson says. "Derek Lawson."

"General."

"Derek, I respectfully insist."

"Then I'll see your Derek and respectfully raise with a Hec."

"Seems you have the stronger hand," Gen. Lawson says. "Retirement treating you good, I hope?"

"Still workin' on this damn tan," Hector replies. "But from what I recall about you, the honor's all mine."

"Major Contreras," Gen. Lawson says as Sev stiffens at attention. "I understand you had an *unsked* exercise today?"

"Just keepin' my men sharp, sir."

"Keepin' your chain of command informed will ensure you have men to keep sharp."

"Yes, sir."

"Shall we, Hec?" Gen. Lawson says to Hector.

"After you, Derek."

As Gen. Lawson and Hector walk, Sev and Maj. Hickson fist-bump.

"Hec," Maj. Hickson says.

"Hick," Sev replies.

The men board a waiting mini. Maj. Hickson drives while Sev rides shotgun. Gen. Lawson sits behind Maj. Hickson while Hector sits behind his son.

"Don't know about you, but not a day goes by I don't recall The Pass."

"Membership has its privileges, I suppose," Hector replies.

Gen. Lawson exposes his arm to reveal a *V* tattoo.

"You gave us hope," Gen. Lawson says.

"And you give *me* hope," Hector returns.

Gen. Lawson looks back at Sev.

"Your old man take credit for anythin', Major?" Gen. Lawson asks.

"Not even me, sir," Sev jokingly replies.

Hector's unenhanced eyes scan Gen. Lawson, who does not appear to have any visible implants or cybernetic enhancements.

"Been-a-min since I've seen a pure organic," Hector says.

"Not entirely," Gen. Lawson replies, pointing at one of his eyes. "I caved on the retinals two years ago. Soldiers gotta adapt."

The mini enters *The Hall of Remembrance*, a large hangar where distinguished Defense and Administrative Club reps are memorialized. The mini drives them through the building. Mourning visitors pay their respects to holographic loved ones either on the walls, in cubicles, or in private rooms. Hector passing through momentarily distracts some of the patrons.

A few minutes later, the mini drives through a guarded corridor and stops before a wall. The ground lowers a few stories. The mini turns 180 degrees and drives until it reaches the vaulted *Framers Annex*. The doors open, and the men exit. They walk past a series of private mausoleums until they reach one digitally marked *Contreras*. Hector's retinal scan opens the door.

"Valet will send a mini when you're ready," Gen. Lawson says. "And we'll be sure to see you off."

"I'm sure you have more pressing matters than babysittin' an old man," Hector replies.

"Not every lifetime you can shake the hands of two legends from the same blood."

"Thank you, sir," Sev sarcastically replies.

Hector and Maj. Hickson chuckle. The general turns to Sev.

"I sure hope, when I read your training report tomorrow oh nine hundred, it'll be more entertaining than your sense of humor."

Sev snaps to attention with a sharp Union salute, a triple tap to the heart with the right hand.

Gen. Lawson winks at Hector then he and Maj. Hickson watch as Hector and Sev enter the chamber and shut the door. Maj. Hickson turns to his superior.

"Mom's gonna flip when I tell her I met Fray-mah Contreras."

"In the meantime, I'm your daddy," Gen. Lawson replies. "Let's go!"

"Sir."

Gen. Lawson and Maj. Hickson take off in the mini.

Inside the Contreras mausoleum, Sev and Hector stand while music and images of Gen. Contreras flash all around them. A hologram of Gen. Contreras, wearing a crisper version of his US general's uniform, appears and smiles at them.

"Hello, Éxi," Gen. Contreras's hologram greets Hector. "Long time."

Surprised, Hector takes a step back. Sev remotely activates a hologram of his grandmother Karla, wearing jeans and a collared shirt, who appears beside Gen. Contreras's hologram.

"Mijo, look at you," Karla's hologram says. "All grown up."

Mesmerized, Hector's eyes widen. "How?"

"G-Pop was easy. But no pics of G-Ma, BMF. So I went chroo some archives to find the right skins. Ask dem anytin'."

Hector walks over to his virtual parents who are both the same age they were during Man Fall.

"Sir," Hector says with a grin and salute.

"Son," his digital father responds with a grin and salute. "Life's been kind to you."

"You think?"

"Your heart's still beating. Isn't it?"

Hector nods, then turns to his holographic mother. "I miss you guys."

"We miss you too. But now we can see each other more often, no?"

Hector nods as his eyes well up, then turns to see Sev holding out a tiny digital chip. "What's that?"

"Mom," Sev says as he hands his father the chip. "But I taught you should be de one to upload her. When you're ready."

Hector hugs his son and responds, "Fuckin' upgrades."

He kisses Sev on the cheek; Sev gently pats his father on the back.

The Wolf

Three hours later, Hector and Gen. Lawson shake hands beside Sev's parked DC. Sev fist-bumps Maj. Hickson then turns to his father.

"I'm right behind you," Hector says.

Sev nods at his father, turns, and salutes the general, then enters his DC. He starts the silent engine and inputs the autopilot coordinates back to Old Summerlin.

Hector and Gen. Lawson observe the citizens milling around, most with cybernetic enhancements on various body parts. For the younger ones, implants have replaced the smartphones now reserved mostly for those who grew up before man's fall.

"In about five *decs* we'll be nuttin' but brains in a tin can," Gen. Lawson says.

"My son thinks that's a good thing," Hector responds.

"And you?" Gen. Lawson asks.

"Don't know what to think anymore," Hector laments.

"That's what happens when you get old," Gen. Lawson jokes.

"At least life goes back to being a bit simpler," Hector replies.

"You miss the old Stars and Stripes?" Gen. Lawson asks.

"Sometimes," Hector answers. "But she wasn't perfect either."

"Well, I still believe in second chances," Gen. Lawson responds.

"I'm on the fence," Hector counters.

"With all due respect, there's only one fence left," Gen. Lawson says as he pulls out his tiny smartphone and fiddles with it. "And the other side ain't pretty."

"We're no supermodel either."

"Well, you need anything, I just sent you my DL."

Hector nods. "And I'm sure you'll know where to find me."

"Another day, Hec," Gen. Lawson says with an American military salute.

Smiling, Hector salutes back. "One day at a time, Derek."

Gen. Lawson playfully rubs his own chin.

"Rugged chops, by the way," Gen. Lawson says.

"Tanks," Hector playfully replies in slang.

Hector hops into Sev's DC. A maglift arrives and carries them back to Valet Gate.

"Fuckin' Hawkin', sir," Maj. Hickson says, smiling as he watches the DC float away.

Gen. Lawson sighs and responds, "Affirmative, Major."

While midair, Hector looks down below to see a strange military caravan parked at another valet lot. Sev looks down on the hoods of the strange caravan: each sporting a spear tip with five points piercing a flaming *C* inside a white maple leaf shaped with a red border.

"Can-Cheez. Long way from home," Sev says.

"Looks like they packed plenty of cojones for the trip," Hec quips.

A large, cybernetic, Native bodyguard sporting a wolf tattoo exits one of the vehicles and opens the rear door. Another tanned Native man wearing foreign skins exits the same vehicle; the redskinned men both look up at Hector and Sev.

"Pop, how come I learn more about De Pass from them, not you?" Sev says.

Hector turns to Sev as the maglift lowers them near the checkpoint.

"What more can I say? Your grandfather put me in charge of over fifty thousand men and women—*civies*. When it was over, we were less than five thousand," Hector replies. "We believed one day we could go back. And we learned the hard way we can never go back."

"Dat's life," Sev asks.

"Dat's karma."

"You sound like P-Doc."

"He's a fuckin' dickhead!"

Traffic slows to a crawl a few miles outside the Hive Zone.

"Great," Sev plays with the display menu. "Accident a few ticks up, looks like."

"Just use your—"

"Bypass code. Yeah, yeah," Sev replies.

Sev transmits his priority code to bypass traffic, but nothing happens.

"You doin' it right?" Hector impatiently asks.

"Course, I'm fuckin' doin' it right," Sev barks.

Sev continues to play with the menu display, when suddenly, an electromagnetic pulse shuts down all commuters, including Sev's DC, within a five-block radius.

Androids appear, firing warning shots above the crowd; people scatter like insects to safety. One of the androids rips open Sev's door and shocks Sev unconscious inside his DC.

Hector quickly opens the small drawer and grabs the magnedisc just as another android tears open his door. Hector then reaches for a gun, but the android snatches it and crumples it like a piece of paper.

The android pulls Hector out of Sev's DC then carries him off. The robot heads toward its getaway commuter when it stops and looks down at the magnedisc stuck to its metal leg.

"Framer Contreras—" the android says as the magnedisc short circuits it.

The android drops to the ground. Another android disengages from the group and rushes toward Hector. However, it's shot in the head by a CG.

Sev wakes as the remaining androids rush toward the CGs, only to be cut down by Hive drones. Sev tends to his unconscious father; CGs surround them.

Teary, Sev looks up at the CGs. "Getta medi!"

Ms. Madagascar

Hector opens his eyes to find himself inside his own meditube as it opens. His blurry vision fights for clarity.

"Ze…" Hector whispers as Toi's happy face comes into focus. She's wearing workout skins. Beside her, a bandaged Sev smiles.

"Nudda day, sleepyhead," Toi greets him softly with a smile.

"Hey," Hector replies. "Was I in a sim?"

"I wish," Toi answers.

"How it hangs, old man?" Sev sarcastically asks.

Hector turns to his son and jokingly counters, "Still heavier than yours."

Hector tries to get up, but Toi pins him down with one hand.

"Rest, yeah?" Sev orders.

"Okie-dokie," Hector replies.

"Syntetic honey tea comin' up." Toi turns to Sev. "Sev?"

"I'm good, tanks," Sev responds.

Sev replaces Toi's hand, so she can leave the room.

"What the fuck happened?" Hector whispers.

"All good, Pop," Sev whispers back. "I hid Mom's chip in your drawer."

"I'm talkin' about the fuckers who jumped us."

"Oh."

Meanwhile, Toi prepares tea in the kitchen when the lights turn red then flash.

"Attention. Executive-level guests have arrived. Attention. Executive-level guests have arrived," Home AI warns. "Please secure any dangerous objects and move cautiously. Failure to comply may result in termination."

Toi looks outside as armed drones escort a Defense Club caravan parked outside the smart home. She walks over to the transparent door display and watches Jaxine and Dyson exit their vehicle.

Conversely, Jaxine and Dyson to see an *infrared* rendering of Toi watching them through the door.

PG Jericho-19 walks up to Jaxine. "*Executive Protocols* initiated, Ms. Director. Area is secure."

"Thanks, Jere," Jaxine replies to the robot as she stares at Hector's home.

"You okay?" Dyson asks.

"Why wouldn't I be?" Jaxine responds as she heads for the front door with Dyson right behind her.

Toi opens the door as Jaxine and Dyson approach.

"Security and privacy overrides initiated. Threat assessment, minimal. The Union appreciates your compliance," Home AI says.

"Don't mention it," Toi mumbles under a fake smile. "Nudda day, Ms. Director!"

"Another day, roomie," Jaxine condescendingly replies. "Now I see why Hec doesn't venture too far from his man cave."

Toi steps out of the way as Jaxine and Dyson enter.

"Please enter," Toi mumbles and shuts the door.

Jaxine motions for Dyson to wait in the living area as she walks straight to Sev standing by the open wellness room door.

"Sev, darling," Jaxine cheerfully greets.

"Ma'am," Sev replies with a salute.

Jaxine tightly hugs Sev; Sev lightly reciprocates with a half-smile and two gentle pats on her back. When they release their embrace, Jaxine's eye contact increases Sev's faux smile.

"At ease," Jaxine orders.

"Yes, ma'am," Sev replies with a nod.

Jaxine proceeds into the wellness room to find Hector still in his meditube.

"And you," Jaxine begins, "are supposed to be stayin' outta trouble."

Jaxine walks over to Hector's side and kisses his forehead.

In the background, Sev turns to see Toi fold her arms.

"Just takin' a little power nap," Hector replies. "Long time no see, Jax."

"Your choice, I recall," Jaxine replies.

"Was it?"

Jaxine turns to Sev and nods for privacy. Sev turns to Toi, shrugs, and closes the wellness-room door, leaving Hector and Jaxine alone. Sev and Toi turn to Dyson, triggering an uncomfortable silence.

"Nudda day," Dyson blurts out.

Inside the wellness room, Jaxine presses a button on her watch.

"Privacy mode activated," Home AI confirms.

Without hesitation, Jaxine reaches for Hector's organic hand. She plants a gentle kiss on his cheek, leaving a faint imprint of lipstick.

"Long time no see," Jaxine says. "For real."

Hector feigns a cough to snap himself out of her trance.

"New eye?" Hector says.

Jaxine nods with a grin. "What good is all this bloody tech if we don't use it to better ourselves?"

"Then why no implant?"

"Like you, I still harbor some…apprehensions about sticking things in my neck," Jaxine answers.

Hector's eyes fix on Jaxine's gold wedding band.

"Speaking of pain in the necks, P-Doc seems to have a little more spring in his step these days."

Jaxine composes herself then replies, "Thoroughly enjoying the fruits of our labors, of course."

"And of course, this ain't a social call."

Jaxine's pleasant smile melts away. "The droids were Kah-Lee, Hec. Their dicks illegally salvaged from a Needles scrapyard."

Hector sits up with Jaxine's help.

"What the fuck do they want with me?"

"I was hoping you could offer insight," Jaxine replies.

"You know I've been outta the game."

"Maybe they didn't get the memo."

"Or maybe you started paying ransoms?"

Jaxine shakes her head. "You're not that special. But the children have been shittin' on my lawn far too long."

"And now they've chosen mine for some reason," Hector counters.

Jaxine nods with a slight grin.

"The Man doesn't act without a reason," she replies.

"Well, I appreciate the concern for my well-being," Hector says. "But my head feels like a Powerball right now. If I recall anythin', I got you on speed dial."

Jaxine remotely opens the wellness room door.

"Tom-Tom and Jerry will keep an eye on you until your security escorts arrive for the celebrations. I'm not takin' any more chances with our Framers. Especially you."

Sev, Toi, and Dyson inch closer to Jaxine.

"I appreciate the gesture but—" Hector retorts.

"You made a deal," Jaxine says. "And the last thing I need to see is your dead body all over the streams. It's not a request."

Hector sighs, then nods.

"Yes, ma'am," Hector replies.

Jaxine leans closer to Hec's right ear and softly whispers, "You broke my father's heart when you walked away, you know."

"He broke mine when he got my father voted off the board," Hector whispers back.

Jaxine pulls back and stands upright, fixing her skins.

"I told you I had nothing to do with that."

"Yes. You did."

Jaxine folds her warms and asks, "It wasn't all bad, was it?"

"It just wasn't meant to be. I guess."

"Another day, Hec."

"Another time, Jax."

Jaxine nods, turns, and exits the wellness room. She walks over to Sev and says, "You need anything—anything at all, Dyson's on it."

"Thanks, Mad-Jax," Sev replies.

Jaxine frowns, then after a very short pause, slowly nods. "Mad... Jax. I like it."

Smiling, Jaxine turns to Toi, nods, then walks past her to the front door.

"Nudda day, Ms. Dir—" Toi replies.

Jaxine exits the house with Dyson in tow. Moments later, Jaxine's caravan drives off. Robotic PGs Jericho-19 and Tom-Tom stand guard as the smart home reverts to its default settings.

"Default systems restored," Home AI says. "Thanks again for your cooperation. Union strong!"

Toi closes the front door. She and Sev enter the wellness room.

"What she say?" Sev asks.

"What she *do*?" Toi replies.

Hector wipes the lipstick from his forehead and cheek.

"Apparently, our new friends were sent by the Children of Kah-Lee."

Toi gasps.

"Framers Day comin' up," Sev replies. "Maybe you should stay home."

"I tried that, son. But if I don't hold up my end, we'll have to move in with you."

"Dare must be sometin—" Toi replies.

"Toi, give us a minute?" Sev asks. "Please?"

Toi turns to Hector who stares at her then nods.

"The roomie will go now," Toi sarcastically replies with a dash of heartache.

Toi reluctantly leaves, closing the door behind her. Sev leans in.

"Pop, I don't like dis?" Sev asks. "You know De Children gonna take anudda swipe at you."

"Well, I'll take my chances with them over the kids at a Green Valley rec center any day."

Sev's implant beeps, and he checks his retinal display.

"Chee," Sev says. "Pop's good, tanks. What you got?"

Sev listens, nods, then sighs.

"Okay," Sev says. "Keep me posted. Union strong."

Sev ends transmit.

"Whoever messed wit' my dick is very good," Sev replies. "Not a trace."

Sev presses his implant.

"Major, dat was fast," Dyson replies on Sev's comchat.

"I want my team wit' Pop on FD," Sev orders. "Pretty please."

Suddenly, an incoming transmission appears Sev's retinal display:

DETAIL REQUEST AUTHORIZED

"Union strong," Dyson says before ending the call.

"Now I babysit you," Sev quips.

Hector shakes his head.

Needles!

Lights flash and sirens wail as Sev's military caravan of heavily armed dicks leave Greater Sin Vegas down the semicongested NevCal Beltway toward the Sector One Border Gate. Tens of thousands of citizens flow between sectors in an organized and heavily controlled manner. Without hesitation, a human border guard allows them easy passage.

Hector observes the dense crowd's cross-sector travel. Citizens arriving from other sectors appear thinner—and occasionally much paler—than those who typically reside within Sector One. Laughter redirects his attention inward.

"Needles!" Sev and Toi shout in unison.

Hector looks outside again to catch the exit display for the Needles Industrial Zone. If you're a janitor, Needles is your pit stop to rep status. This former dusty settlement now serves as the Union's main distribution and repurposing megacolony for everything from metal to bone. These days, nothing goes to waste. Absolutely nothing.

Toi turns to see Chino quietly napping.

"Dis beats de metro for real, yeah," Toi says.

"Yeah. And it only cost me an arm," Hector deadpans while raising his bionic arm.

After a brief silence, everyone laughs. Smiling, Hector turns his attention again outside.

Pedestrians swarm the ground like ants. Rows of megascrapers conceal the horizon.

"Sah-bee says New Vick get twice de size in de last five years," Toi says.

"I only recall blood, guts, twisted metal, and the smell of burnt flesh," Hector remarks.

Screams draw everyone's attention outside. Hector sees a gauntlet of cheering, scrawny citizens. Above them, media drones track the caravan's journey toward the New Victorville Bloc.

"Dis for you, Pop," Sev replies. "How you feel?"

"Like a sittin' duck," Hector replies as he scans the crowd with his organic eyes.

Sev pats his father's shoulder. "Don't worry. Crowd control will kill anyone before dey get to dis door."

"Dat make no sense. Can't sit *and* duck at de same time," Toi says.

Hector and Sev look at each other, then burst into laughter.

"A duck was a bird," Hector replies.

"Oh. Like a pidge?" Toi asks.

"Yeah. Only ducks quack," Hector replies.

"Fuck you! Birds don't talk," Toi asks.

"Not dat kinda *quack*," Sev chuckles.

"It means to feel exposed," Hector adds. "With no protection."

"Oh," Toi says. "Den why not say sittin' pidge?"

Hector pours two SinWater shots and hands one to Toi.

"Why not? To sittin' pidges," Hector toasts.

"To sittin' pidges," Toi toasts.

They drink. Toi places her hand on Hector's knee. Hector places his organic hand on top of hers. They smile at each other. Hector shakes his head.

"My dad. My mom. Uncle Rod. Uncle Manny. The Volunteers. They were the real heroes. I'm just fuckin' lucky."

"And we lucky too, yeah," Toi says.

Toi turns to Sev.

"Damn right," he adds.

Toi plants a kiss on Hector's lips. They remain entangled as Sev rolls his eyes.

"For Union sake, wait till we get de room," Sev snaps.

New Victorville

Sev's military caravan cruises through Sector Two, the Death Valley Sector (or D-Sec), en route to the New Victorville Bloc. Inside Sev's DC, Hector recalls a time when his family fled the same town, known simply as Victorville back then.

A visibly shaken Karla sits with Hector inside the Chinook as it prepares for takeoff. Gen. Contreras arrives.

"You guys okay?" Gen. Contreras asks.

Karla nods as she clutches onto Hector who looks around.

"Wait, where's Uncle Rod?" Hector asks.

Gen. Contreras looks at Karla, whose eyes swell with tears. Gen. Contreras bends toward Hector.

"Uncle Rod's gonna stay behind to help the wounded. He'll meet us in Vegas, okay?"

Hector nods.

Gen. Contreras looks up at Karla for assistance.

"Let's pray for Uncle Rod, mijo."

"I'll be right back," Gen. Contreras says.

Hector and Karla silently pray.

Gen. Contreras heads to the cockpit as the Chinook rises, heading east.

Hector pulls out his digital binoculars and looks out the window as various soldiers scramble below. Aiming at the horizon, he zooms in. Fires rage in the far distance as a group of futuristic-looking fighter jets dart west toward California.

Snapping out of his daydream, Hector looks out at the New Victorville landscape. Reborn from the ashes is a bright metropolis akin to a New York City, pre-destruction, on steroids.

Chino continues his power nap.

Toi reads messages on her retinal display.

Sev watches his father staring out the window.

"All good, old man?" Sev asks.

"Looks like another planet," Hector replies.

"Only one I been on," Sev says.

Toi turns off her retinal display and turns to Sev.

"Guys, I really need to pee."

"For real?" Sev asks.

"My pipes are gonna burst," she begs.

"I could use a piss too, son," Hector replies.

Sev sighs then enters a command into his implant. Yawning, Chino wakes.

"We dare yet?" Chino asks.

"Request for route change authorized," Sev's DC confirms. "Confirming relief point coordinates and lockdown. Confirming SOF tactical coordination with local law enforcement. ETA, eight-point-five-six minutes."

With *show-of-force* weaponry on full display, the dick caravan takes the next exit. Sirens and sonic-disrupter cannons instinctively instruct citizens and commuters to part for Sev's caravan to pass unimpeded.

Inside Vitchenko's DC, Angel watches Vitchenko fiddle with a small electronic device.

"What dat?" Angel asks.

"My *clearcurt*," Vitchenko answers. "Like a mini *clearop.*"

The small device short-circuits, shocking Vitchenko's thumb. Vitchenko sucks his thumb to reduce the sting. Angel laughs.

"Maybe we get you some clear formula and a clear bib, yeah?" Angel jokes.

Defense Club troopers, the Union's civilian law enforcement officers, set up barricades a block away to prevent citizens from venturing too close.

Sev's caravan passes a heavily guarded checkpoint. They roll into the New Victorville *Community Zone*, a heavily guarded, mixed-use gated community spanning nearly a third of the city and caters to high-ranking reps. Sev's caravan parks outside one of the Defense Club's live/work towers in the neighborhood.

"Current threat assessment minimal. EDT, fifteen minutes," Sev's DC confirms.

The DC timer beeps, starting the countdown. Area completely secure, Hector, Sev, and Toi exit Sev's DC. The rest of the security detail exits their DCs, including short, pale-skinned Linguistics Corporal Recard Murphy; muscular, olive-skinned Specialist Raffie Klondike; and lanky, dark-skinned Specialist Chalk Gamby who help form a perimeter.

A trooper leads Sev, Hector, and Toi inside the building and down a short hall, walking past dozens of Union propaganda to a private bathstall.

"Twelve minutes," Sev says. "Don't do anytin' stupid, yeah?"

"Like what?" Hector asks, puzzled.

Sev catches himself.

"My bad, Pop. Just a habit to say."

Hector flashes his son a semiskeptical look.

"Just keep the engine runnin'," Hector replies.

Hector grabs Toi's hand as they head into the bathstall.

"And no fuckin'," Sev yells. "Pretty please!"

The bathstall door locks. Sev leans against the wall between a digital aerial display of the entire New Victorville Bloc. Beside it, a display of citizens suspected of either petty criminal acts or work violations such as unauthorized absences to tardiness. Sev and the trooper hear *faint giggles* from inside the bathstall. They glance at each other; Sev fidgets.

"Nudda stall?" Sev asks.

The mute trooper holds up four fingers.

Using his implant, Sev remotely transmits four thousand socreds to the trooper. Receiving transfer confirmation, the trooper presses his wrist implant. Suddenly, the Bloc map display slides open to reveal a secret bathstall.

"Tanks," Sev says as he adds ten minutes to his DC's countdown timer and enters the bathstall.

The Pinnacle

Sev's caravan pulls into one of the Pinnacle Hotel's premier valet lots designated for high-level guests and dignitaries. The Pinnacle Hotel and Commercial Zone's digital displays boast one of its key marketing draws: accommodating elites from three of the four rival governments on the continent. The lone exception being the Southern Cross Empire.

Hector, Sev, Toi, and Chino exit the DC. Defense Club personnel and hotel drones coordinate the smooth transition of everyone's luggage inside. Exiting the Pinnacle, General Manager Waltrichard McHendy enthusiastically greets his new arrivals.

"Nudda day, Nudda day! Real-time honor," McHendy begins. "Waltrichard McHendy, GM. But please…call me Witty!"

The heavyset, black-skinned manager who might have passed for a charismatic, African dictator a century earlier chuckles as he walks straight to Toi, grabs her now yellow-gloved hand, and gently air-kisses it. Toi blushes.

"Nudda, day, Witty. I'm Toi."

A small hotel drone carrying a smaller case follows close behind McHendy, who salutes Sev. When McHendy stops at Hector, the hotel drone beeps and opens the case. McHendy reaches into the small case and pulls out a right-handed glove emblazoned with the letter *P* encrusted with jewels. He puts on an impression glove and extends his right hand to Hector.

"Fray-mah Contreras, it would be a big, big honor if I could add your prints to my prized VIP collection of extremely special guests," McHendy asks. "I assure you, this glove's completely sanitized."

Hector hesitates, then replies in a playful tone, "Why not?"

Hector shakes McHendy's gloved hand.

McHendy nearly passes out from excitement. He removes the glove and lowers it back into the small case, which secures, labels, and dates the memorabilia for McHendy's private collection. The small hotel drone then scurries off.

"Never taught dis dyin' orphan would one day shake de hand of a true hero," McHendy confesses. "Tanks!"

"Just don't let me catch that shit on eBay," Hector jokes. "Yeah?"

"Pard?" a puzzled McHendy asks.

"A little Old Nation humor," Hector replies.

"Right. Please forgive my overjoy."

Toi interjects, "Very, very nice place, yeah."

Hector points to Sev. "And this is Major Contreras, my... *PIG*"

Sev's puffed chest deflates as McHendy's eyes dart from Sev to Hector and back.

"You must be so proud," McHendy says to Hector.

"He has moments," Sev deadpans. "Call me Major. To avoid confusion, of course."

"Okie-dokie, Major. Now let's get everyone some good air, yes?"

Vitchenko supervises the detail outside while McHendy leads Hector, Sev, Toi, Chino, and Angel inside.

The GM and his very special guests enter a private VIP corridor. McHendy stops everyone, making sure they're all still before using his implant to activate the floor, which glides them down the hall.

"Welcome to De Pinnacle, where our guests get only de best," McHendy cheers.

The floor carries them through a virtual corridor. To their left, digital copies of photos taken across the Old Nation BMF rotate within antique-looking frames from the early nineteenth century. The wall to their right morphs into a one-way window, enabling them to view other guests milling about the main lobby.

Angel scans the main lobby while scratching his short blond hair. Something catches his attention, prompting him to tap Sev on the shoulder and subtly nod him toward the area of interest. Sev turns to the main lobby to see Crayton and Wishbone conversing among a group of men. Using his retinal display, Angel silently relays instructions to the rest of the team outside.

The window display to the left morphs into a commercial ad for the U-Stream while vilifying the Dark Stream, known as the D-Stream, or simply *De D*, a shadow network that bypasses government-controlled firewalls and tracers.

"I can get used to dis," Toi replies.

"We do offer a variety of extended-stay packages," McHendy responds with pride.

"Sure you do, Witty," Hector says.

Two robotic arms carrying champagne glasses lower from the ceiling; Hector and Toi each grab a glass. The arms retreat back into the ceiling, which then transforms into a sunny blue sky with a few random clouds. The floor stops at a dead end. Using his implant again, McHendy remotely triggers a *bing* sound, and the wall in front of them slides open, exposing a secret cave. Everyone enters, and the cave avalanches shut behind them. Inside the dark cave, the floor lights up around them and transforms into a stone platform.

"Elevating," the Pinnacle AI says.

The stone platform lifts them through a hole that opens up above the cave. They then find themselves rising from underground and up the side a cliff beside a gigantic waterfall to their right. Crashing water, birds flying, animals grazing in the distance, and the gentle breeze make it difficult to decipher what's real. As they slowly float upward, Hector and Toi hold hands.

"I got you," Hector comforts Toi.

"I got you," Toi responds with a fixed gaze on Hector.

Sev rolls his eyes.

A group of giraffes graze in the distance.

"Dope lift, yeah?" McHendy asks.

"This… A-free-ca?" Hector asks.

"Very good, Fray-mah," McHendy acknowledges. "The former Republic of Zim-baby-wee to be more precise. Like most governments, dey fell to de Xenos during Man Fall. Currently, de Lagosian Federation remains de last major government on de continent."

"For now, anyway," Sev mumbles.

"For de more curious, guests with *vee-rooms* can enjoy access to premium Union archives. Our resident historian Professor Pillsbury Snowman recently acquired historical files from a deceased citizen whose blood father was an Old Nation reporter during Man Fall. We took de liberty of recreating her stories for mass consumption."

The stone platform stops at a wooden gate to their left at the top of the cliff. The gate opens to a waiting hotel drone holding a tray with two more drinks. Hector and Toi replace their empty glasses for the full ones as they pass the hotel drone.

"I am impressed, Witty," Hector says.

"Dat's what she said," McHendy jokes.

"Bet dat never gets old," Sev sarcastically whispers into his father's ear.

Toi gasps as McHendy leads the group away from the waterfall and through brush. They arrive at a clearing to see a dirt path between two rows of cabins. Lifelike, virtual monkeys scamper and swing in the distance.

"Love it," Toi exclaims. "Love...it!"

"Welcome to our safari suite! Should you wish a change of scenery—or anything else—Henri, your *convirt,* will assist. *Luego!*"

McHendy waves. The group watches as McHendy retreats back into the brush.

"Aloha," Henri greets.

Everyone turns back to see Henri, a suave, dark-skinned Frenchman dressed in posh safari attire. Sev turns back to see the stone platform lower McHendy and the hotel drone down until they vanish.

"*Yo soy* Henri, your con-vair. Anything you want, I provide."

"Good to know, Henri," Toi playfully responds.

Hector, Sev, Chino, and Angel all roll their eyes.

"Should we?" Henri asks with his virtual arm extended.

"Should you insist," Toi replies.

"Should I throw up?" Hector sarcastically asks.

Toi playfully locks arms with Henri as they walk toward the cabins. Hector and Sev follow while Chino and Angel scout the perimeter.

"Cocktails start at eighteen thirty," Henri says.

Digital names appear on each cabin. Toi runs up to her and Hector's cabin labeled CONTRERAS / MADAGASCAR.

Toi opens the door to find their luggage waiting inside.

Angel turns his attention back to the waterfall to see both Vitchenko and Specialist Raffie Klondike riding up the stone platform.

Sev watches Hector and Toi enter their cabin then finds the one with his and Chino's name above it. He walks toward it, when another cabin grabs his attention labeled VROOM.

"Care for a demo, Major?" Henri asks.

Startled, Sev pulls out his sidearm and aims it at Henri's face. "What de—"

"Pardon moi. No intentions of elevating your heart rate," Henri responds. "Perhaps you prefer to access Hah-lee?"

Sev holsters his sidearm.

"I prefer to access your security protocols," Sev responds. "S'il vous plais."

"Of course. Consider it…"

Ignoring Henri, Sev turns and heads to his cabin.

"Rude," Henri mumbles under his breath.

Sev stops but doesn't turn around.

"Say somethin', convirt?" Sev asks.

"Transmitting the access codes, Major."

Smiling, Henri suddenly experiences a series of strange glitches just before vanishing.

Sev turns back in Henri's direction but sees only Chino, Angel, Vitchenko, and Raffie conversing. He shrugs then heads toward his cabin.

Vroom

Thirty minutes later, Toi exits her and Hector's cabin and heads toward the stone platform. As she enters the brush, Spc. Raffie Klondike taps her on the shoulder. Startled, Toi instinctively grabs Raffie's hand and flips him to the ground.

"Easy!" Raffie mumbles. "I'm your protection."

"Seems you need mine."

She helps Raffie up, then flashes Sev, who's laughing at them from the front of his cabin, both middle fingers.

"Not bad," Raffie says.

"Six-point-seven-tree *comrate*," Toi replies.

"Damn. Pretty hi rate for a—"

"Roomie?" Toi interjects.

"Civvy," Raffie finishes.

"Identify," Toi orders.

"Specialist Raffie Klondike, ma'am. Your shadow today."

"Try to keep up, Shadow!"

Toi jogs through the brush with Raffie right behind her. Hector exits his cabin to see Sev spying Raffie chase after Toi as they head toward the stone platform.

"Major."

Sev turns to Hector and replies, "Framer."

"Gonna check out that vee-room while we got some time," Hector says.

"Right behind you," Sev replies.

"I'll be fine," Hector says.

"'Cause I'll be right behind you," Sev counters. "Sir."

"Whatever."

Hector and Sev walk to the vroom. Hector pauses by the door.

RON HORSLEY

"Pop?" Sev asks.

"Just preparing myself for any upgrades."

Hector and Sev enter the pitch-black vroom. The door shuts behind them. Suddenly, they find themselves standing in the middle of a futuristic Times Square that no longer exists.

"What Bloc is dis?" Sev asks with the eyes of a child opening presents.

"New York. I think," Hector answers.

"New York City, circa 2105. It was the largest metro in the former United States of America, commonly referred to now as the Old Nation," Holee, an attractive, scantily clad, holographic female says as she appears behind them. "Another day, Founder. Major. I'm Hah-lee."

The two men turn from startled to enamored in seconds.

"Nudda day, Holee," both men answer simultaneously.

"How can I assist?"

Hector and Sev turn to each other again. They shake their heads.

"Just here to feed the brain, Holee," Hector replies.

"Would you like to stream?" Holee asks.

Hector and Sev burst into laughter.

"Too easy," Sev chuckles.

"Any new Union archives from Man Fall?" Hector asks.

"Accessing Union archives," Holee says.

A list of files appear beside her. Sev eagerly presses one. Hector turns to him.

"Aren't you on duty?" Hector asks.

"Yeah."

Suddenly, Times Square transforms into the front lines of a massive battle that pits the remnants of North American military might against the Lorian invaders.

Hector and Sev are surrounded by explosions and flying bodies when they hear the booming voice of a male narrator.

"Cajon Pass," the narrator begins. "Once a lifeline too many, now our line in the sand!"

The men watch as a Lorian command post gets vaporized by laser-guided missiles created by man with the help of reverse-engi-

98

neered Lorian tech. Miraculously, tens of thousands of human soldiers force the remaining Lorians into retreat. After pausing to assess and confirm victory, exhausted cheers and gunfire scream into the polluted air.

"After six months of carnage, the first of many victories," the narrator says.

"I know that voice," Hector says. "An entertainer, I recall…"

"Sound like a fairytale," Sev jokes.

Suddenly, Hector and Sev appear in the middle of a Pacific Military Command Center somewhere between the Cajon Pass and Victorville.

A virtual Gen. Contreras surveys the battlefield. However, unlike Hector's real father, this digital replica has Gen. Contreras's face placed on top of a younger, muscular body sporting an arm tattoo of the Sin Vegas Union's original insignia.

"Don't recall that," Hector says.

"Pop," Sev says.

Hector spots a suave, ripped Hispanic soldier running up to his father. The soldier has a Philippine flag on his pristine uniform with the last name "CAMPOS" over his left breast.

"Guess that's Uncle Manny," Hector says.

Virtual Manny stops in front of virtual Gen. Contreras.

"Forces confirm a full retreat!"

"They're leaving The Pass?" virtual Gen. Contreras asks.

"They're leaving the West Coast!"

"Where the fuck are they going?"

"Who the fuck cares?" virtual Manny says. "They're gone, sir!"

Loud cheers roar across the desert. However, virtual Gen. Contreras takes the nearest seat to take it all in.

"They're not gone," the virtual general replies. "But DC is. And the Pentagon—NORAD. Manila. London. Nairobi. Buenos Aires. Beijing. Sydney. So what the fuck do we do now?"

"What we always do, sir," virtual Manny answers as he salutes. "Press on!"

All the surrounding soldiers salute the virtual general; he reciprocates.

"What a bunch of bullshit…" Hector snaps. "My mom used to watch shit like this when I was a kid!"

Suddenly, Hector and Sev find themselves inside a virtual recreation of Gen. Contreras's Chinook frozen midair above the McCarran-Reid International tarmac. They watch a virtual rendition of Karla comforting young Hector as he looks out the window. Hector and Sev look out to see Gen. Contreras and the Japanese officer facing each other—frozen in time.

"The blood we spilled fighting each other for land, only to lose the planet," Hector says. "What does that say about us?"

"We only human," Sev replies with a shrug.

Hector chuckles; his smile dissipates.

"I wish you didn't have to live like this," Hector says.

"You gave me a good life, Pop. You gave us all a good life."

"Good?" Hector responds. "We used to roam the planet. Now we trample each other, dependent on machines—and aliens—for survival."

"Been dat way before Man Fall too, yeah?" Sev replies. "Not everyone can hide in Old Summerlin. So we fight."

"Fight for what?" Hector asks. "The right to become cyborgs instead of foodies?"

"The right to survive. For our kids. And grandkids."

"Stop program," Hector commands. "Main menu."

The vroom returns to its default settings as the file menu pops up.

"Maybe you need some rest, yeah," Sev says.

"I'm good," Hector replies, flipping through the list.

"Come on, Pop."

Sev pulls on Hector's arm, so he can't select another file. However, Hector switches to his cybernetic arm. Sev then grabs that arm. The two struggle until Hector accidentally elbows Sev's chest with his enhanced elbow. However, Sev barely moves. Hector turns.

"Why don't you check the perimeter, Major?" Hector says.

"For real?" Sev asks.

"That's an order," Hector answers.

Sev releases his father, salutes, and replies, "Yes, sir."

Sev leaves the room. Hector sighs and turns his attention back to the main menu. He slowly reaches into his pocket and partially pulls out Zerina's chip when Holee reappears. He tucks the chip back into his pocket.

"Pardon, Framer Contreras, but I detect high stress levels."

"I'm fine, Holee. Just a minor family dispute."

"Might I help recall our vrooms offer a variety of ways to help our guests release tension?"

Holee nods behind him. Hector turns to see a spotlight shining on a massage table. He turns back to see Holee smiling at him.

Old School

Toi and Raffie pass through VIP identity scanners as they enter the Pinnacle's Consumer Village, an enormous plaza modeled after an eighteenth-century Eastern European seaside village that consists mostly of digital retail facades with no store interiors. Rather, digital displays function as simulated windows that rotate between faux store interiors, store inventory, virtual store managers, commercials, and propaganda. Thousands of citizens pack the enclosed shopping center.

"Every sector dis crowded, Rocky?" Toi asks.

"Ray-fee," Raffie answers. "We de lucky ones."

Raffie spots a couple of women walk past them. The women, wearing chic visors and yellow Administrative Club skins, smile at him. One of the women is taller and thinner and has much paler skin than the other. Their giggles momentarily distract Raffie.

"Never seen a racha before, Ratty?"

"I see plenty, ma'am. And it's Ray-fee."

Weaving through citizens, Toi and Raffie pass several windows until they reach a display for the store Old School. Toi stops.

"Dis de shop," Toi says.

Suddenly, a digital redhead named Tiara appears in the Old School window display.

"Sis, you look like you got a few socreds to burn," Tiara says to an unresponsive Toi.

"No tanks. Just waitin' for a friend," Toi replies.

Toi and Raffie pass by the first window.

"Tired of boring Club skins?" Tiara asks, again to no avail.

Toi and Raffie pass the second window.

"Tired of fittin' in?" Tiara continues as she laughably tries to squeeze into tight clothing.

Toi and Raffie pass the third window.

"Tired of being seen as just anudda...*roomie?*" Tiara asks, finally grabbing Toi's attention.

Toi stops, turns, and walks up to Tiara.

"Den bitch, it's time to go Old School," Tiara says to Toi. "And let you...be *you!*"

"Hmmm...what you tink, Rat-feet?" Toi says, eyes still on Tiara.

Tiara's eyes, which also function as retinal scanners, blink as they discreetly upload Toi's profile. Smiling, Tiara motions Toi to remotely link her implant to Tiara. Toi complies.

"Nudda day, Ms. Madagascar," Tiara whispers. "Looks like you've been authorized a room credit of two hundred tousand socreds! Please note credits are only valid on property and any remaining auto expire at checkout."

"Toi! Dat you, bitch?" Sabrine playfully yells.

Toi and Raffie turn to see an excited Sabrine runs over and bear-hug Toi. Raffie's retinal scan confirms Sabrine's identity. Toi and Sabrine scream as if it's been a while since they had seen each other in the flesh.

"What a sight for sore *retscans*," Sabrine says.

"Oh, Sah-bee. Too long," Toi replies.

"I miss you—and de space and fresh air of de *Hive-Sec!*"

Sabrine turns to Raffie and smiles. Though trying to maintain professionalism, Raffie grins.

"Sabrine," Toi says. "Dis Ray-fee."

Toi winks at Raffie.

"Call me Sah-bee," Sabrine says.

"Call me whatever de fuck you want," Raffie replies.

Grinning, Toi rolls her eyes.

Sabrine

Toi and Sabrine sit at a table in a replica European seaside café on a long-forgotten French Riviera while Raffie watches nearby. Raffie spies the other tables of citizens chatting away, easily identifying their respective clubs, home sectors, and bodyguards while Toi and Sabrine dine on a plate of small flavored protein cubes.

"Not bad," Sabrine says.

Toi leans closer.

"All real Xeno shit," Toi whispers. "Not dat lab shit!"

Sabrine continues chewing.

"Fuckin' good, yeah," Sabrine replies.

They sip on small—and pricey—glasses of 100 percent pure, unrecycled water, which they augment with small *hydrotabs*.

Their table display shows 3D renderings of each other wearing the clothes they recently purchased at Old School. The display also reveals that the items will be packaged and shipped to their respective homes within a few days.

"Almost a dec now, yeah," Toi says.

"Started on de Strip, now we here!"

"Chroo dat, sis."

Sabrine sips water.

"How are you? For real?" Sabrine asks.

"What you mean?"

"C'mon, Tee," Sabrine replies. "Don't need no retinal scan to see you."

"All good, sis."

Sabrine places her left hand on Toi's right hand from across the table.

"Okay. But we don't age young. A lease—"

Toi pulls back and interjects, "Don't worry about me, yeah?"

"Just sayin'," Sabrine replies. "You come so far. Work so hard. Fought so tough. And friend so many. You deserve security."

Toi's eyes water.

"Tanks," Toi says. "I know you mean good. But we oxy. For real."

"Okay, let's switch streams," Sabrine says. "Ready for de big day?"

"Just happy to get outta Old Summerlin," Toi replies. "And into some new skins."

They giggle when Sabrine's alarm buzzes through her implant. Sabrine sighs.

"Wish we had more time, girl," Sabrine says after reading her retinal display. "Tanks for de rooms. And de skins."

Toi presses a button on her digital table that allows her to pay the seventeen-thousand socred tab with her room credits.

They rise, hug, and exit the café.

"Tanks," Sabrine continues.

"Good to see you real time, yeah?" Toi responds.

They continue to walk. Sabrine tears up, then chuckles. They stop at Sabrine's entry gate.

"Recall dat liddle doll you had?" Sabrine says.

"Madonna," Toi replies.

"Yeah," Sabrine says. "Don't know why it popped in my head. Guess I miss doze days."

Sabrine's implant buzzes again. She hugs Toi. Both are in tears.

"Love you, bitch, yeah," Toi says.

"Love you, bitch," Sabrine replies. "Only a call close."

Raffie watches the two women say their goodbyes when his eyes dance over to a window display that momentarily goes dark between ads. During this moment, Raffie catches Bic's reflection watching them. Raffie turns quickly. However, Bic's nowhere to be seen among the clutter of pedestrians.

"Lay-ta, Ray-fah," Sabrine jokes as she wipes away her tears then waves.

Raffie simply nods with a slight grin and replies, "Nudda day, Sah-bee."

One eye on his surroundings, Raffie forces himself to give Toi just enough time to see Sabrine vanish into the crowd. He hands Toi a small sanipad so she can wipe her face as he gently escorts her back toward their VIP Gate.

The Man

Bare chested and wearing traditional samurai garb, Hector finds himself in a virtual rendering of an ancient Japanese temple. Traditional Japanese music plays faintly in the background, along with the sounds of a calming stream just outside.

Holee enters dressed as a geisha and slowly walks toward him. Her body briefly glitches, though both parties ignore it.

"You like, Hec-san?" Holee asks.

"Me like, Hah-lee-san," Hector replies while nodding.

Taking Hector's left hand, a giggling Holee leads him down a hallway where virtual rice-paper walls project various commercials and pro-Union propaganda. One ad even promotes an upcoming Lottery, the Union-sanctioned fertility draft for reps.

"Lots of tension," Holee says.

"Lots on my mind," Hector replies.

"Fortunately, my programming comes with a wide variety of stress relievers."

Hector turns his head slightly with suspicion.

"We being recorded?" Hector asks.

"Do you wish to be?"

"Fuck no," Hector tries to rise.

Holee calms him back down and replies, "Rest assured, in accordance with both your grandfathered status and penal snitch codes 43920 and 49392, what happens here stays here. Unless you explicitly consent otherwise, I serve at your absolute and confidential pleasure."

"Good to know," Hector says.

Holee brings Hector into a sensual massage room. She disrobes and walks behind him. Her eyes flicker as she undresses Hector and caresses his body.

In reality, a smiling Hector sits in the vroom chair...with an erection.

Back in the virtual temple, Holee leans close to Hector's ear.

"Do I have your attention now, Framer Contreras?" Holee seductively whispers.

Holee helps Hector onto the message table facedown. She rubs his shoulders.

"Fuck yeah," Hector says.

The music stops—and so does Holee—while Hector remains facedown.

"Oxy," Holee says.

Suddenly, restraints lock Hector's legs and arms—including his cybernetic one—to the table. The table then transforms into a chair. He faces a smiling Holee standing across from him.

"What the... Sev? Sev!"

"Wasting good air, Hec," Holee says in a warped voice.

"Not the happy ending I had in mind."

"I gave Holee a coffee break, so we could have a little privacy."

"Angel, if this is one of your pranks," Hector warns.

"This ain't no joke, Framer Contreras. And if I wanted you dead, I could've done it back at the Hive. Yes."

Hector studies Holee's demeanor, as if trying to locate her puppet strings.

"Who the fuck are you?" Hector asks.

"Take a wild guess."

"I'd like to use my second lifeline," Hector quips.

"I disabled the safety settings in the room. No guardian to save you this time. So I'd choose your next two words very carefully."

Hector briefly hesitates. "The Man."

Holee stands up straight and yells, "Damn right! The muthafuckin' Man."

She looks down at Hector as the vroom goes completely dark.

"Hey. Just tell me what the fuck you want."

"What I want…is for you to wake the fuck up."

"I don't understand."

"Tick-fuckin'-tock."

A low growl rumbles through the room and Hector's chest. Suddenly, a giant naked Lorian charges at him.

Armed, Sev bursts into the room with Chino right behind him. There's no monster. Chino inspects the vroom.

"Pop?" Sev calls out.

Toi enters the vroom. "Hec?"

Hector finds himself back in reality, constrained to the vroom chair. The chair releases its restraints, freeing Hector. Hector removes his helmet to see Toi and Sev tending to him. Hector tries to rise on his own, yet still a bit disoriented. Sev and Toi help Hector maintain balance as the vroom chair slides back into a closet. The closet door then shuts.

"All good," Chino says.

"I got you, Pop," Sev says. "You good?"

"Just get me the fuck outta here," Hector replies. "Please."

Sev and Toi walk Hector outside the vroom.

"What happened?" Toi asks.

"The whole floor had some kinda power surge," Sev yells. "Where de fuck's—"

Suddenly, Henri appears outside while Holee appears just inside the vroom doorway.

"Big sorries," Henri says. "Seems we've encountered a minor glitch."

"Glitch?" Sev rhetorically asks.

"Minor?" Toi rhetorically asks.

"Seems?" Hector rhetorically asks.

"Apparently, a malfunction with one of our power generators triggered an emergency reboot to all electrical systems on this level. However, no security breaches have been detected."

Sev's retinal display scans Hector's heart.

"Pop, your heart rate's chroo de roof," Sev says.

"Yeah, no shit," Hector replies.

"What you doin' anyway?" Sev asks.

"Yeah," Toi chimes in.

"Just…recallin' memories," Hector answers. "Next thing I know, Holee turns into a fuckin' Xeno."

"Forgive, Framer Contreras. I don't recall what got into me," Holee says.

"It was almost me!"

"No worries, Framer," Henri interjects. "I will attempt a program reconstruction to render what transpired."

Hector silently gulps and asks, "You can do that?"

Henri's multiple attempts fail.

"Apparently not, unfortunately. All vid files since you arrived were cleansed from the system a few minutes ago," Henri says.

"Cleansed?" Sev asks. "By who?"

"Sorry, Major. I'm unable to indentify," Henri replies.

"Chee, everyone's eyes up," Sev orders.

"Got it, boss!"

"Mad sorries, Framer Contreras," Henri says.

"Don't beat yourself up, Henri," Hector replies. "You tried."

Sev briefly turns to his father before turning to Henri.

"De power generator serves only dis tower?" Sev asks.

"Correct, Major," Henri replies.

Holee vanishes as Specialists Raffie Klondike and Chaulk Gamby arrive and enter the vroom.

Toi turns to Hec.

"Let's get you back to de room," Toi asks.

Hector nods.

"Sir," Raffie cries out as he runs toward them holding something. "Found dis on de floor.

Hector and Sev's eyes widen as Toi grabs Zerina's chip.

"What's dis?" Toi asks.

Sev snatches the chip from Toi and replies, "Dat's mine. Must've dropped it on my sweep earlier. Tanks."

Toi shrugs. She and Hector head back to the room. Henri trails behind until McHendy, nearly out of breath, appears from the brush and shoos him away. Henri quickly vanishes as McHendy walks up to Hector and Toi.

110

"Biggest, biggest sorries, Fray-mah Contreras," McHendy whimpers.

"All good, Witty," Hector replies.

"Another sincere token of our gratitude, everyone in your group will receive two water creds for de trouble."

"Very kind of you—" Hector begins when…

"Four," Toi interjects with a hint of disinterest. "Including de security team."

"Tree," McHendy counters after swift consideration. "Nontransferable."

"One *tran*, two non," Toi counters back after swifter consideration.

Hector and Sev observe the back and forth with piqued interest.

"No fuckin' wit' dis one," McHendy agrees. "Henri and Holee, you wish to reboot?"

"No. We wish to give second chances," Toi replies as she turns to Hector. "Yeah?"

Hector nods, then deadpans, "Sure do."

Likesmart

Soft music plays in the background. Chewing on a taste pill, Toi stands partially naked in her cabin's luxury bathstall with the door open. Staring at her reflection, Toi uses her implant to remotely change her eye color. She hears a series of beeps before a section of a bathstall wall slides out. She browses through a selection of colored lips, nails, and a wig she ordered for the evening. Another small wall section slides open for her to spit her taste pill saliva into. She keeps her mouth open wide as a dental scan shows no signs of infections or cavities.

"Perfecto," Toi says.

"Toi!"

"Yeah?"

Hector appears wearing only a towel. These days, Toi pays more attention to his cybernetic arm than the scars crisscrossing his semi-toned body.

"Where we gonna store all that shit you bought?"

"Don't worry," Toi says. "I recycle de old skins, yeah?"

"One for one?"

"Uh-huh," Toi replies.

"Pinky swear," Hector playfully demands as he holds out his right pinky.

"Fuck," Toi responds while holding up her right pinky.

"For real."

"Okay! Pinky swear."

They briefly lock pinkies to seal the deal.

"Thank you…and please hurry up," Hector says. "Man Fall didn't take this fuckin' long."

The doorbell rings.

THE GREATER UNION

"Dat's for you," Toi bellows in the background. "For tonight!"

Hector turns to the door.

"But I already brought my—"

The bell rings again.

"Get de fuckin' door, yeah?"

"All right! Fuck."

Hector opens the door to find Cpl. Recard Murphy holding a package with the Pinnacle logo on it. His attention momentarily redirects to Vitchenko patrolling the area as Spc. Chaulk Gambino escorts the hotel drone back through the brush to the stone platform.

"We...have...inspected the package and everything appears... to be in...or-der. Sir," Murph says.

Hector's taken aback by Murph's perfectly spoken English considering his age.

"Murphy, right?"

Murph salutes. "Corporal Ree-card Murphy, sir."

"I recall. Not many people left who speak—" Hector says.

"Old Nation's tongue?" Murphy proudly answers, before realizing he cut Hector off. "My bad, sir."

"At ease," Hector replies. "In my day, we spoke plain old English."

"I took Old Nation Studies in de Academy. Tell me, please. Were tings back ago really dat...*clean?*"

"Not everythin', kid."

"Stall's yours, Hec," Toi yells.

"Good talkin' to you, Murph."

"Likesmart, sir," Murph says has he salutes.

Murph turns away as Hector shuts the door.

Inside, Hector walks over to and opens the package. He pulls out formal Defense Club skins consisting of pants, a V-neck shirt, and shoes—similar to twenty-first century sportswear. Attached to the package, a digital note:

WELCOME! XOXOXO

Shaking his head, Hector smiles.

Fresh Meat

Arms locked and wearing matching formal skins, a clean-shaven Hector and stylish Toi exit the cabin to cheers and whistles from Sev and his men. Toi soaks up the adoration.

"All right, all right," Hector replies.

"Ready for prom, yeah?" Sev jokes.

"Ready to eat," Toi says.

"I can eat a fuckin' horse," Hector says.

"Dat why only pills and goo left for us, yeah?" Chino sarcastically asks.

"Touché," Hector concedes.

"Okay, pill pop-pahs and goo drop-pahs. We on de clock," Sev barks.

Cpl. Recard Murphy and Spc. Chaulk Gamby stay behind and patrol the virtual jungle while the others board the stone platform lift and descend the cliffside. Virtual moonlight flickers on the virtual waterfall.

Upon reaching their designated level, the occupants wait for the front door to open. However, a camouflaged rear door opens. Hector, Sev, Toi, and Chino turn and exit through the rear door while Raffie continues down to the main lobby.

Hector, Sev, Toi, and Chino arrive at a reception area where VIPs wait to enter a large ballroom. McHendy waves them over.

"Now *dat* is a pow-ah couple," McHendy says.

"Thanks," Hector replies.

"Too much, Witty," Toi replies.

"And big sorries again for earlier," McHendy says. "Anytin' you need me to assist, hollah."

"Water over the cliff, Witty," Hector responds. "For real."

Smiling, McHendy escorts them past everyone waiting in line and heads straight up to two large, fully armed cyborg troopers. After a quick scan, the troopers grant them access. McHendy motions them all inside but stays behind.

"Catch you inside," McHendy says.

Hector and his group enter an enormous virtual ballroom filled mostly with VIPs from Sector Two. Attendees erupt with applause at Hector's entrance while a brief video montage of Hector's past military and political exploits appear on all the displays.

Stomach growling, Hector nods with gratitude and quickly fist-bumps lucky citizens as he makes his way down the greeting line. Sev and Chino strategically roam the ballroom.

Enamored with the reception, Toi soaks in the breathtaking opulence. Old Nation paintings and antiques adorn the walls. Amusingly, most of the valuable artwork includes preserved pornographic magazines, children's art, and random commercial products. Even the metal chairs and tarp-covered metal tables resemble a former public-school lunchroom.

A robotic DJ plays soft, uneven beats under warm lighting. The formal club skins worn by guests are reminiscent of twenty-first century casual sportswear.

"Amazin', yeah?" Toi rhetorically asks.

"Yeah. Amazin' how fast we forget," Hector mumbles.

"Citizens, let's welcome de man of de hour," the robotic DJ introduces. "De one. De only. Director Brax-ton Filly-bussss-tah!"

To his own entrance music and video, the scrawny twenty-something Section Two Director Braxton Filibuster appears with two scantily clad models—one male and one female—on each arm as the crowd cheers.

Entering the room, McHendy makes a beeline for Dir. Filibuster, rips him away from his escorts, and delivers him to Hector while the escorts follow a few steps behind.

"Fray-mah Contreras, dis our beloved Directah Filibustah," McHendy says.

Hector and Dir. Filibuster fist-bump each other.

"Fray-mah," Dir. Filibuster says.

"Direc-tah," Hec replies. "Nice setup."

"Tanks, bro. Oh, before I forget, Fray-mah Titts sends hellos."

"Blast from the past. What's that shifty bastard up to these days?"

"Livin' de dream. Like you, yeah?"

"Tryin' at least," Hector responds. "Topaz still in Old Rancho?"

"Long time ago. He livin' Tarzana Beach for years now."

Hector leans closer and whispers, "Any trouble with the Kah-Lee lately?"

"Doze fuckers make trouble everywhere," Dir. Filibuster answers then pauses. "Don't worry, bro. Troopers don't play out here. And needa do de *TEDs*."

"So I've seen," Hector says.

Dir. Filibuster turns his attention to Toi.

"And. Who. Dis?" Dir. Filibuster asks as his sticks out his fist.

As Toi sticks out her fist, Dir. Filibuster grabs it, gently unfolds her fingers, and slowly shakes her hand.

"Toi," she answers with a warm smile.

"Sexy outfit...for a sexy roomie."

Toi slowly pulls her hand back.

"Tanks," Toi replies with a lukewarm grin.

Dir. Filibuster turns back to Hector.

"Betta have dis under lease, Fray-mah," Dir. Filibuster says.

Hector's stomach growls again.

"All due respect, Director, if I don't get something in my stomach soon, I'm gonna tear apart the closest piece of meat I can get my hands on," Hector replies.

"Guess I betta keep back, yeah?" Dir. Filibuster says with a smile.

Hector nods and replies, "Another day, Director."

Smiling, Dir. Filibuster nods.

"Nudda day, Fray-mah," Dir. Filibuster replies, then nods at Toi.

Toi flashes Dir. Filibuster a fake smile.

"Happy to make de intro," McHendy says.

Dir. Filibuster and his two escorts leave to mingle with other guests.

A waiter walks by with glasses of filtered water. McHendy takes one. Hector grabs two glasses. He hands one to Toi.

"Seems nice," Hector mumbles as he takes a sip.

Toi takes a sip of her water. McHendy sips from his as well.

"Dis some good shit," Toi says.

"Pure double-filtered water," McHendy replies.

"I'm only good enough for two filters, Witty?" Hector asks.

"Uh…" McHendy stammers.

"I kid," Hector admits with a smile.

McHendy exhales and smiles.

"So unreal peeps used to waste liters of dis shit," Toi says.

"Once upon a time dis shit was free," Hector replies.

"Yes, we know. De good old days," Toi jokes.

Servers coast around with trays of processed insects eagerly snapped up by famished guests. Hector, Toi, and McHendy grab some hors d'oeuvres and wash them down with more double filtered water.

Toi spots a group of roomies chatting in a corner of the room.

"Meet you at de table, yeah?" Toi says, heading over to the group.

"Oh…kaay," Hector replies.

Toi easily ingratiates herself into the group while Sev silently instructs Chino to keep an eye on her.

"Fray-mah, would you mind if I—" McHendy says.

"All good, Witty," Hector replies.

McHendy nods then disappears into the crowd.

Escorted by Sev, Hector grabs a few rat-meat hors d'oeuvres from a roving waiter en route to his table then sits.

"The more shit changes, it's still shit," Hector says.

Sev uses his retinal display to silently check in with his men. Nothing to report from anyone. He looks over at Chino, who silently directs his attention to the door.

Crayton and Wishbone enter the room with female escorts. Crayton spots Hector and Sev.

"Dat's him," Wishbone says.

"Tanks," Crayton sarcastically replies.

"I taught he was bigga, yeah?"

"Told you I never see him in de flesh till now. Only reason we in dis shithole. C'mon before de show starts."

After dropping off their escorts, Crayton and Wishbone head toward Hector's table.

Sev stands in between Hector, Crayton, and Wishbone.

Chino cautiously roams in the background while remotely communicating with the rest of the team.

"Colonel," Sev greets. "Nice surprise."

"Major," Crayton replies. "Fray-mah, a true on-ah!"

"Pop, dis is Col. Crayton Stak and Lt. Wishbone Jonas. 331st Group. Mesquite Outer Garrison."

"Big, big honor, Fray-mah. Sir," Wishbone says.

"Union strong," Hector replies. "Three thirty-first, huh?"

"Tweens," Sev explains.

"I serve de Union chroo boat Unrests," Crayton brags.

"De Second for me," Wishbone gleefully adds.

"I now recall a Stak. P-Bloc Siege," Hector replies. "You look like a pup. Maybe your father?"

Crayton and Wishbone proudly smile.

"Dat's me, sir," Crayton chuckles.

"Col. Cray-Cray help your fah-dah pacify de entire *Zona-Sec*!" Wishbone proudly trumpets.

"Stak," Hector replies. "Yeah, okay. So you're the dickhead sergeant who got half his men killed for nothin'?"

Crayton and Wishbone's smiles evaporate.

Sev turns to Hector and says, "Wait, what? Why I'm hearin' dis now?"

Hector turns to Sev and replies, "Son, when you get to be my age, some things slip through the cracks."

"You only in your sixties, Pop," Sev counters.

"Some go faster than others."

Crayton's eyes turn red. Clenching his fist, he looks around at the oblivious gathering. Wishbone covertly waves his superior back to reality with a brush of his hand like a magic wand; Clayton's fist unclenches.

"De P-Bloc Siege is a must study," Sev replies. "It's on de fuckin' exam!"

"Did I write the fuckin' exam?" Hector counters.

Crayton and Wishbone's eyes dart from Hector to Sev during the back and forth.

"You didn't recall de name Stak?"

"I had a lot on my plate in LA, okay?" Hector snaps back. "And the data networks back then weren't exactly the most reliable."

"Hey," Crayton interjects. "I saved de fuckin' Bloc!"

"Thanks to my father's men who got there in time," Hector counters. "Or you'd be one of the fallen."

"So we boat have your poppa to tank," Crayton says.

"I got no problemo wit' dat," Hector replies. "You?"

Tension thickens around them, though Hector could care less.

"Colonel, my pop needs a recharge," Sev interjects. "Elders, yeah?"

"Yeah," Hector adds. "Sometimes when I don't eat, I get a little cray-cray."

Crayton chuckles.

"Nudda day, Fray-mah," Crayton says.

"Another day, Colonel," Hector replies, then turns to Wishbone and says, "And whoever the fuck you are."

After a brief stare down, Crayton pulls Wishbone back to their table.

"Fray-mah," Wishbone replies. "May-jah."

An oblivious Toi arrives at the table. She sits and turns to Hector.

"Makin' new friends, yeah," Toi says.

"Something like that," Hector deadpans.

Crayton and Wishbone sit with their dates. Using his implant, Wishbone activates his aural enhancer to eavesdrop on Hector's table. However, a high-pitched sound nearly blows his eardrum out, and he immediately shuts it off. Wishbone silently grimaces.

"Dumbass," Crayton says.

A grinning Crayton looks over at Sev grinning back at him, when the background music stops and the lights dim. A screen flashing a series of propaganda images appears. It stops on the Sin Vegas Union government logo. Everyone in the room gives the Union salute.

"S-V-U! S-V-U! S-V-U! S-V-U," attendees chant while tapping their hearts.

"Citizens, show gratitude to our sixth Union leader," the robotic DJ yells over the PA. "Our highest rep, forged from the ashes of mankind's hubris with the sole purpose of restoring humanity to greatness. Please welcome our beloved president and chief executive officer, Dock-tah Terrence Geeeeee!"

A hologram appears of Terry, an older gentlemen propped up with the help of two cybernetic exo-legs preventing his confinement to a wheelchair. Terry places his right hand over his heart as multiple Sin Vegas Union flags wave behind him; light reflects off the gold wedding band on his ring finger.

"P-Doc! P-Doc! P-Doc," citizens chant.

"Good evening, fellow citizens. It is with great humility that I address you tonight. As we venture into this new *millen* with excitement and hope, we must never forget those whose courage, vision, and sacrifices helped create one of the largest, most advanced, and civilized societies left on the entire planet. For them, we will make this inaugural Framers Day celebration an event generations will recall for centuries. A tribute befitting of those who worked tirelessly to form this great Union. And we all know that those who work hard?" Terry pauses.

"Shall always be rewarded," everyone shouts in unison.

Terry's hologram bursts into tiny squares that reassemble into a giant LED screen. A promotional and patriotic video for the upcoming Framers Day celebrations plays to loud music:

The video glorifies not only the bloody battles against the Xenos, but also the ensuing atrocities. It also touches on the evolution of the Sin Vegas Union government from the Las Vegas Worker's Union prior to man's fall into one of the only five advanced societies occupying Old Nation territory.

More clips introduce a special group known as the Framers Union: fifteen men and five women that include Hector, Gen. Contreras, Professor Topaz Titts, Dr. Liseli Stormblood, and Maximilian Harper Coltraine. The clip is akin to watching action movie clips for each member.

"Dear citizens, you have worked faithfully to preserve a society to be envied," Terry's voice-over continues. "And as you show your appreciation to Framers past and present, the Union shall continue to show its appreciation for your unwavering loyalty and dedication to a common cause. Recall, everyone's contribution ensures the survival of our species."

The displays show a map identifying the five sectors that make up the Sin Vegas Union:

1. GREATER SIN VEGAS (SIN-SEC/HIVE-SEC)
2. DEATH VALLEY (D-SEC)
3. ARIZONA (ZONA-SEC)
4. SOCAL (SO-SEC)
5. NORCAL (NO-SEC)

The video concludes with the eruption of applause. The lights come on as guests take their seats. Waiters resume serving an assortment of plant-based foods and desserts that look more like frail works of art than sustenance.

"'Bout fuckin' time," Hector says.

"Damn right," Toi adds.

Hector turns to Sev.

Suddenly, a giant hologram of Jaxine appears.

"Not so hungry now," Toi mumbles.

"Another day, citizens," Jaxine begins. "Although I'm unable to physically join your sector festivities, be sure that the Hive remains vigilant against those that would do us harm from without and within. And as thanks for the sacrifices you continue to make for the prosperity of our great Union, your directors have sponsored a special treat to show their appreciation for your service. Those who work shall always be rewarded. Bon appétit!"

Jaxine's hologram disappears.

Waiters enter the ballroom carrying trays of steak pellets, which they serve to everyone. One waiter approaches Hector's table.

"*Real steak?*" the waiter asks.

"You shittin' me," Hector replies, practically drooling over the pellets.

"Sir, I assure you this is the real deal. And for the record, we only serve Xeno feces—not human."

The waiter places the real steak pellet in front of him.

Toi turns to Hector and smiles.

"Looks like someone hit de crackpot," Toi says.

"Jackpot," Hector corrects.

"Crackpot better, yeah," Sev retorts with a wink to Toi.

Smiling, Toi winks back.

Another waiter places a steak pellet in front of Toi, followed by other waiters who offer Sev and Chino a sample.

Sev sniffs his steak pellet and replies, "Wow!"

Chino takes a whiff as well and adds, "Dis smell bedda den rat!"

"And tastes better," Hector responds while chewing.

McHendy walks by Hector's table.

"All good?" McHendy asks.

"All fuckin' good, Witty," Hector replies. "Where'd you get this?"

"Genetic descendants of cows dat survived Man Fall—and de chaos after. Deez very hard to get. So if you take, you must finish under penalty of law!"

"Well, you know I ain't fuckin' goin' to jail tonight," Hector replies.

"Enjoy," McHendy says as he takes off again.

"If you insist," Toi replies with a stuffed mouth.

"Membership def de privilege," Chino says.

"For real," Sev replies as he chomps down on his steak pellet.

Hector calls over a waiter.

"Sir?" the waiter asks.

"Seems four of our guests caught a bug."

"Oh dear."

"Could you send four of your entrées up to the jungle suite, pretty please?" Hector requests. "The Major here will transmit your tip upon arrival."

"Of course, Framer," the waiter replies.

"And don't forget dessert," Hector adds.

The waiter nods, waits for Sev to send him the names, then takes off.

"Tanks, Pop," Sev sarcastically says.

"I got you, son," Hector replies.

Meanwhile, a cybernetic waitress serves Crayton, Wishbone, and their dates then walks away. She spies on Hector's table while heading toward the kitchen. Her retinal scans record them when she accidentally bumps into McHendy.

"Watch where de fuck you goin'," McHendy hisses.

"Big sorry, sir," the cybernetic waitress says.

McHendy orders a security drone over to them. The security drone scans the cybernetic waitress. After momentary static interference, a green light declares a negative scan for malfunction or infection.

"Back to work," McHendy responds. "Or I'll ship your rusty ass to Needles!"

"Yes, sir," the cybernetic waitress complies as she nods and scurries off.

McHendy sighs then mumbles, "Good help so hard to fine deez days."

FRAMERS DAY

Extra Crispy

Lying naked and sweaty in bed, Hector and Toi breathe deeply as they look up at the twinkling stars.

"I'm happy we came," Hector says as he gets up.

"We can cum again, yeah," Toi jokingly replies as she pulls him back in bed.

"I meant from Ol' Summerlin."

"Dat too," Toi replies. "Wish we could stay."

"Yeah," Hector responds. "Sorry if I've been a dick."

"No worries," Toi replies, reaching for his crotch. "Recalls can be hard too."

Hector chuckles and turns to her. The sun rises above them and digital versions of birds long extinct sing as they dart across the ceiling.

"Another day," Henri's preset wake-up call annoyingly repeats.

"Sleep," Hector orders the virtual wake-up call.

Hector gets back up and says, "Gotta drop a few bombs."

Hector turns toward the luxury bathstall; Toi blurts out, "I never wanna replace Zerina. I just…"

Hector turns back to her and responds, "Let's get through today. Tomorrow we real talk over breakfast. Yeah?"

Toi cracks a smile.

"Okie-dokie," Toi replies.

Hector enters the luxury bathstall. A second later, the doorbell rings.

"Tell Sev I want my bacon extra crispy," Hector yells.

Toi gets out of bed, slips on her robe, and walks over to the door. She begins to activate the door's display. However, she changes her mind and simply opens the door to see a giddy Sev holding two glasses of a thick, red concoction.

"Happy Framers Day," Sev says, handing her one of the glasses.

"Happy Framers Day," Toi replies. "Dessert so early?"

"Try it."

Toi downs some of the liquid; her eyes light up as she says, "Wow!"

"Cranberry sauce," Sev replies with an affirming nod.

"Cranberry?"

"Today we call it Framers Day," Sec responds. "But de Old Nation called it Tanksgivin'."

"Tanksgivin'?" Toi sarcastically asks. "Like tanks for givin' us dis shithole planet?"

Sev grabs Toi's glass then sets both glasses down on the nearby table. "Hungry?"

"For real," Toi replies. "Of course, he wants his shit extra crispy."

"I'll give him extra crispy," Sev jokes as he pretends to draw his gun then reluctantly places the order. "And what you want?"

"Same ting de last six years," Toi replies.

Sev nods and says, "You know, Pop went chroo nine roomies."

"I know."

"I mean de man…he was never satisfied—"

"T-M-I, yeah?"

"Satisfied wit' his heart," Sev interjects with a sigh. "Pop may not tell me everytin'. But I know he loves you. He just actin'…stoo-pid?"

Toi's eyes water as she chuckles.

"Stub-bun," Toi says. "But same ting."

"Hey, I interview many citizens. So I know you for real."

"Tanks. You too."

Sev and Toi hug each other when they hear a series of gentle beeps coming from Sev's implant.

"Breakfast gettin' cold, old man," Sev yells toward the luxury bathstall.

"In a min!" Hector yells from the bathstall.

Toi dries her eyes.

"See you outside," Sev says.

As Sev turns, Toi asks, "Coltraine for real too?"

Sev turns back to Toi and laments, "One time ago."

Turning back again, Sev leaves to check on his men who rotate between eating breakfast and patrolling.

Two hours later in the Pinnacle's valet lot, Angel directs the rest of the team to finish prepping Sev's military caravan for departure.

Chino helps Toi into Sev's DC, then enters behind her.

Sev stands guard beside Hector who fist-bumps McHendy.

"Another fuckin' day, Witty," Hector says.

"Nudda fuckin' day, Fray-mah," McHendy replies. "For real, you truly inspire!"

"Call me Hec."

McHendy's eyes widen.

"Please revisit, Hec."

"Long as you're buyin'," Hector says with a devilish grin.

McHendy slightly grins without clear confirmation.

"Major," McHendy says with a nod.

"Witty," Sev responds with a nod.

Sev helps Hector into the DC then hops in beside Chino and shuts the door. He gives the order to roll out. Chino taps Sev on the shoulder while looking outside.

Sev spots Crayton and Wishbone exit the Pinnacle and watch the caravan depart. He gives Crayton a half-hearted salute as his DC passes them on the way out. Crayton and Wishbone reciprocate the insincere gesture.

McHendy activates his comchat.

"Dare gone. Show? No show for me. I got enuff shit to deal wit' here. No need to go for a show," McHendy says as he reenters the hotel. "Yeah, yeah. Union strong."

Thousands of citizens cheer as Sev's military caravan departs from the Pinnacle.

Clearwall

The DCs rumble nearly a dozen blocks then into the *Contreras Landing Arena*. Hector looks up to see his name flashing above, then turns to Sev who nods and smiles.

"Surprise," Toi says.

"We callin' it *De General's House*," Chino adds.

"Tink G-Pop would like?" Sev asks.

"He'd definitely be impressed," Hector replies.

"Fuckin' oxy, yeah," Toi says.

Hector looks out at the endless sea of citizens holding signs and cheering as the caravan passes.

Standing in front of the enormous facility, a giant hologram of Gen. Contreras, wearing his inaugural Union military skins, greets the crowd.

Hector looks up; his father's hologram smiles down on him. The image briefly triggers *a childhood memory of a smiling Gen. Contreras, wearing his United States military uniform, looking down at young Hector.*

"I need a drink," Hector says.

Sev hands Hector a glass of filtered water and smiles.

Hector smirks at his son then forces a sip.

Toi spots a female citizen holding a sign:

FRAMER CONTRERAS, (RE)LEASE ME!!

Rolling her eyes, she huffs. Chino holds a cup of filtered water out in front of her.

"Sometin' stronger, yeah," Toi replies.

Hector's eyes widen as they approach the humongous stadium. Media drones hover around them. Tens of thousands wait in line for entry.

Sev spots a few dozen *vpods* for dedicated citizens without stadium access codes to experience everything inside via virtual reality.

"Hottest codes in de Sec," Chino adds.

"Reminds me of the Big Game when I was a kid," Hector says.

"Dey had Pow-ah-ball den?" Chino asks.

Hector chuckles while shaking his head.

"Different sport," Sev replies.

"Our Powerball was a lottery for credits," Hector adds.

"To breed?" Chino innocently asks.

Hector gently nods and replies, "You could say that. Winners got hundreds of millions of socreds."

"You lucky to get half a woman's egg for dat," Chino counters.

Hector, Sev, and Toi laugh as Sev's military caravan pulls into their designated parking area. Everyone exits. Toi looks around in awe.

"How many dis fit?" Toi asks.

"Two hundred fiddy-five tousand," Chino replies.

"Fuck me," Toi says.

"Only if you play your cards right," Hector jokes.

"Dat Old Nation talk bedder mean *yes*," Toi replies.

Entering through a VIP gate, the group walks unimpeded past adoring citizens and into a private lift. One of the walls morphs into a display that shows the arena—as if it were open air. As they rise, they see an electrified crowd pouring into the stadium.

Toi points to the bigview, an enormous digital display above the arena.

The bigview shows video clips of Union propaganda featuring Hector and Gen. Contreras while a VJ plays fast electrobeats to pulsating lights.

The lift stops and opens at luxury level two. The occupants disembark. Security drones patrol the level. Service drones escort them through the busy corridor and stop at the Framers suite, a luxurious room with a room occupancy of a hundred people. Hector and his entourage enter. Although not as opulent as their dinner party, the suite looks like the deck of a yacht looking out at a sea of people. Actual digital images of various Framers, including Hector, throughout the Union's relatively brief history, rotate around digital walls.

There also autographed memorabilia from major events, including Powerball, on display. Floors are cleaned almost immediately upon detection of spills. Upon Hector's entry, guests applaud for a few moments before continuing their own conversations.

"Ho-lee shit," Hector says.

Toi elbows him.

"Pop," Sev admonishes.

"Sorry," Hector replies. "Old Nation habits die hard."

Hector turns to see a magnificent view of the arena's crowd. He walks closer, then stops at the clearop, a large wall of nearly impenetrable, thin, plastic-like material overlooking the arena. This state-of-the-art, transparent material allows guests to see and hear the experience without direct exposure to the elements...or projectiles.

Human and robotic wait staff serve artificially flavored SinWater cocktails along with cooked vermin, insects, and genetically modified hors d'oeuvres.

Hector makes the rounds, slowly succumbing to the adoration thrown his way. The same feelings he imagines his parents experienced when Gen. Contreras became one of the Union's original Framers.

Sev brings Hector back over to the clearop. Hector looks out at the bigview that projects an old family portrait of himself as a child sitting on Karla's lap. His father, dressed in his former United States Army uniform, stands behind them with his hand on Karla's shoulder.

Another iteration of this family portrait appears. However, this one consists of a young Sev sitting on his mother Zerina's lap while Hector stands beside them.

Hector instinctively turns to Toi, as if seeking her approval. Toi smiles and nods as a waitress approaches. Hector smells something familiar. He turns to see the waitress holding a tray of fruity drinks.

"Orange or grapefruit?" the waitress asks.

"Both please," Hector replies as he takes a glass of each.

"Shift change comin'," Sev says. "You all good?"

"Oh yeah," Hector replies.

"So fuckin' good," Toi says.

Sev grabs Chino, and they exit the Framers Suite. They see Cpl. Murphy and Spc. Gamby a few yards down the hallway walking toward them and wait.

"Lifetime contracts?" Gamby says in disbelief.

"For real, bro. And no options," Murphy replies.

"No wonder de Old Nation go down," Gamby says. "You never catch me in no lease. Forget about uh…what you call it?"

"Mare-edge," Murphy replies.

"Yeah. Forget dat mare-edge bullshit," Gamby replies. "And what de fuck marriage mean anyway?"

"Old Nation speak for suicide, yeah?" Murphy jokes.

They stop at Sev and Chino by the Framers Suite door.

"How's de Lounge?" Sev orders.

"Radder have some more dem cow steaks from last night, boss," Murph replies.

Gamby peeks inside the suite.

"Maybe dey got some here," Gamby adds.

"Sorry, boys. No takeout dis time," Sev says. "You see anytin' strange, I don't care. You call, yeah?"

"Yeah, boss," Murphy and Gamby simultaneously reply.

"And no SinWater," Chino adds. "Murph!"

"Why me?" Murph asks.

"Cause dey know I hate dat shit," Gamby replies.

"You missin' out, bro," Murphy says.

"Gotta recharge," Sev says. "Eyes open!"

Murph and Gamby nod and enter the Framers suite. Sev and Chino walk down the hall.

"Ray-fee," Sev calls over his comchat.

"All good, boss," Spc. Raffie Klondike replies via comchat. "But I really gotta piss."

"Hold for five, Ray-fee," Vitchenko confirms.

"Compren-day, Sarge," Raffie replies.

Cpl. Murphy and Spc. Gamby monitor Hector and Toi, respectively. Toi places her empty glass on a roving waiter's tray and notices Hector with two more glasses. She snatches his grapefruit juice and finishes it in two gulps.

Hector's taken aback as Toi burps.

"Grapefruit better," Toi says.

"Tink?" Hector sarcastically replies.

Toi glares at Hector, who slowly drinks his orange juice in a stalling tactic. They both look around to see that the fruit juices are a hit with everyone. Guests marvel at the taste. Hector finishes his juice when Dir. Braxton Filibuster and his scantily clad models approach him.

"Fray-mah," Dir. Filibuster says. "Bin-a-min since you had real froot, yeah?"

"Oh, yeah-wait. Did you say... *real?*"

"Uh-huh."

"Real fuckin' oranges?" Hector asks in disbelief.

"And grapefruit?" Toi chimes in.

Dir. Filibuster gleefully nods; Hector prepares to fist-bump him.

"Tanks to our first trade agreement with de SoCrows," Dir. Filibuster replies as he extends his first to meet Hector's.

However, Hector quickly retracts his fist and counters, "Those racist assholes? They must be really fuckin' desperate!"

Dir. Filibuster leans in to one of Hector's ears.

"Who ain't deez days?" Dir. Filibuster whispers.

The music stops. Everyone turns their attention toward Hector.

Toi latches on to Hector's organic arm.

Dir. Filibuster leans back between his dates and smiles.

"Fray-mah! Fray-mah! Fray-mah," everyone cheers.

Everyone gives Hector the Union salute, then applauds.

"Nudda day, Fray-mah. Roomie," Dir. Filibuster says.

"Another day, Director," Hector replies. "Toi."

"Director," Toi replies.

Dir. Filibuster exits the room with his model escorts in tow.

Hector looks at the clearop. He watches the tail end of an exhibition Powerball match unfolding on the court below between P-Bloc from Zona-Sec versus NV-Bloc from D-Sec, the home team. Following NV-Bloc's friendly victory, there's a mock banishment of the losing team captain through the demarcation line to the delight of adoring fans. Soon after, horns blare throughout the stadium.

"Citizens, lend your eyes and ears," the announcer screams. "Streaming all sectors. Live from de Hive. De one. De only. Our beloved—and fearless—president and CEO, Dr. Terrence Geeeeeeeee!"

Fireworks and applause across the Union are livestreamed with Terry's face on every functioning digital platform.

"Another day, citizens," Terry begins. "Tonight, we celebrate a special group of reps. Reps that pulled us from the brink of extinction."

Again, the crowd roars.

"Tonight, please show mad respect for our great Fra—"

Without warning, the U-Stream feed cuts out.

"Tech diff?" Toi smirks.

Hector looks out to see the entire stadium illuminated with emergency lighting.

Simultaneously, citizens celebrate throughout the arena. In another VIP section, Sabrine and her co-tens Keno and Danori Rikardsen order shots of SinWater. They toast.

"I taught de captain can't come back," Sabrine says.

"Dey can if dey survive de No Man's Land for six mons," Keno replies. "But so far no one comes back."

"Tanks again for dis, Sah-bee," Danori says. "Best night so far!"

"And will only get bedder!" Keno adds. "Tanks!"

"Tank me later, yeah," Sabrine replies.

The three touch glasses and down their shots.

In the Framers Lounge, Hector spots something blinking in the distance. The blinking grows larger until Hector realizes that they're military aerial drones—firing at each other.

The aerial firefight moves closer toward the stadium. Faint warning alarms around the Bloc grow increasingly louder.

"Dis for real?" Toi calls out.

Hector pulls her down to the floor.

Hacked, three of the four robotic security drones go rogue and open fire on select guards in the suite while purposefully avoiding any unarmed citizens. However, the other two robotic security drone open fire on everyone and everything with reckless abandon.

Their comchats not working, Cpl. Murphy and Spc. Gamby engage the second pair of robots in the ensuing firefight, and the pair of combatants riddle each other with laser bullets and collectively drop to the ground; blood drains from both Cpl. Murphy and Spc. Gamby.

One of the robots uses infrared scanners to visualize a heavy firefight outside the Framers Suite. It then provides cover for the second robot heading for Hector, who shields Toi on the ground.

"Sev?" Hector orders Toi.

Toi replies, "No connect."

Hector spots Spc. Gamby fatally bleeding out beside him. He grabs Spc. Gamby's gun and aims at the robot providing cover fire when the second robot snatches the gun away and destroys it.

"Not ag—" Hector says.

The second robot delivers an intentionally gentle punch to Hector's face, knocking him out with minimal damage. It catches a falling Hector and carries Hector toward one of the solid walls on the other end of the suite where the third robot has been using its dragon, a high-powered laser torch that melts metal into goo then cools almost as quickly. While other hacked robots from neighboring suites herd more unarmed citizens safely into the Framers Suite, the second robot carrying Hector prepares to enter the dragon's hole upon completion.

Toi lifts her head to peek at the action when she notices Hector's no longer with her.

"Hec?" Toi asks. "Hec!"

Toi spots the second robot carrying an unconscious Hector waiting for its partner to finish the dragon's hole. Psyching herself up, she rises, clenches her fists, and charges toward Hector.

The first robot turns to intercept Toi when it's hit by a few laser bullets fired by another guard. Damaged, the first robot falls, but manages to hit the guard who shot it. However, as that guard dies, he involuntarily fires a single laser bullet that hits Toi in the gut.

Clutching her gaping wound, Toi collapses. She catches a glimpse of the second robot carrying Hector through the dragon's hole then passes out.

Not So Suite

Sev and Chino stop a few yards from the Executive Lounge entrance. Inside, high ranking citizens and their guests enjoy food and drinks while enjoying the arena performances. Angel and Vitchenko exit the Executive Lounge and head toward them. They meet up just outside the entrance.

"Boss, Cray-Cray and Wishbone jumped de Bloc," Angel says.

"When?" Sev asks.

"Tirteen hundred," Vitchenko answers. "Soon as dey checked out."

"Dey goin' back to Hive-Sec?" Chino asks.

"Don't know," Angel replies.

Sev turns to Chino.

"Lawson?"

Chino activates his retinal display.

"San-jo-zee," Chino answers. "Dey party in dat new stadium up dare."

"Why Cray-Cray come all de way here for one night?" Sev asks.

"Maybe to meet Pop?" Vitchenko asks.

"Yo," Chino says. "Just lost my fuckin' stream!"

The others check their network connections. After a few moments, they recheck.

Vitchenko turns back to the Executive Lounge. Everyone there seems to be having the same connection issues.

"Pop-" Sev begins when...

Outside, Raffie takes an unscheduled piss behind on of the DCs. Dick in hand, he looks up at the sky. His eyes widen just as drone missiles slam into his parked convoy.

Back inside, explosions rock the arena's foundation. Alarms blare. Chaos ensues. Suddenly, the Executive Lounge's metal doors shut, locking in its occupants; gunfire and screams pierce through the metal doors.

"Murph! Gamby!" Sev screams into his comchat.

Sev and his men draw weapons and sprint down the corridor when another explosion jars them again. People pour into the corridors as hacked *SDs*, or security drones, attack anyone with a weapon.

"Dey been hacked," Vitchenko shouts as he blasts one of the drones into scrap metal.

Sev and his men fire on the remaining SDs. Vitchenko gets hit in the arm with a laser bullet, though he appears to feel no pain. A couple of the SDs left standing nearly overpower them when there's another explosion behind them.

A handful of surviving cybernetic soldiers blast through the Executive Lounge doors and join Sev and his men in the fight. Together they help take out the two SDs before they can do any further damage. Sev raises his hand.

"Who de ranking officer?" Sev yells.

A heavyset, dark-skinned soldier in his late thirties covered in full tactical gear and a cybernetic eye steps forward and salutes with one of his electronically enhanced arms.

"Sgt. Babcock Swayzee, sir!"

Swayzee and the other cyber soldiers scan and confirm Sev as their new commanding officer.

"Fray-mah Suite," Sev orders as he charges down the hall.

Swayzee turns to his men.

"You heard de Major," Swayzee replies. "Union strong!"

Sev and his group reach the hall outside the Framers Suite when they're greeted with a hail of laserfire by two more hacked SDs guarding the door. Sev orders a return volley of firepower back at the heavily armored battle drones.

The SDs close in on Sev and the remaining men when the Framers Suite doors open. The SDs turn their attention to the doors. The Framers Suite SDs exit and immediately open fire on their hacked counterparts, destroying them. When the dust settles, the

Framers Suite SDs stand down, granting Sev and his men safe passage inside.

Sev runs inside the Framers Suite. Dead bodies carpet the floor, including Murph and Gamby.

Chino, Angel, Vitchenko, and Swayzee enter right behind Sev.

"Angel! Chenk," Sev says, pointing to Murph and Gamby.

Angel and Vitchenko rush over to their fallen comrades.

"Murph," Angel says, running over to his fallen friend.

"Gamby," Vitchenko says, checking the soldier's vitals.

"Pop! Toi," Sev yells.

"Boss!" Chino yells.

Sev turns to see Chino pointing to a group of frightened bystanders cowering in a corner. Sev and Chino rush toward the adjacent room as more friendly SDs walk past them and form a protective barrier in the hallway and by the clearop, which has partially deteriorated from bombardment. Sev locates the dragon's hole. He discovers a deep shaft leading down into darkness. Screams echo through the shaft when all lights and displays turn back on. Sev punches another small hole into the wall.

"Hec," Toi faintly calls out.

Sev turns to see a bloody Toi. He rushes over to her, pulls out his small tube of Nanorem, and tends to her stomach wound.

"Toi?" Sev says.

"Dey took him."

"I know. You gonna be fine."

"I... I try..."

Toi's eyes close. Sev gently taps her face for a reaction, to no avail.

Angel rushes over to them.

"Medics on de way," Angel says.

"Toi? Toi?" Sev asks.

A series of minor explosions take place outside the suites. People scream. Swayzee calms everyone down. Sev silently instructs his men to aim at the door.

Chino, Vitchenko, and Swayzee slowly move to the door and listen. Nothing but silence on the other side. Chino signals Swayzee to open the door on a count of three, so Vitchenko and the other can shoot whatever's outside.

One... Two... Three!

Swayzee opens the door. Vitchenko jumps out to find that their mechanical saviors have destroyed themselves. Smoke fills the halls.

The SDs by the clearop also self-destruct, releasing smoke.

"Angel. Chenk. Find Ray-fee," Chino orders.

Angel and Vitchenko sprint down the hall when, as they head out, Terry appears on every working display, including the damaged bigview outside.

"Citizens, remain calm. Order has been restored. Help is on the way," Terry repeatedly reassures the people as the video loop echoes through the stadium.

Clenching a metal fist, Sev fixates on a nearby monitor as his eyes turn bloodshot.

Meh-jah

Ree sits inside a *hubble*, the Lorian's bubble-shaped equivalent of a vroom. Inside, she combs through centuries of secretly recorded atrocities her species has inflicted upon humans. She focuses on short video clips that float around her as a three-dimensional collage. Among them, are…

A naked, drugged and pregnant young female—among dozens of captive women of all races confined to a gestation recliner as she gives birth. Wearing a strange helmet surgically affixed to her bald scalp, she ignores her newborn as metallic limbs from the recliner gently lower the baby onto a conveyor belt between her bloody legs and cut the woman's umbilical cord. The conveyor belt spirits her baby away from the mother. Though catatonic, the woman sheds a tear.

Another clip shows a group of Lorians toying with a defenseless twelfth-century European couple. After brutally beating them, they rip both humans apart by their limbs and consume their raw flesh.

A third clip among the group shows a Japanese family wearing Lorian halos plugged into each member's heads used to domesticate their human pets. The family's alien master leads them through a Lorian metropolis neighborhood where they stroll past other Lorians and other domesticated humans.

Ree rearranges the clips in various sequences when flashing lights followed by a series of pulsing beats echo around her, signaling an incoming transmission. She instructs the hubble to accept.

The hubble transforms into a virtual replica of the caller's location. Skulls and vertebrae from various species rest on shelves among other intergalactic trophies. A holographic rendering of Lorian High

Commander Mjar appears in the foreground as he playfully flays and consumes a naked and squealing teen male human.

"Daughter," Mjar begins. "I must recharge while we converse."

"Father, I understand your motive."

"You seek transport from that filthy meat rock?"

"I called to bargain," Ree replies.

"Your humor is welcome."

"This matter is important."

Mjar finishes his meal, burps, then replies, "Continue."

"Poachers increasingly violate the demarcation."

"Terrans are popular—and delicious. A prized commodity!"

"A commodity that risks extinction."

"We can breed more."

"Not enough to satisfy our growing consumption."

"Perhaps you should plead with your Terrans," Mjar growls. "Because of them our people have so few alternatives there."

"Father, you know Terrans are sent—"

"Daughter, I know hunger. And I know pain."

"As do I," Ree counters. "And the Terrans."

"We saved the Terrans—yet they continue to consume."

"We are more common than you care to admit," Ree replies.

Frustrated, Mjar summons over a container occupied by a female human captive. He yanks her from the container, and rips and consumes her as she squeals. The unfortunate woman's blood squirts from Mjar's mouth. Ree redirects her optics while her father sucks the human flesh from its bone.

"You are persistent...and my offspring. I will petition for increased enforcement and higher penalties. In exchange, there will be a moratorium on new preserves," Mjar says. "Daughter, you accept this bargain?"

"Father, I must accept," Ree answers.

"Terrans beyond the demarcation remain fair game."

"Understood," Ree agrees.

"Converse with your mother. She misses her firstborn. For Loria!"

"Father, I will. For Loria!"

"End transmission."

Ree's virtual environment morphs back to its previous state. She finds herself staring at an image of another helpless, pregnant young woman confined to the gestation recliner while a helmet covers her head.

The Man Cave

Deep within the bowels of the Hive, Jaxine and Terry exit a lift and walk down a bustling corridor. PGs Peters and Tom-Tom shadow Jaxine while both PGs Kindle Wilis, a muscular female cyborg, and her robotic partner DAF-47, shadow Terry.

"Two hundred miles...to fuckin' nowhere," Terry snaps.

"We scanned every inch of those tunnels," Jaxine replies.

"And?" Terry asks.

"Bloody fuckers are good," Jaxine answers. "Hate to admit."

They arrive at the door of the *Presidential Man Cave*, the Hive's war room. The four PGs stand post as Terry stops and turns to Jaxine.

"So...this nuisance, as you call them, not only have access to our heavily encrypted network, murdered eleven Framers—grabbin' three on our very first Framers Day in heavily populated Blocs—but they've also cloaked tunnels that empty into the middle of the fuckin' desert?" Terry barks. "No prints? No hair? Not even a fuckin' drop of sweat?"

"It would appear so."

"It would appear I'm starring in an episode of *D-N-A: Sin Vegas!*"

Terry's eyes turn bloodshot as he stares daggers at Jaxine, who gulps at the sight of Terry's bulging neck veins.

"We'll find them, Mr. President," Jaxine says.

"Anyone else, you'd be in a fuckin' tube to Needles," Terry barks.

"I'll find them," Jaxine pleads. "I swear."

Jaxine holds up her left hand, displaying her gold wedding band. The redness in Terry's eyes dissipates; the bulging veins recede back into his neck. Terry holds up his right hand, showing off his own gold wedding band. Their ring hands interlock.

"My bad, honey." Terry smiles. "It's these fuckin' wires in my head."

"Maybe you should have Shima—"

"No! No more fuckin' implants. No more fuckin' upgrades," Terry snaps.

"We'll stick with pills. Okay?"

"I could use a drink."

"We all could," Jaxine says.

Jaxine stares down Terry, albeit not quite as intimidating. Terry slowly nods. Jaxine opens the door. Holding hands, they enter the Man Cave and shut the door, leaving their PGs outside.

At the opposite end of the room, Dyson chats with Terry's voluptuous aide, Corin Atwalter. Jaxine and Terry walk over to the large round table with ten empty chairs in the middle of the room. They pass the empty chairs lining the walls and stand in front of their respective seats with digital nameplates. Jaxine sits to Terry's immediate left.

Corin presses a button on the wall, and out comes two glasses of pure water. She grabs both glasses and places them on the table in front of Jaxine and Terry

"All sectors linked, Mr. President," Corin says.

"When you're ready, Ms. Director," Dyson says.

Dyson presses a button on his virtual console. Digital names of the other six board members light up in front of each empty seat at the table. Suddenly, the lights dim as holograms of Interim Sector Two Director Lampost Cooper, Sector Three Director Yindora Zu, Interim Sector Four Director Wynten Mones, and Director Metamucil Ferouk appear in their respective seats from Jaxine's immediate left. To Terry's immediate right are four empty chairs respectively designated for Gen. Lawson, Gen. Tegashito, Gen. Monahan, and an unidentified empty chair furthest to the right.

A bell rings; everyone gives the Union salute.

"A moment for our fallen," Terry orders.

Everyone bows in silence.

"Union strong," Terry says.

"Union strong," everyone else parrots.

Terry sits; the others follow suit.

"Before commencement, I'd like to acknowledge our interim directors. Lampost Cooper and Wynton Mones whom I'm happy to say has the board's full confidence," Jaxine opens.

"Meta, you good?" Terry asks.

Dir. Ferouk, bruised and wearing a cast, clears his throat.

"Alive, tanks," Dir. Ferouk replies. "Revised casualties at ten tousand six hundred seventy-tree an countin'. Fifty-six tousand wounded.

"The amphitheater?" Terry asks.

"Heavy damage, but nuttin' dat can't be fixed before de new year," Dir. Ferouk replies.

"Our condolences, Meta," Jaxine adds.

"Jacques was a good man," Terry says. "Can't imagine what it's like to lose a child."

Jaxine lowers her head.

"Tanks, Mr. President," Dir. Ferouk answers. "De Man's head on a plate will ease de pain…a liddle."

Terry turns to Interim Dir. Mones.

"Wynten, anything on Topaz?" Terry asks.

"Still no trace of Fray-mah Titts, Mr. President," Dir. Mones replies. "But we traced a hacked signal to a U-Z building under renovation in de Inland Empire Bloc. Unfortunately, De Children booby-trapped dare tech and suicided."

"Waive all work absences and tardies," Terry order. "Standard compensation for employers negatively impacted. Double The Man's bounty to one hundred million socreds. Yindora?"

"With all due respect, Mr. President," Jaxine interjects. "Bounties have yet to inspire meaningful cooperation."

"You of all people should know everyone has a price," Terry counters. "With all due respect, Ms. Director."

Everyone turns to Sector Three Director Yindora Zu.

"A crash-pad raid in de P-Bloc uncovered a partially damaged e-tab. IT's still workin' on it. We found a lone female organic inside. She *su-eed* before we could apprehend her," Dir. Zu responds.

"Sector casualties?" Jaxine asks.

"Tirdy two tousand dead. Seventeen tousand four hundred six-ty-one wounded,"

"What about Framer Igloo?" Jaxine asks.

"We found traces of his DNA outside Sun Devil Coliseum," Dir. Zu answers. "Wherever he is, he gonna need a med, and I got all medis here on watch."

"Mr. President," Dir. Cooper says. "Our IT agents found a second program dat was uploaded chroo de same backdoor one min after de first. Dey share some coding, but de second one targeted more specific tech den de first. And dey appear to operate…independent from each udder."

Jaxine turns to Dir. Cooper and responds, "Independent?"

Dir. Cooper nods and continues, "Witnesses recall seeing some of de hacked tech actually fighting each other."

"De enemy of my enemy?" Dir. Ferouk rhetorically interjects.

"So we've got another terror group to deal with?" Terry asks.

"Maybe a splinter cell?" Dir. Zu opines.

"Fuckin' fantastic," Terry sarcastically replies.

"Deez programs were embedded de U-Stream. But dis second one been upgrading over many more years. De code goes back to de U-Stream's creation," Dir. Cooper explains to collective gasps.

"Impossible," Jaxine responds.

"Hola! We've been livin' the fuckin' impossible," Terry counters. "Pause meeting!"

Corin uses her retinal display to pause the meeting.

"Meeting paused, Mr. President," Corin replies.

From the respective board members' points of view, the holograms of Jaxine and Terry freeze in place.

Back in the Man Cave, Jaxine and Terry confer while their guests' holograms are frozen in place as well.

"Dye, I want a full audit," Jaxine asks.

"Yes, Ms. Director," Dyson replies.

"Clear my schedule for the next three days!" Terry orders. "And get Shima to the table!"

"Yes, Mr. President," Corin replies. "Calling Gen. Tegashito right now."

After a few seconds, Gen. Tegashito's hologram appears.

"Mr. President?" Gen. Tegashito asks.

"Tell me you've made progress."

"We're gettin' real close—"

"You've got two fuckin' weeks. I suggest you make them count," Terry growls.

"Mr. Pres—"

Terry cuts off the transmission; Gen. Tegashito's hologram vanishes. Jaxine gulps.

"Resume meeting," Terry commands.

Corin reanimates all the guest holograms.

"All set, Mr. President," Corin replies.

"I want all your best techs workin' OT," Terry barks. "If I don't see progress, heads will fuckin' roll. Reconvene tomorrow, eleven hundred. Union strong!"

"Union strong!" everyone shouts in unison.

Terry ends the transmission, and the holograms vanish. He turns to Jaxine.

"I want files on all reps with Hive access going back to U-Stream launch."

Jaxine turns to Terry.

"We're talking tens of thousands…possibly hundreds—" Jaxine replies.

"Then get the fuck to work!" Terry yells.

"Yes, Mr. President," Jaxine says with a curt nod.

Jaxine exits the room with Dyson right behind her. Corin walks over to Terry.

"Mr. Pres—" Corin begins.

"Just… I need a minute," Terry says, pointing to the door.

Corin hightails it out of the Man Cave. The door shuts behind her.

In a fit of rage, Terry throws shit around the room. He kicks a chair into pieces with his cybernetic legs, takes a deep breath, composes himself, and exits the Man Cave.

Bedside Manners

Toi lays unconscious inside an open meditube. Bruised and cut, but not broken, Sev sits beside Toi in a private mediroom within a heavily guarded Defense Club medical facility, or medi. A long table with dozens of synthetic flowers sits by the window. There's a gentle ring. Sev turns the door display transparent to see Gen. Lawson patiently waiting on the other side with Maj. Hickson behind him holding yet another bouquet of synthetic flowers.

Gen. Lawson stares straight at Sev, nods, and rhetorically asks, "Permission to enter?"

Sev uses his retinal display to slide open the door. Gen. Lawson grabs the bouquet from Maj. Hickson, enters, and places them on the table with the others while Sev stands at attention and salutes.

Remaining in the hall, Maj. Hickson simply nods his condolences. Sev returns the gesture. Gen. Lawson stares outside at the massive amounts of pedestrians below, then looks up at the clouds.

"At ease, son," Gen. Lawson orders. "How's she holdin' up?"

"She'll live."

"The president and board convey their deepest sympathies," Gen. Lawson adds.

"Wit' respect, sir. I could use a little more den sympathy," Sev replies.

"Privacy override 6Q Delta 29 Sefora. General Derek Filmore Lawson," Gen. Lawson commands. "Initiate."

Suddenly, the room enters a privacy mode where neither sight nor sound can penetrate. A meditube cover lowers on top of Toi's bed, which creates a casing that allows Toi to rest and heal peacefully while giving Sev and Gen. Lawson complete privacy.

"Privacy override initiated," Medi AI acknowledges.

"We traced one of the programs the hackers used to a series of abandoned relay stations within twenty miles of each Framers Day event—except for the Hive," Gen. Lawson says.

"More than one virus?" Sev asks.

Gen. Lawson focuses on Sev's faint reflection in the window.

"Apparently a second, much-older program was embedded in the U-Stream. Dormant until now."

"But de Hive stopped direct connect to de stream years ago," Sev recalls.

"Praise the Union," Gen. Lawson replies. "But seems the Hive wasn't the target."

"Framers," Sev says.

"Eight of the living eleven deleted. Along with your father, Harkin Igloo and Topaz Titts are the only MIAs breathing. And with them being grandfathered, they…"

"Can't be traced," Sev answers.

"NorPac has offered their assistance. Seems everyone on both sides of the fence want this merger to happen."

"Maybe not everyone," Sev replies. "Still no ransom?"

Gen. Lawson turns to Sev and shakes his head.

"But Gen. Tegashito has endorsed the *TEDs*."

Sev's eyes widen and replies, "They'll fuckin' get Pop killed!"

"Major, may I remind you hundreds of thousands are already dead?" Gen. Lawson snaps back.

"No disrespect to de fallen, sir."

"Once P-Doc and Devore record their finsigs, the new government will issue a declaration of war on the Kah-Lee, placing the entire Union on restricted lockdown until the threat is eradicated."

"My team's ready, General," Sev says.

"You mean what's left of it, Major?"

"Locked and loaded, sir."

"Son, if I could, I would," Gen. Lawson replies. "But effective immediately, Dir. Coltraine has personally requested you and your men be given seven days leave—"

"Sir—"

"With ten water creds each," Gen. Lawson interrupts. "Very generous considering her requests are never requests, Major. You of all people should know that."

Gen. Lawson slowly walks toward the door.

"Permission to speak with Jax directly, sir."

Gen. Lawson turns to face Sev and snaps, "Permission fuckin' denied, soldier. And given the last time your daddy dipped into her well, you will refer to Dir. Coltraine's title in my presence. Understood?"

"Sir. My bad."

"Look, I want him back too. But I ain't lettin' you tear ass all over the Union! We'll handle it. At least your father had the sense to bag a dead fuckin' Xeno *before* he thought to question authority. End privacy override!"

"Privacy override deactivated," Medi AI says.

Sev salutes.

"Major, cherish your time off," Gen. Lawson says. "It might be a while before any of you get another."

"Sir."

Gen. Lawson opens the door to see Maj. Hickson waiting at attention. When Gen. Lawson reaches the doorway, he stops with his back still to Sev.

"Maj. Hickson will see to it your fallen comrades get heroes' send-offs and all registered next of kin generously compensated."

"Union strong," Maj. Hickson replies.

Gen. Lawson exits and walk down the hall. Sev and Maj. Hickson make eye contact.

"Hick," Sev greets with a nod.

"Hec," Maj. Hickson replies with a nod.

Maj. Hickson then follows Gen. Lawson down the hall. Sev turns to see Toi still resting in her now uncovered meditube. He sighs.

The B Team

Sev enters Vitchenko's mediroom a few doors down. He spots Vitchenko chatting with Chino and Angel. Sev closes the door behind him.

"Genetic match for Ray-fee by the convoy." Sev sighs.

The men lower their heads.

"How is she, boss?" Vitchenko asks.

"Still better looking dan you," Sev replies.

"Dat ain't no challenge," Angel jokes.

"Asshole," Vitchenko retorts. "Doc says I check out tomorrow."

"Good," Sev replies.

"Next move, boss?" Chino asks.

"Seven-day leave," Sev replies. "Ten water creds...each."

The men perk up with excitement.

"Tranny or non?" Angel asks.

"Does it matter?" Sev fires back.

"Any *jizz* on Pop?" Chino asks.

"Only he and two udder Fray-mahs taken alive, but one of dem MIA. De rest wit' de fallen," Sev replies.

A collective sigh fills the room.

"Can't wait to get outta dis fuckin' place," Vitchenko begins in a coded response to throw off any unknown listeners. "Got a friend in La-La I can look up."

"Anyone we know?" Angel asks.

Vitchenko shakes his head and answers, "But I vouch."

"I got some peeps I can check on too," Angel cryptically replies.

"Lucky you," Chino responds, indicating his lack of any leads. "Got no fam. And lost touch wit' old friends long ago."

"You not alone," Sev says. "How 'bout a liddle a boys trip?"

"I'm down," Vitchenko agrees.

"See de sights. Breed heavy recycled air," Chino says. "Why not?"

"De cock tour party," Angel jokes.

"Chenko, de five of us can rideshare wit' you?" Sev asks.

"Uh, boss?" Vitchenko responds. "We only got four."

Sev opens the door; Sgt. Swayzee enters.

"Nudda day, fellas," Swayzee greets with a respectful nod.

Chino, Angel, and Vitchenko turn to each other in bewilderment.

The Children of Kah-Lee

Heavy rain pours down on the battlefield. A severely wounded Lorian warrior, wearing a badly damaged mechsuit, victoriously screams in defiance of the enemy. It stomps its way across a carpet of human and robotic corpses toward a twentysomething Hector—with both his real arms—lying on his back in acceptance of his fate.

In his final act, Hector pulls out a magnegrenade with his right hand and activates it. However, the rain causes it to slip from his hand and roll toward a mortally wounded soldier only a few feet away. Hector turns to reach for the magnegrenade when the Lorian beast stomps on Hector's right arm as it passes. Hector's painful scream barely registers with the large beast.

Simultaneously, the mortally wounded soldier manages to attach both his and Hector's magnegrenade to the Lorian's metallic boot as it passes between them. Hector follows the monster with his eyes and sees large spots of exposed back flesh through its mechsuit. Moments later, the magnegrenade's detonation causes limited damage by blowing a hole through the alien giant's boot heel while in midstep. When the monster's now-exposed heel hits the ground in stride, it slips backward on the muddy earth. Falling on its back, the alien warrior not only crushes the mortally wounded soldier, but also fatally impales itself on sharp, twisted metal wreaked by its own havoc.

Miraculously, Hector survives by mere inches as reinforcements arrive. When comrades call out for survivors, Hector screams until a bright light shines on him. He passes out to the sound of a clicking noise that snaps Hector back into consciousness. He's confined to a bed in the middle of a vroom set up to look like a typical child's bedroom. Hector turns his attention to the clicking sound.

Using one hand, Bic plays a word game on an e-tab that also monitors Hector's vitals. Bic clicks his green Bic pen with the other hand. A cup of water with a straw sits between Bic's tapping feet.

Hector struggles to rise, but his hands and legs are restrained by flexible, interwoven Lorian metal fibers. Not even his bionic arm can free him.

"Sleepin' Fray-mah wakes," Bic says with a grin.

"You Holee?" Hector asks.

"You still lookin' for a happy endin'?"

"Depends on the release you offer."

Bic sets down his e-tab. Hector recognizes the green pen's Bic logo from a world long gone. Realizing Hector's fascination with his green pen, Bic tucks it away.

"My mom's," Bic says. "She died during Man Fall birthing me. No real pic of her. But when I was old enough, my unk helped me draw her face with dis. I use every fuckin' drop of…"

Bic struggles to find the right word.

"Ink?" Hector replies.

Bic grins. "Use all dis ink makin' her face when I was a boy. Only ting left of her. And my unk."

"We all lost a lot, huh…" Hector inquires in a raspy voice, fishing for a name.

Smiling, Bic nods. He grabs the cup of water by his feet and holds it in front of Hector's mouth.

Grabbing the straw with his lips, Hector takes a few sips. His cracked lips and dry throat soak up the refreshing fluid when Bic pulls away the straw.

"Easy, Fray-mah," Bic instructs. "Good news for you. Your son and roomie still live. Dey recover in a New Vick medi."

Looking around the room, Hector winces.

"You expect me to thank you?" Hector asks.

"I expect you to drink more," Bic replies. "Slow, please."

"If you insist."

Bic feeds Hector the rest of the water and places the empty cup back on the floor.

"Not de good shit you have," Bic asks. "But it's all we got."

"So you De Man or what?"

Bic chuckles. "Just a lost child of Sin who found a home in Kah-Lee."

"Well, Mr. Child, I'm retired," Hector says. "Seems propaganda is my only value to the Union these days."

"You market yourself too low, Fray-mah," Bic replies.

Bic rises and heads for the door.

"You know the Hive never pays ransoms," Hector counters.

"No one talkin' ransom but you, Fray-mah," Bic's voice echoes as he exits the room.

A Kah-Lee guard slams the door shut.

Hector looks around to see his vroom cell has now transformed into a high school principal's office converted into Gen. Contreras's private office. The general works at his desk while Hector lays helplessly confined to a couch nearby as if seeking his father's consult.

"What the..." Hector mumbles.

Hector's eyes lock in on a photo taped to a wall of his younger self and his parents taken before most of the planet knew what a Xeno was.

Gen. Contreras's hologram enters, slamming the door behind him. Hector turns.

"Just tell me what you fucking want," Hector barks.

An incoming vidchat pops up on the general's laptop. Gen. Contreras accepts; Karla pops up on-screen.

"Hey," Gen. Contreras says. "Everything okay?"

"Sorry to interrupt, but..." Karla trails off.

"I know," Gen. Contreras replies. "Truth be told, that beautiful face of yours keeps me going. Éxi still having trouble sleepin'?"

"He misses his father," Karla answers. "I miss him too."

"Why don't you guys come down to the base next week? I'll arrange a mini staycation for his birthday."

"We'll take whatever we can get," Karla replies. "I'm proud of you, my love. We all are."

Someone knocks on the door.

"Gotta go. Love you."

"Love you too—be safe," Karla replies.

They blow each other kisses before ending the transmission. Gen. Contreras turns to the door.

"Come in!"

The door opens. Manny Campos's hologram enters and shuts the door behind him.

"Hey, Manny. I know we haven't had a chance to talk about Desiree and Pacifica—" Gen. Contreras begins.

"Hec," Manny interjects.

Gen. Contreras pauses, then replies, "They're here. Finally!"

"Five hundred just landed at Nellis," Manny says.

"Five?" Gen. Contreras trails off in disbelief. "And the other three fuckin' thousand?"

"About a thousand stayed behind at Fort Campbell—against orders," Manny says.

"AWOL?"

"Xenos. Apparently, those men bought the rest just enough time to evac."

"Fuck," Gen. Contreras replies. "And the other two?"

"Xeno attack just outside of Denver, sir," Manny replies. "Sir, communications are breaking down."

"From the Pentagon?" Gen. Contreras asks.

"From the East Coast."

Gen. Contreras slams the desk then leans back in his chair, places his hands on his head, and sighs.

"We still have sats. There's gotta be something," Gen. Contreras says.

"Also, British Ambassador Finwood Devore arrived last night in Mesquite with his family. He and Mayor Coltraine are close friends. The grew up together," Manny replies.

"Good for them."

"The Devore family was on one of the last transports to make it out of DC. They barely had time to take a shit in Houston when the Gov. Stanswill ordered the state's evac. By the grace of God, they managed a Special Forces escort to Mesquite."

"More likely by the grace of DeBeers," Gen. Contreras deadpans.

"By the time Devore's plane touched down, DC, New York, and Miami all went dark."

"NORAD? The nuke codes?" Gen. Contreras asks.

"Not a peep since that aftershock hit two days ago," Manny replies. "Around the same time Recon Delta reported heavy smoke in that direction from a camp fifty miles southwest of Grand Junction."

"Delta's current location?"

"It's been over thirteen hours since they last checked in," Manny answers. "Their third missed since then."

"C'mon...think, dammit! There's gotta be...something... someone," Gen. Contreras says.

Manny takes a deep breath then walks over to Gen. Contreras.

"Hec..." Manny somberly begins. "Never in a million years did I imagine saying what I'm going to say. But we gotta face facts. *There's no more US.*"

Gen. Contreras's first tears since his brother died race down his face. Manny turns his head toward Hector and looks straight at him.

Suddenly, the holographic program ends. Everything around Hector vanishes—except for Manny's hologram, which morphs into a living, older, battle-weary version of Manny complete with leathery face and bionic limbs.

"Only...*us*," Manny continues. "Kamusta ka, Éxi?"

Hector and the *real* Manny stare at each other. Manny smiles; his eyes water.

"*Manny?*" Hector asks.

"In the flesh," Manny replies. "Or what's left of it."

"Fuck...me," Hector replies.

"That's what Holee said," Manny quips.

Vanguard

Still healing from old—and new—wounds, the naked Lorian poacher wakes to find itself in a large, pitch-black cavern deep underground. The dazed, massive creature adjusts its ocular light filters as dim lighting suddenly fills the cave. The Lorian poacher identifies four small objects about fifty yards away, quickly closing the distance in half before they stop. It belts out a horrific growl that transmits an uneasy sensation though a human's internal organs.

The objects, two male and two female cybernetic soldiers, don sleek, silver battle skins with the letter *V* over their hearts. Their implants blink faintly through their flesh. The soldiers' nanohelmets, developed with Lorian tech, form over the soldiers' heads. They charge at the poacher, using their speed and agility to frustrate the large beast.

The Lorian poacher manages to kill one of the male soldiers with a lucky swat from one of its four flailing arms.

The three remaining soldiers regroup. They charge again, firing specially designed hybrid weapons at their giant adversary.

Severely weakened, the Lorian poacher stumbles, then falls.

The soldiers cautiously move on top of the monster for the kill, firing at will as it screams in pain. As they penetrate the extraterrestrial beast's tough flesh, one of the female soldiers gets snatched by one of the poacher's grapplers, and her head is chomped off from her body. During this moment, the final two soldiers strike dual death blows, finally killing the Lorian poacher.

Sugar Bunker personnel and invited reps erupt with cheers. The *V* logo on the remaining two soldiers' chests illuminates. The victorious soldiers raise their arms in triumph when the male soldier starts twitching and coughs up blood. Cheers dissipate into gasps as the twitching male soldier convulses and falls. The convulsing soldier's nanohelmet activates, protecting his head just before impact with the ground. Unfortunately, blood pours from the soldier's nose and mouth, partially filing the nanohelmet, which reflexively deactivates to prevent sanguine drowning, allowing the coagulating plasma to spill onto the ground while the male soldier continues twitching.

Unemotional, the female soldier mercilessly puts her comrade out of his misery with a laser bullet to the head and chest. Standing alone, she deactivates her nanohelmet. After awkward silence, the crowd showers her with overwhelming cheers. She proudly raises her fist in defiance of any remaining compassion for her fellow man and shouts, "Union strong!"

"Union strong," the boisterous audience repeatedly chants.

"Privileged citizens, we give you...*the Vanguardian*," Gen. Lawson triumphantly announces over the intercom.

Without warning, the female soldier's head explodes. Her limp, headless body crumples on top of the dead Lorian poacher.

Collective jaws drop, followed by a moment of silence.

"Clean up, Bay Six," Gen. Lawson says.

Medics rush in. Some spirit away the human corpses while others use surgical lasersaws to strategically dissect the Lorian poacher in easier-to-carry pieces. Once the medics exit, janitors in hazskins enter to clean up the mess.

Later, Capt. Theroux drives a mini back to Tunnel One with Gen. Tegashito riding shotgun with Jaxine and Terry in back.

The minis exit and cruise down a tunnel. They pass through two tunnel checkpoints that lead into an enormous warehouse packed with liquid-filled tubes containing fetuses. The minis cruise between two rows of the tubes as lab techs carefully inspect each one. Although the fetuses are in various stages of life, they all have minuscule blinking devices embedded in their transparent brain stems. However, 90 percent of the tubes display a steady yellow light, an indication of tangible progress.

Gen. Tegashito turns. "Just got word one of our techs in Fresno may have found what we need."

"May is either a month or a female," Terry quips. "Not an action or consequence."

Gen. Tegashito nods and looks forward again.

Jaxine turns to Terry and whispers, "You saw what they could do. That's bloody progress if you ask me."

"I saw them barely beat a naked, handicapped, dying animal," Terry responds. "You call it progress. I call it unacceptable. And your commentary wasn't solicited."

Wakey! Wakey!

A savory smell jolts Hector from his sleep. Wearing a strange metal bracelet on each wrist, he finds himself sitting in an unrestrained chair at the head of a table covered with organic food which includes...*real bacon?*

Manny sits at the opposite end of the table from Hector.

"Just in time! To your left is Luna," Manny says. "Don't let that sweet, innocent face trick you. She can be one nasty bitch."

Luna, a fit and seemingly ageless for a woman in her late sixties, smiles.

"Only when I have to be," Luna replies.

Sitting to Luna's left, Invoice nods and greets, "N-D, mang."

"That's Invoice. Next to him, Jolly," Manny continues, "and you've met my right hand, Bic."

"We go back a bit," Hector sarcastically replies.

Bic sits to Jolly's left and Hector's right. He flashes a warm grin to Hector in an effort to distract from the gun under the table he has pointed at Hector.

"You don't have to worry about me leaving just yet," Hector says.

"De more I worry, Fray-mah, de less dey have to," Bic counters.

Sitting to Manny's left, Jolly quietly studies Hector.

Manny bows his head and closes his eyes. Bic, Invoice, and Luna follow suit.

Luna opens with a strange blessing of words mixing various religious references since forgotten—or forbidden—in this new world order.

Head down and eyes closed, Invoice stealthily grabs a piece of food from the table and stuffs it in his mouth. A skeptical Hector makes eye contact with an emotionless Jolly quietly staring back. Bic keeps his head down and eyes closed—but his gun under the table remains fixed on Hector, finger still on the trigger.

Luna lifts her head up.

"Ah-min," Luna says.

"A-men," Manny and Bic both reply.

"A-men," Jolly and Invoice both reply.

All three stare at Hector in awkward silence.

"I know it's hard to believe, Éxi," Manny says. "But you're among friends."

"Am I?" Hector replies.

"When...in... Ro-ma," Jolly says.

All eyes silently remain on Hector.

"A... A-me... A-men," Hector replies, exhaling has if a giant weight's been lifted from his shoulders.

"A-men!" Manny, Bic, Jolly, and Luna yell.

"A-fuckin'-men!" Invoice yells.

Everyone gives Invoice the stink-eye for his blasphemy.

"Fuckhead," Bic grumbles.

Manny and Luna both reach for some food.

"Okay, dig in," Luna shouts.

Bic, Invoice, and Jolly grab random samples of food.

Hector immediately targets what appears to be bacon. He inspects it, then pulls the bacon slowly to his mouth then hesitates and looks around. Luna swipes the bacon from Hector's hand, bites half of it off, then tosses the rest of the bacon onto Hector's plate.

"I made it myself," Luna quip, staring at Hector as she eats.

Hector looks down at his plate and eats the other half of bacon; he stops chewing.

"Somethin' wrong?" Manny asks with a devilish grin.

Hector eyes widen.

"This *real*," Hector replies.

Manny smiles.

"You really wanna know?" Manny asks.

Hector shrugs then continues chewing on the bacon. He then samples some of the other food on the table. Luna intentionally coughs at Bic, forcing him to reluctantly holster his weapon while eating. Eyes darting around the table, Jolly silently studies the interactions. Hector reaches for some more food to put on his plate as Manny chuckles.

"After all these years," Manny says. "Never thought I'd see you again."

"Makes two of us," Hector replies. "Uncle Man."

"Well, I'm truly sorry we have to meet like this," Manny says.

"And the innocents you murdered?" Hector sarcastically asks. "Sorry for them too?"

"We can chat more once you've gotten your strength back," Manny says.

"I'm feelin' pretty fuckin' good right now," Hector replies defiantly, raising his metal bracelets.

Suddenly, the metal bracelets drag Hector's wrists back down to the metal arms on his chair. Everyone stops and stares daggers at him, including the service drones catering.

"Yes, I am De Man," Manny replies. "That what you want to hear?"

"How 'bout you're fuckin' bananas?" Hector asks.

"Bananas?" Jolly whispers to Bic who silently cuts him off.

"Your Pop—" Manny begins.

"Don't! Please…don't," Hector interrupts.

"Fuck I won't," Manny snaps back. "Just because I wasn't a drop in your daddy's nuts doesn't mean we're not family!"

Clearly disadvantaged, Hector relents.

"Fine. All ears… Unk," Hector says.

"You know your father needed the backing of the Workers Union."

"They had the men and the resources," Hector replies. "He had their loyalty and respect."

"Yes. In the beginning," Manny counters. "But unfortunately, greed did not die with the Old Nation. So he came up with this fuckin' crazy idea to form a secret movement as a fail-safe of what's now to come."

"Bullshit. My father would never support a terrorist. Let alone *be* one."

"Of course, *we're* the terrorists," Manny says.

"If the Framers Day Massacre fits," Hector replies.

"Dessert anyone?" Luna interjects.

Hector turns to see Luna holding a bowl of apples in front of him. At first, he leans back as if to decline the offer. However, his stomach growls and his taste buds get the better of him. Hector grabs an apple.

"Luna, you're killin' me here," Hector sarcastically responds and takes a few bites.

"Welcome," Luna replies with a smile.

"Why me? Why now?" Hector asks with a mouthful of apple.

"We need you," Manny answers. "And we're running out of time."

Hector finishes the apple and places the core on his plate.

"For what?" Hector asks.

After a brief pause, Manny rises, grabs another apple, and tosses it across the table to Hector. Hector easily raises his left hand to catch the fruit.

"Our walk," Manny replies.

Suddenly, the metal bracelets drag his hands back to the chair arms and unlock in place. Everyone watches as Hector slowly rises. Manny walks over to Hector and bear-hugs him. Feeling all eyes on him, Hector cautiously embraces Manny.

"You know... I could kill fuckin' you right now," Hector says.

"Well, it wouldn't do anyone any good if we're both dead," Manny replies.

They separate, and Hector follows Manny out of the room.

Bic grabs two more apples, puts them in his pockets, and follows them out with Invoice right behind him.

Jolly grabs and consumes the remaining food from Manny's plate—including the apple core. Luna glares at Jolly with her arms crossed; Jolly rubs his belly and burps.

"Needles!" Jolly says with a smile.

"Liddle asshole," Luna lovingly responds.

La-La Land

A long train of connected DCs slows as it approaches a So-Sec Border Gate scanner. As the train passes through it, a series of scanners identify all the military personnel inside each DC. Halfway through, two of the DCs detach from the train and continue down another track to a *pit stop* for further inspection. The remaining DCs reattach into a train and continue into Sector Four. The train cruises through the redeveloped Cajon Pass, one of the few areas preserved after man's fall, when it passes a digital exit sign:

CAJON PASS MEMORIAL—3 MI

Inside Vitchenko's large DC attached to the train, Sev and Chino compare notes on their e-tabs. Although it's spacious for the five men, the DC still looks as if it can barely Vitchenko's massive frame. Angel naps while Vitchenko fiddles with an electronic device. Swayzee looks outside using his retinal display. He spots a large group of people wearing colorful NorPac skins. They're taking photos in a designated area littered with bones, trash, and twisted metal preserved from *La Exodus*. An administrative guide herds the group back onto their specially outfitted DC train.

"First time from de Hive-Sec?" Vitchenko asks.

Swayzee stays focused on the group outside.

"Looks jus like de trainin' sims," Swayzee opines. "But witout de tourists."

Swayzee turns to see Vitchenko working on his electronic device.

"Dey won't be tourists for long," Vitchenko says. "Dey gonna be one of us."

"Where you from, Sarge?" Swayzee asks.

Suddenly, Vitchenko's DC detaches from the rest of the train and proceeds down a connecting route. The rest of the train takes on three new DCs before continuing on to its next destination.

"When de Xenos attack de Mudderland, my preggo granmudda escape to de Old Nation. She have my Ma in Bayland where Ma have me. I get citizenship af-tah de Second Unrest den I move to Norte Vegas. You?"

"Centennial Bloc. Mum's a processing exec in Needles—"

"Needles!" everyone else cheers.

"Dad's a janitor," Swayzee continues, "My sista a roomie up in No-Sec."

"She sign a lease?" Angel jokingly asks.

"Okay, boys, collar up," Chino interrupts.

Chino reaches into his small backpack and hands everyone a *camonek* to wear around their necks, concealing it under their skin collars.

"Deez may work on Troopas and sec cams, but not Lawson," Swayzee comments.

"I got deez modified," Chino explains.

"By who?" Swayzee asks.

"Don't ask, won't tell," Chino replies. "So just put it on."

Vitchenko's DC enters the Sidekick Hotel's main parking garage and parks in his designated stall.

Swayzee remotely checks into a hotel suite using his retinal display.

"We're checked in, sir," Swayzee says.

"Last chance," Sev says. "Nice pad wit' water creds waitin' upstairs."

Sev looks around, but no one hesitates.

"How 'bout a long game of po-kah?" Angel says as he activates his retinal display.

The men grab their backpacks and exit Vitchenko's DC. Vitchenko secures the vehicle. They walk out of the Sidekick's garage and blend into a very crowded—but immaculate—street where citizens swarm like ants in an orderly chaos. They arrive at a Metro station for both elevated and subterranean public transport.

While most citizens travel underground, higher-ranking club reps are afforded elevated access that offers both a little more space and slightly faster service.

Sev and his team head underground. Metro facial scanners at the entrance acknowledge the false profiles transmitted by their camoneks. The men wait on a crowded platform for their tubecar while janitors ensure the Metro's cleanliness.

Armed robotic and cybernetic troopers canvas the station, walking past digital screens that display some form of Union propaganda, including...

...tributes to the Framers Day Massacre, then...

...a hefty reward for information leading to "De Man" with a question mark symbol imposed over a dark silhouette.

An automated Metrotube arrives. The doors open. Citizens disembark. Sev and his men board with other citizens in an orderly fashion.

"Doors closing. Doors closing. Doors closing," the Metrotube AI warns over the PA.

The doors shut, and the Metrotube zips through the tunnel at lightning speed.

Inside, windows double as video displays while *tubecams* watch over the passengers. Citizens focus on their retinal displays, e-tabs, or both while Sev and his men blend in. Thirty minutes later, the Metrotube arrives at the team's stop.

"Westwood Pier, Los Angeles Bloc. Doors opening. Westwood Pier, Los Angeles Bloc. Doors opening," the Metro AI warns. "Martial law approaching. Doors closing. Martial law approaching. Doors closing. Next stop..."

Sev and his men exit the Metrotube and head aboveground. They pass a digital timer counting down to martial law. The men navigate a seemingly endless sea of citizens walking the streets. Above them, elevated commuters automatically stop and slide to one side, making way for medical, law enforcement and delivery cruisers that continue unimpeded. Security drones and closed-circuit cameras blanket the neighborhood.

"Dey gotta lotto in dis sector or what?" Swayzee sarcastically asks.

"How can sometin' look so clean and still smell like shit?" Angel adds.

"You tell me, Lieutenant," Sev says.

Angel sniffs under his arms. Swayzee looks around as if it were his first trip to the amusement park.

"Time for a trainin' sim update, huh, Sarge?" Vitchenko asks.

"Looks so," Swayzee replies.

Vitchenko reads his retinal display showing their intended location only a few yards away.

"Almost dare," Vitchenko says.

"Sure you trust dis dude?" Angel asks.

"Mo' den you," Vitchenko shoots back.

"Dat hurt, bro," Angel replies.

They walk a few yards until they reach the Sunset Marketplace, a large building the size of an entire city block. Hundreds of janitors continuously clean and repair every inch.

"You talkin' now," Swayzee says with excitement.

Vitchenko leads them right past the Borat Condos' robotic security guard.

"Not here," Vitchenko explains, pointing to the adjacent entrance. "Up dare."

The men arrive at the Sunset Café a few doors down. Window displays turn transparent, allowing pedestrians to see patrons eating and drinking inside. A bouncer guards the entrance.

"Identify," the emotionless bouncer asks.

Vitchenko transmits his reservation code to the bouncer, who grants them all entry. Inside, a hostess leads them through the crowd to room 15. They enter. The hostess closes the door to their private room then heads back up front.

"Anyone see a menu?" Angel asks.

Suddenly, a secret door opens and out pops Hennessey Munro, a pale-skinned female with hypnotically gray eyes and a thinly toned frame partially covered in tattoos. All but Vitchenko instinctively turn their weapons on her.

"Stand down," Vitchenko forcefully whispers.

The men lower their guns.

"She's a ra—" Swayzee begins as Chino elbows him in the ribs before continuing. "Ra-eally preddy lady."

"Late, Eve," Henn says before Vitchenko can warn her not to call him that.

"Eve?" the men collectively respond.

"For Ivor," Vitchenko explains.

"What-evah you say, Eve." Chino chuckles as he spots Vitchenko's cold gaze, clears his throat, and says, "I mean, Sarge."

"Henn, men. Men, Henn," Vitchenko introduces.

"Let's go, men," Henn barks.

Sev and Chino use their cybernetic eyes to scan Henn for her credentials. Their retinal analysis confirms Henn's false male profile.

"You heard de womman," Sev says.

Vitchenko shrugs. Henn ushers them through the secret door, and Sev walks through first. The others follow with each nodding to Henn as they pass.

Henn eye-fucks a sheepish Swayzee as he passes by. Bringing up the rear, Vitchenko passes, gently tapping Henn's shoulder. As Vitchenko passes, Henn grabs his arm with the laser bullet wound as she retinal scans it.

"Gonna need some more Nanorem," Henn says.

"I'm good," Vitchenko replies with a grin.

Henn gently slaps Vitchenko's ass while guiding him through the door.

"*Groundas*," Henn quips as the secret door shuts behind her.

Seconds later, the hostess returns with new customers to occupy room 15 as if oblivious to its original occupants.

Happy Birthday!

Hector and Manny walk down a corridor with private, sound-proof rooms on each side. Inside every other room, small groups of people sit plugged into virtual reality via helmets or implants. One or two people in the adjacent rooms monitor each groups' activity.

Manny points to the different rooms as they pass and identifies, "Powerball. Electro Concert. Nightclub. Park. Fake avatars enable us to infiltrate public venues through both streams."

"Where'd you get the IDs?" Hector asks. "Needles?"

"And a few other places," Manny replies.

Hector follows Manny through an enormous underground cavern. He looks up to see the torn and/or partially burnt flags of humanity's former nations hanging across the smooth ceiling with wounded pride. Hector looks on as Kah-Lee soldiers work and train under strict supervision. Upon seeing Manny, the Kah-Lee faithful stand at attention as Hector and Manny pass by.

"How many of there are you?" Hector asks.

"After the Second Unrest, your father worried about the direction of the Union," Manny replies, intentionally ignoring the question. "But the old guard was lost to war or Mother Nature, gradually replaced by those with more…questionable motives."

"He never mentioned any of this to me," Hector says.

"It was a source of friction between he and your mother. Right up until she…"

Hector and Manny continue walking while the Kah-Lee faithful resume their tasks.

"What happened?" Hector asks.

"It was only a matter of time before *we* needed to be dealt with," Manny replies. "So your father inspired the idea you see before you."

"Insurrection?" Hector replies.

Manny chuckles. "Preserving humanity. Each day more Xenos arrive while our remaining sanctuaries grow more crowded. We can only build so high…and dig so low. Do you know there's nearly nine million Rachas who will live their whole lives having never seen the sun? Now *that's* bananas!"

"You still haven't told me why all those citizens had to die."

"Nothing I could do about that," Manny replies.

Hector stops. Manny stops and turns.

"How 'bout not fuckin' murder them?" Hector says.

"I can't apologize for what I didn't do."

Hector pauses. "My bad. Guess I just imagined all those dead bodies at the arena."

"There's no disputing what you saw. Just what you believe."

Manny gets Hector to keep walking.

"And you want me to believe you're trying to prevent a coup and not start one?"

"As opposed to you believing we would kill everyone but you?" Manny replies. "Opo."

Manny and Hector stop at a guarded door which the armed guard opens. Manny leads Hector inside the dimly lit room.

"Again with the fuckin' vrooms?" Hector sarcastically asks.

The vroom lights up into a three-dimensional rendering of an underground Union base similar to Sugar Bunker.

"Apparently, the first zeezees we discovered many years before the Xenos made their formal introduction to the world," Manny says. "Your great-grandfather was one of the first who tried to warn us."

"My father said everyone thought he was nuts."

"Not everyone. Not the ones who were tryin' to create their own zeezees decades before Man Fall," Manny asks.

"Men have been trying to control men since creation," Hector replies. "It's a dictator's wet dream."

"Well, unfortunately for us, that wet dream is much closer to reality," Manny counters. "Activate: vlog tango, bravo, six, bulot, sayonara."

"Password required," the vroom AI replies.

169

"Another trip down memory lane?" Hector asks.

"Don't take my word for it," Manny answers. "Hec said if we ever met like this, to make sure you, quote, look after your baby brother. But he only had one child—"

"Spirit?" Hector blurts out.

"Password and voice recognized," the vroom AI confirms.

One of the walls morphs into a video display showing a freeze frame of an aged and worn-down Gen. Contreras in Defense Club skin.

"Who the fuck's Spirit?"

"My Uncle Rod's puppy," Hector replies. "He got it for me the day I was born."

"No one said anything about no dog."

"Apparently, he got some kind of disease. He died before I even left the hospital," Hector says. "But Uncle Rod would bring it up every now and then. Except for the last time we saw him. He stayed behind in Victorville. I never even got say goodbye."

"I met him once," Manny laments. "Good man, like your father."

Hector notices the video date and time stamp.

"That's my birthday," Hector mumbles.

"Yes. He recorded it two months before his passing," Manny replies.

"And three years after yours," Hector retorts.

Hector turns his head to Manny, then back toward the display.

"Happy birthday, son. Not sure where or when you'll see this," Gen. Contreras begins. "God willing, you won't see this at all. But if you are watching this, I'll start by saying I love you with all my heart. You and your mother, of course, have been the few bright lights in this never-ending darkness we now live in. Know that everything I did was to protect the both of you—and our people—from both the monsters out there…and the ones among us."

Hector turns to Manny, who nods at him.

"When my grandfather learned about the Xenos, he could only imagine the worst. With help from some friends, they developed a supersoldier program designed to give us a fighting chance.

It was during this time when he discovered a covert program called Vanguard. When he got too close to the truth, his own government forced him into hiding. By the time my father and I learned the truth, all hell had already broken loose," Gen. Contreras continues. "Now, I don't know how, but it appears that someone within our new government was able revive Vanguard. What I do know is that Vanguard not only has the potential to enhance human capabilities, but it could also be used as a back door to total population control."

"That doesn't sound good," Hector mumbles.

"So far, all but a handful that we've sent to infiltrate this mysterious cabal has disappeared. And now I fear that any further moves will put you and your mother in grave danger. Your Uncle Manny's one of the few left I completely trust. And Manny...always good to see you, brother."

Manny smiles.

"Éxi...or is it Hec now?" Gen. Contreras asks with a smile. "Son, for the past thousand years, our family has served on the front lines—it's in our blood. And I pray you understand, as our fathers did, that our reward for helping shepherd humanity is the survival of our lineage. And vice versa!"

Manny's eyes burn with unshed tears at the sight of his fallen friend.

"And I trust you know we can't do that as mindless drones, now can we?" Gen. Contreras continues. "So I'll end on this note: Right or wrong doesn't matter anymore. There's action or reaction. And I'll always regret not having more time with you and your mother."

There's a knock at Gen. Contreras's door.

"Dad," a young Hector screams behind the door. "You said no working on my birthday!"

"I'm not, little buddy," Gen. Contreras answers as he stares at the camera and smiles. "You got this, son. Love you."

The video ends. The lights brighten. Hector turns to see Manny holding out a pair of old, tiny digital binoculars—Hector's from the Chinook a long time ago. Hector takes the deepest breath he can to control his rising heartbeat. His hands tremble for a split second before he regains control. Hector exhales forcefully then says, "Saw a lot of fucked-up shit through these."

"Well, get ready to see more," Manny replies.

Crash Pad

Henn leads Sev and his team through an underground maze of lightly populated tunnels. Suddenly, the faint echoes of sirens wail through the dimly lit halls.

"Martial law," Swayzee confirms.

"Gotta move, groundas," Henn says.

"You leadin' us to de core or what?" Chino sarcastically inquires.

Henn takes them down a shorter tunnel and stops at a dead end. She places her palm on a camouflaged sensor; a rock wall slides open. She leads them through; the rock wall closes behind them. They walk through a corridor to the end where Henn opens another sliding door that leads to an underground safe house. She enters with Sev and his team. Once everyone's inside, she closes the door. Lights flicker on. Water drips from an old pipe. The walls are cracked and grimy. Bug boxes in every corner of the safe house have flickering lights.

"Mos def puts de crash in crash pad," Angel quips.

"Seven hours to rest, pussies," Henn replies as she turns away. "Den long days ahead."

"Henn—" Sev says as he grabs Henn's shoulder.

"Boss," Vitchenko blurts out half a second too late.

Henn grabs Sev's arm in a stalemate to Sev's surprise.

Angel rushes over, but Henn kicks him to the ground.

Chino and Swayzee converge on Henn, who puts a gun to Sev's head while pinning Angel to the ground with one foot. With her free hand, she pulls out a sawser grenade set for instant detonation upon release.

"No touch," Henn says. "Never. Touch."

"Henn, chillax," Vitchenko says.

"Chenko, calm your bitch down, bro," Angel barks.

"Shut de fuck up, Angel," Vitchenko replies.

"My bad, Henn. For real," Sev says. "Just sayin' tanks."

"Boss meant no dis," Chino adds. "Chenko's friend our friend too, yeah?"

"I vouch for dem, Henn," Vitchenko pleads.

Staring at Vitchenko, Henn reluctantly disarms the grenade and holsters her weapon.

"Shitter and sanipads, o'dare. Sleepers…skins, dare," Henn says. "Rations, dare."

"SkyHawk?" Vitchenko asks.

"Workin' on it," Henn replies. Not like orderin' Xeno shit." Henn snaps.

"What's dare?" Angel asks, pointing to Henn's room.

"Dare's off limits," Henn replies. "Eve, parlay?"

Vitchenko follows Henn into her room. The doors lock. The others look around and at each other.

"Union strong, Evie," Angel howls at the door.

Chino turns to Swayzee. "Sarge, ever fuck a racha?"

Swayzee shakes his head and asks, "You?"

"Oh yeah. But if you don't satisfy dem for tree straight hours, they fuckin' kill you, bro."

Swayzee shares a puzzled look then asks, "For real?"

"I still here, yeah?" Chino cryptically answers.

"Fuck dat mean?" Swayzee counters.

"Fuck you tink?" Chino replies.

Swayzee shakes his head in frustration while Chino unpacks some of his gear on a table. Sev plops himself on the couch next to the table. "Chee, first watch."

"Yeah, Boss," Chino replies.

"I got shitter," Swayzee says.

"I hope we got vents," Angel replies.

Sev closes his eyes. "I'll got second."

"Sweet dreams, boss," Chino replies.

"She got any rat meat in dis bitch?" Angel says.

Chino shakes his head and replies, "Just you!"

An hour later, Sev sits up and looks around the room. He rolls over and activates the table display set to a D-Stream channel. He clicks through the channels reporting...

Martial law taking effect in all but Sector One.

Updates on the Framers Day Massacre, including critics' skepticism following the Hive's public announcement that Hector, Framer Titts, and Framer Harkin Igloo all remain in critical condition while under armed guard at separate, undisclosed medis.

A conspiracy theorist hypothesizing that the Children of Kah-Lee are working for the Xenos.

Chino walks up, holding out a small flask of SinWater. Sev grabs it and takes a sip. He hands the flask back to Chino.

"Pop's a lot of tings," Chino says. "Tough muddafucka's numero uno."

"Anytin' from Coltraine or Lawson?" Sev asks.

Chino takes a swig then hands Sev back the flask.

"Sure dey got udder bugs to fry," Chino replies.

"Doze guards," Sev says. "De ones dat save us..."

"De Hive re-get control, yeah?"

"Den why suicide?" Sev rhetorically asks.

They turn their attention to Henn's room as faint grunts of passion emanate from within. Sev takes a swig of SinWater then hands the flask back to Chino, who also takes a swig.

Jumping Jax

Back in the Man Cave, Jaxine and Terry sit across from the holograms of Generals Tegashito, Lawson, and Monahan. Dyson and Corin sit behind Jaxine and Terry, respectively.

"Based on the new sat images, it appears the Lagosian Federation fell less then forty-eight hours ago," Gen. Tegashito says. "Which means the Xenos now control roughly 60 percent of the African continent and its resources."

"And reduces the African Alliance to a handful of tribal communities," Gen. Lawson says.

"The Vermainians have offered secondary citizenship to any Africans brave enough to cross the Atlantic. As do the SoCrows," Jaxine adds.

"But with a lot less strings attached, I imagine," Terry quips.

"At dis rate, no free man will walk on African soil within one *gen*," Gen. Lawson says. "Maybe two."

"An entire continent now one big slaughterhouse," Gen. Tegashito says.

"I wanna chunder," Jaxine replies, shaking her head. "They're taking our land. Water," Jaxine replies. "They won't stop."

"Did we?" Gen. Monahan rhetorically asks.

"They'll turn us all into fuckin' rachas," Terry says. "Those of us left, anyway."

Out of the corner of her eye, Jaxine spies Dyson and Corin secretly flirting by rubbing each other's pinkies. Jaxine turns her attention back to the current discussion.

"Any more good news?" Jaxine asks.

"We received an encrypted transmission from the GDR High Command confirming a successful coup over the Sao-Rio

Government," Gen. Lawson answers. "They intend to honor all existing pacts to avoid any trade disruptions."

"Not many fish left in the sea," Terry replies. "Nukes?"

"It'll take a fuckin' miracle," Gen. Lawson responds.

Jaxine turns to Terry.

"Even if we got them online, two nukes would just *really* piss them off," Gen. Tegashito says. "Assuming they even get off the ground."

"We wouldn't last a week," Gen. Monahan replies.

"So Vanguard remains our best option," Terry responds.

"As it stands, it's our only one," Jaxine replies.

"Keep workin' those nukes, Derek. Sooner or later, they'll be better to have and not need," Terry replies. "Regardless, it's all to shit without this merger."

"Just crossin' *i*'s and dottin' *t*'s, Mr. President," Jaxine says.

"I hope so, Ms. Director," Terry replies. "For all our sakes. Union strong!"

"Union strong," everyone else parrots with the Union Salute.

All three generals' holograms vanish. Jaxine and Terry are alone with their aides. Terry turns to Jaxine.

"So what the fuck does he want now?" Terry asks.

"One last meeting," Jaxine answers. "Just the two of you."

Terry stares lovingly at his spouse's hypnotic eyes; he melts.

"Son of a bitch pulled this on purpose," Terry says. "Now I feel like throwing up."

"He was your best friend," Jaxine replies.

"Now you are."

"He's still hurt."

"Hurt?" Terry says. "If he's hurt gettin' his dick wet all fuckin' day, I can only imagine what his depression must feel like!"

"We're in the final stretch. Just kill two birds with one stone. You don't have to mean it," Jaxine replies.

"You drive a hard bargain," Terry says.

"That makes two of us," Jaxine counters. "Dye!"

Sans hesitation, Dyson rises and replies, "Yes, Ms. Director."

"Union strong," Jaxine says.

Corin helplessly watches Dyson follow Jaxine out the door, which shuts behind them.

Terry turns to an emotionless Corin and smiles.

"Union strong," Terry mumbles.

Long Beach Island

On a windy, deserted island off the Pacific coast, Hector uses his old digital binoculars to scan the Union's heavily militarized *Pacific Coastal Fortifications*. Among the heavy artillery are a series of water-desalination plants barely treading the grossly elevated sea level. Hector also spots two Lorian ships darting across the upper atmosphere in opposite directions.

Hector and Manny lay beside each other under a cloaking tarp infused with Lorian tech, blending them into the environment. Using modified zoomers, Manny tracks a squadron of Defense Club aerial drones patrolling the mainland coast.

"If this is about those surfing lessons you promised, water's way over the bridge at this point."

"Definitely do not miss the sarcasm," Manny reluctantly chuckles.

"Well, I'm only here as long as you need me," Hector replies.

Manny's timer quietly vibrates.

"Here we go," Manny says.

Manny trades Hector's digital binoculars for his modified zoomers. He directs Hector's line of sight high above the coastline.

"Gonna tell me what I'm lookin' for?" Hector asks.

Manny uses Hector's fingers to instruct him.

"Okay, press this button and hold it down."

"You De Man," Hector jokes.

"Just press the button, smart-ass," Manny orders.

Hector presses and holds down the zoomers' small button.

"Okay, now what—the fuck!" Hector says. "They movin' their whole fuckin' planet to the moon or what?"

Hector's eyes widen, then swell with water. His jaw slightly drops. Dejected, he lowers his head then hands Manny back the modified zoomers.

"Not exactly," Manny says. "We believe they're using the moon as Earth's border customs."

Manny hands Hector back his digital binoculars, then scans the coastline with his modified zoomers. He spots two Defense Club aerial drones heading toward them.

"Game fuckin' over, isn't it?" Hector asks.

"Will be if we don't bounce *right now*," Manny says.

Manny pushes Hector into a small crack in the earth then crawls in behind him while the tarp provides cover. Manny then uses a false stone to conceal the crack.

Moments later, the two DC aerial drones casually scan the island, which is littered with rusted scrap metal and a few decayed bones.

Lights from one of the aerial drones shines on a bloodstained, partially torn billboard laying on the ground:

SCOVER LONG BEACH ISL

Underground, Manny uses an old manual lift to lower them both deep into the earth.

"Well that was educational," Hector deadpans.

"I thought so too when a friend showed me many years ago," Manny replies.

"Pop?"

"No," Manny answers. "Though your father did see this coming a mile away."

Manny stops the lift at the bottom and opens the door for them to exit. They're greeted by waiting Kah-Lee soldiers who escort them down a long hallway.

"I'm too old for this shit, Manny," Hector admits.

"And that makes me?"

"As Toi would say, pidge shit cray-cray."

"And where can you hide when the whole world goes to shit?"

"Asks De Man who lives underground," Hector counters.

"What about Sev? Ocho? Your precious Toi?"

Hector raises his cybernetic arm.

"I did my time," Hector snaps. "We both did."

Manny pulls up part of his shirt, exposing cybernetic wires meshed with battle-scarred flesh across his body.

"We did your father's time," Manny snaps back. "*This* is our time."

"That man's long gone."

"No. He's just tired and scared like the rest of us," Manny counters. "And like the rest of us, he's gotta pick a club."

Manny leads Hector down the hallway with their armed escorts.

"Speaking of rest, where's that fuckin' mini?" Hector pleads. "My feet are killin' me."

Pillow Chat

Lying in bed, Vitchenko watches Henn inside the bathstall, wiping down her very pale, fit, tattooed body with scented sani-pads before tossing them into a recycle bin, or *recbin*, that contains disinfectant.

Henn grabs an unopened packet of sanipads and tosses it to Vitchenko.

"Still a ball buster, yeah?" Vitchenko says.

"What you tink?" Henn replies.

"Dis friend…wit' de *jizz*…"

"We tag-team off and on for years," Henn says with a smile. "Contacts in every sector. Very good fighter."

"Tougher den you?" Vitchenko asks.

"Tougher den you," Henn replies.

"Can't wait to meet him."

Smiling, Vitchenko gets up and carries the packet of sanipads with him to the primitive bathstall. Henn notices Vitchenko's pouch beside his clothes. She opens it and pulls out a clearcurt disc.

Minutes later, Vitchenko wipes himself clean and tosses the soiled pads into the recbin. He exits the bathstall. Henn walks over to him, checks the laser bullet wound on his arm, then sprays it with Nanorem.

"Tanks," Vitchenko says.

Vitchenko and Henn exchange smiles. Henn grabs Vitchenko's clothes and places the Nanorem on the counter.

"Mama done wit' you, Evie. Recall your hydrotabs."

"Chenko around de fellas, yeah?"

"Go see Papa now," Henn says.

Henn tosses Vitchenko his clothes. As Vitchenko dresses, Henn opens her room door to find Sev and Chino standing by the door, pretending they weren't listening in. Henn gently escorts Vitchenko out of the room.

Henn shuts the room door. Sev and Chino turn to Vitchenko.

"What?" Vitchenko shrugs.

"Nada," Sev and Chino simultaneously reply with a shrug.

Back in her room, Henn prepares her tactical gear. She inserts a counterfeit Defense Club trooper access badge into her armband pouch. After taking a hydratab, Henn presses her implanted comchat. Her retinal display requests confirmation to record and transmit a message.

"No delays anticipated," Henn whispers into her comchat. "Payment will be wired on delivery as agreed."

Henn sends the transmission and sighs.

Bedridden

Toi regains consciousness in her mediroom; a blurry, dark silhouette stares at her.

"Hec?" Toi murmurs.

As Toi's vision clears, she discovers it's actually Hilga smiling down at her. Toi reflexively backs away in pain.

"Easy, Toi," Hilga says. "It's Hil."

"Where's Hec?"

Hilga looks down.

"You can't recall?" Hilga asks.

Toi rubs her head and looks up at Hilga.

"Dey took him!"

"Calm, we know. But still no ransom."

"Fuckin' Children," Toi says. "How long?"

"Four days."

"Four fuckin'… Sev?"

"He's fine, Toi. Dey put him and his boys on leave," Hilga says. "Right now, you need to breed…and focus. Dare you go. Breed… focus…"

Toi takes a few deep breaths then says, "I try to stop dem. I really try…"

"No shit. You all over de stream," Hilga whispers with a smile.

Toi tries to get out of bed, but she's too weak.

"I gotta get—"

Hilga helps Toi back into a more comfortable position.

"More rest," Hilga interrupts. "When you betta, de Hive wanna know what you know."

"I just wanna go home. I want Hec."

"Oh, Toi…"

"What? Hil?"

"Dey say if Hec die, you lose de home."

Toi pulls away and asks, "Who say?"

Hilga looks over at a large, colorful bouquet of synthetic flowers on the table. Toi notices Jaxine's name and title embedded on the vase.

"She said witout a lease—"

"She's de fuckin' board director," Toi interrupts.

"Big sorries, my dear," Hilga replies. "But cherish de silver clouds."

"What fuckin' silver clouds?"

"Well, as a rep, you can go wherever de fuck you want now," Hilga answers.

"But I don't wanna be a fuckin' rep," Toi barks. "I wanna be...*a fuckin' rep?*"

Hilga smiles and gently hugs Toi.

"Welcome to de club, sista," Hilga says. "Max benefits. Live in any sector—but who de hell wanna choose outside de Hive-Sec? All tanks to de fuckin' board director."

Tears seep through Toi's closed eyes.

"Wow. Sah-bee gonna..." Toi trails off as her eyes widen. "Hey, please check my friend and her co-tens. Keno and Danori Rikardsen."

Hilga activates the mediroom e-tab, which starts at the main menu.

"Online," Hilga says.

"R-E-T-A-N-G-A," Toi spells out.

Hilga types and repeats, "Okay. Re-tan-ga..."

Hilga reads the report. After a few moments, her bottom lip quivers.

"What?" Toi asks. "Hil?"

Hilga looks up.

"Your friends...dey all check out de medi dis mornin'."

"If she go home, why not call me?"

Hilga's eyes water as she slowly shakes her head.

"Not home. Needles."

Toi processes Hilga's words for confirmation. She lowers her head and sighs.

"Needles?" Toi sobs.

Hilga hugs her.

Rise and Shine

Sev, Chino, Angel, Vitchenko, and Swayzee wait in awkward silence. Vitchenko notices the others purposely avoiding eye contact with him.

"Fuck you all," Vitchenko playfully growls.

The men finally make eye contact with him and laugh. They stop in unison as Henn exits her room in a sleek, but deadly tactical skins.

"Birdie's in de nest," Henn announces.

The men stand at attention.

"Let's roll," Sev replies.

"First, we gotta off-road," Henn says.

"Off where?" Sev asks.

"To meet my friend...de one wit' jizz on your Pop," Henn responds.

"Betta be some good fuckin' jizz," Swayzee chimes in.

"Good enough to wanna vet you all first," Henn replies. "Only give jizz face-to-face."

"Better not be no fuckin' racha trap—" Angel says.

Suddenly, a *torchblade* appears right between Angel's eyes, its searing metal hovering an inch from his face before snapping back into Henn's *torchglove*.

Sweating from both heat and fear, Angel slowly raises his hand.

"Sorry, Henn. De boy's a liddle slow," Vitchenko says.

"Cool it, Angel, yeah?" Sev orders.

"Yeah, I'm cool," Angel replies. "We cool, sista?"

"Dat's pretty fuckin' cool," Swayzee interjects.

Sweat drips from Angel's brow, his body frozen in place.

"We cool now," Henn says. "But we gettin' real fuckin' warm, grounda."

"Compren-day," Angel concedes.

Henn deactivates her torchglove and lowers her hands.

"So where we goin'?" Sev asks.

"*Subclarita*," Henn answers with a smile.

"Rachaville?" Swayzee rhetorically asks before spotting Henn's glare and correcting, "My bad. We cool!"

"You boys want homeschoolin'? Or you want jizz?"

"Your friend…you vouch?" Sev asks.

"More den you, grounda," Henn replies with a grin. "And Eve."

"Chenko…please," Vitchenko forcefully begs.

"Gear up," Sev replies.

Everyone prepares to leave. Vitchenko walks up to Sev.

"Boss, Henn's—" Vitchenko whispers.

"You vouch, I vouch," Sev interjects.

Sev and Vitchenko lock eyes.

"Your pop, my pop," Vitchenko counters.

Sev nods then walks away just as Henn joins Vitchenko.

"Dunkin' arm betta?" Henn asks, tossing Vitchenko his pouch.

Vitchenko effortlessly catches the pouch with his previously injured arm.

"I can dunk you now," Vitchenko replies.

"Welcome," Henn says.

Henn walks past Vitchenko, patting him on his injured arm. Vitchenko slightly winces, opens the pouch, and pulls out a clearcurt disc. He inspects it, looks at Henn, and smiles. She nods back with a grin.

Angel walks up to Vitchenko.

"Let's go, Ro-mee-oh," Angel wisecracks. "Jizz now, biz later."

Queen Bee

Naked, Jaxine sits back as a thirtysomething Hector goes down on her in their former bedroom. Jaxine looks to her right, her gaze fixed on a digital projection of her much younger self and Hector during a happy moment. As she gyrates closer to climax, a bell rings. She tries to ignore it, but the persistent bell keeps ringing. She looks down at young Hector as he flickers, then transforms into…

…a fully clothed Dyson going down on her. Wearing only virtual glasses and the top half of her work skins, Jaxine sits in an office chair split open at the legs. Smiling, Dyson peeks up at her, erroneously confident in his performance. However, Jaxine's blank expression confirms his delusion. She gently kicks him out of the way so she can reconnect the chair legs back into recliner mode.

"Sometin' wrong?" Dyson asks.

Dyson rises; Jaxine reaches into a drawer and pulls out a few sanipads.

"Something's always wrong," Jaxine replies.

Jaxine slides the chair closer to her desk console. She accepts the incoming priority call from NorPac's Subprime Minister Alexi Goatee.

"Lexi, how's it hangin'?" Jaxine asks. "No worries. Everything's set for the Red Woods. He'll be there. For real. Will Archon be taking… Oh? You sure about that? You know those bloody *Islanders* are…uh-huh…"

Dyson enters a meticulously elegant bathstall that rivals the Pinnacle and quickly grooms himself. As Jaxine wraps up her brief call, she cleans her privates, grabs her pants from the floor, and puts them back on. She turns and tosses her used sanipads when the window display grabs her attention. The pristine green valley takes her back to a time when *a young Jaxine playfully sings in the car with her father, Maximilian, and birth mother, Amandla, as they drive past the White House sometime before man's fall. Between radio songs, a brief news report updates listeners on the strange, unidentified objects detected many light-years away that appear headed toward Earth.*

"Some are saying they could be extraterrestrials," Amandla says.

"A load of tosh," Maximilian replies. "Probably meteors or comets."

Amandla nods to a smiling Maximilian then turns to her young daughter happily confined to the rear driver side seat.

"And is my little Jumpin' Jax ready for our new arrival?" Amandla playfully asks, rubbing her swollen belly.

Jaxine snaps out of her daydream to see a faint reflection of her dark pupils piercing through the virtual landscape, another reminder that all good things come to an end. She turns to her virtual console. After some thought, Jaxine turns toward the window display again.

"Activate Hive-Stream," Jaxine orders. "On mute."

The window display connects to the Hive-Stream, the Hive's heavily encrypted, private network system that runs somewhat parallel to the U-Stream. A newsfeed provides updates on...

...the Framers Day Massacre...

...upcoming NorPac merger talks...

...brief global events...

...the recent lotto results...

...and a commercial for Ed Sherman's *Li'l Marco's Space Adventures*, a highly anticipated children's streaming series premiering Union-wide on Jan 14.

Jaxine hesitates before ordering, "Priority access override. Victor Zebra 56 Sigma. Director Jaxine Elizabeth Coltraine. Initiate."

"Priority access override confirmed," Hive AI replies.

"Framer Hector Contreras's residence," Jaxine orders.

The display switches to an outside sec cam in front of Hector's smart home. The sec cam swirls across the street as static interference obstructs her view of the tan-skinned Native and his larger, tattooed companion walking behind a reck parked directly in front of another smart home. The static interference dissipates as the cam swerves back to Hector's front door to reveal opened Pinnacle containers waiting at their designated pickup spot.

Jaxine pauses. She swerves back across the street to the parked reck. There's now a perfectly clear view of a janitor compacting and loading unwanted containers onto the reck. A second janitor reattaches the waste module to the outside of the smart home. Both janitors then proceed next door on foot while the unmanned reck follows.

The sec cam swerves back to Hector's front door. The Hive AI remotely—and covertly—displays a partial infrared rendering of a sobbing Toi curled up on the living-area couch, surrounded by the spoils of her Pinnacle shopping spree. The display also shows Toi screening—and refusing—incoming calls.

Rattled by momentary empathy, Jaxine then orders, "Major Hector Contreras's residence."

The window display switches to a sec cam situated across the street from Sev's high-rise condo in North Sin Vegas, or *Norsin* for short. It zooms into Ocho's bedroom as he attends virtual home-school with his back to the unobstructed window. A holographic poster for the upcoming Ed Sherman's *Li'l Marco's Space Adventures* streaming series plays on the wall above him.

The sec cam zooms out, then pans over to the living-area window to spy Hilga pacing as she chats with Rusani Cutwater over her LiveLink.

Jaxine taps into her transmission line.

"He and de boys are payin' respects to dare fallen. Okay, I will tell him. You too. Night, Rue-see," Hilga says before ending her LiveLink call.

Hilga tries to LiveLink Toi but gets forwarded to her voice mail.

"Toi, it's Hil. Please call—"

"Find Major Contreras," Jaxine orders.

"Tracking last-known coordinates," Hive AI replies.

The window display again switches to a hallway sec cam outside Angel's hotel room door. Hive AI sets the door to an infrared rendering of Sev and his men casually playing cards in the living area.

Suddenly, an incoming transmission notification with Gen. Tegashito's profile pops up on the display. Jaxine accepts the call as *audio only.*

"You callin' with good news, I hope?" Jaxine commands.

"Pickin' up lots a chitchat in So-Sec. Mostly in and around the you-zees," Gen. Tegashito says.

Eyes still on the display, Jaxine sees Sev and his men continue their card game when something catches her eye. She magnifies the display on an infrared rendering of Swayzee. Dyson exits the bath-stall to see Jaxine pointing him to the door; he quickly exits.

"I'd focus on Vanguard," Jaxine asks.

"Always to the point," Gen. Tegashito replies.

"Just how you like it."

"We're only human, Jax."

Jaxine replays a few seconds of the card game; a glitch in the display shows part of Swayzee's warm hand vanish, then reappear.

"You'll be something else entirely if you can't deliver a finished product soon."

Jaxine types in a command. Hive AI quietly analyzes Sev's card game. A digital report pops up on-screen, revealing that all the men inside are actually part of a military-software program designed to fool infrared sec cams. Her eyes widen.

"I know I'm maxed out here, but I'm gonna need more time—" Gen. Tegashito says.

"One second, Shima," Jaxine interjects as she puts Gen. Tegashito on mute. "Retrace Major Contreras's movements from Sector Two gate."

Jaxine unmutes her call while Hive AI replays Vitchenko's DC traveling from the sector gate and into the Sidekick Hotel parking garage.

"Sorry, Shima," Jaxine says. "I was lookin' for somethin'."

The display shows the DC parked in a corner of the lot just out of sec-cam visibility. The display switches to various sec cams outside, picking up static interference on virtually every feed surrounding the Sidekick Hotel.

"Anythin' I can help find?"

"Actually, Major Contreras."

"Hec's boy? Don't tell me you two are f—"

"I granted him and his men paid leave for their loss," Jaxine counters.

"Right. My bad."

"Now they've all gone off the grid," Jaxine replies.

Brief silence.

"They're looking for your ex," Gen. Tegashito says. "Just have Derek recall them."

Jaxine pauses, crosses her arms, then replies, "A pawn who can make it across, can lead you to victory, or stymie a loss."

"Your father did have a way with words."

"The MOG, the one who bagged the Xeno for you."

"Crayton."

"Have him report to Sector Four immediately," Jaxine order.

"Yes, ma'am. So where were—"

Jaxine abruptly ends the transmission and leans back in her chair.

"Last visual confirmation of Major Contreras: Sidekick Hotel," Hive AI says. "Last visual confirmation of Captain Ma-cow: Sidekick Hotel. Last visual confirmation of Lieutenant Spot-zee—"

"End inquiry," Jaxine snaps. "Terminate privacy override. Display Old Cali beach."

"Priority access override terminated," Hive AI responds.

The window display becomes a coastal view; ocean waves crash the Malibu shore as the sun sets.

"Where the fuck you goin', Sev?" Jaxine ponders.

Hy-fer

Ree enters Nooz's medical pod. Hyfor's optics dart between an unconscious Nooz and a floating, holographic display.

"Status?" Ree asks.

"Stabilized," Hyfor replies. "Friend, I wish to converse."

Ree walks over to Hyfor and looks at a portable display that shows a Lorian satellite image of the entire Sin Vegas Union territory.

"There appears to be social unrest within the preserve," Hyfor says.

They watch as a series of explosions appear in various parts of the Union.

"Although Terrans have a history of conflict and violent transfers of power, they have become more docile since the resettlements," Ree responds.

"And more adept at repurposing our tech," Hyfor adds.

Ree watches as Hyfor scans conflict areas where all the Framers Day public events are being held. She observes the small greenish triangles along with red dots across Union. However, there appear to be no red dots within a fifteen-mile radius of the Hive.

"See that?" Hyfor asks.

Hyfor points to the dots as they systematically vanish, though very few manage to escape Union territory.

"Shit," Ree says.

"We continue to underestimate their intelligence," Hyfor responds.

However, Hyfor also highlights a few greenish triangles that have managed to move about somewhat freely, though none occupy Sector One—yet.

"The experimental protein trackers Nooz received from the home world have shown success," Ree states in reference to the greenish dots.

"Side effects still limit its use. It will take a few generations to perfect. And look at this," Hyfor says, pointing to the NorPac Federation's southern borders.

"Increased intercolony traffic," Ree states. "And border settlements."

"Yet no signs of hostilities," Hyfor adds.

"Perhaps they are converging?" Ree replies.

"This phenomenon appears to be somewhat common on this planet," Hyfor replies. "When resources are scarce, rival groups will either conflict or cooperate."

"I have conversed with Mjar," Ree says. "He will petition leadership for more resources. Should these colonies merge, we will amend the northern demarcation."

"You still believe our strategy will influence sympathy among the collective?" Hyfor replies.

"My birth mother has studied Terran communication for quite some time. Specifically, their use of light and sound to incentivize specific tasks—or none at all."

"Perhaps we should let the Terrans rule," Hyfor barks.

"Friend, I acknowledge your distress. But we swore an oath to this cause," Ree says. "As did Nooz."

"I agree," Hyfor replies. "I speak with anger."

"You speak with truth," Ree counters.

"Friend Reh-ee. You have my loyalty," Hyfor declares.

"Friend Hy-fer. You have mine," Ree replies.

Lights blink on the portable display.

"Something has crossed the demarcation," Hyfor states.

"Poacher?" Ree asks.

"Too small," Hyfor replies. "Likely Terran."

"Likely dead, if left unaided," Ree says.

Hyfor turns to Ree and says, "It appears a detonation within the preserve has generated an unusually strong signature. The object was on a course for one of the Three Villages…then vanished."

"A cloaked attack?"

"Though anything is possible with these Terrans, readings indicate a steep climb followed by deceleration and descent."

"A test of some sort, perhaps," Ree concludes. "Can you calculate—"

"Here are the coordinates," Hyfor interjects. "Not too far outside the demarcation."

"I will address it," Ree says. "Stay with your mate."

"You go alone?"

"We cannot spare current resources. Do not fear. My lineage will protect me from poachers."

Ree heads for the exit.

"And the Terrans?" Hyfor asks.

"I will bring caution," Ree replies as she exits.

The White House

Terry and Generals Monahan, Lawson, and Tegashito take turns hitting golf balls in a virtual twenty-first century outdoor driving range—and they all suck. Sipping on SinWater, the two men laugh at each other's embarrassing swings as if they were old college buddies. Soft electronic beats fill the vroom.

"Fuck that baby Hitler!" Gen. Monahan shouts. "If I could go back, I'd kill de mudderfucka who made dis game!"

After another crazy shot way off the mark, Gen. Monahan steps down.

Terry steps up to the tee.

"I'd fuckin' put baby Hitler to sleep," Terry says. "No hesitation!"

Terry swings and makes good contact with the ball.

"How are my Vanguardians lookin', Shima?" Terry asks.

"Wouldn't you rather have soldiers whose heads don't fuckin' explode on the battlefield?" Gen. Tegashito asks.

"Depends on when they explode," Terry counters. "I'm getting tired of seeing red and yellow lights. I want those fucking tubes green!"

After a few hits, Terry steps away from the tee to make room for Gen. Tegashito.

"If it's not the Xenos, it's the fuckin' Man," Gen. Lawson adds.

Gen. Tegashito hits his virtual ball, which sails widely off course. After a few balls, he takes a seat.

Gen. Lawson steps up as a virtual ball appears on the tee. He swings and misses.

"Fuck," Gen. Lawson barks at the ball.

Gen. Lawson swings again. This time he connects. The ball floats into the air and lands straight on the White House lawn a few yards from the hole. Gen. Lawson's score briefly floats over the ball before disappearing. He then takes a seat.

Gen. Monahan steps up to the tee again.

"And I thought our air was fucked up," Gen. Lawson says.

"We ruled Earth once. We'll do it again," Gen. Tegashito says.

"Maybe. And dat's if we had every man, woman, child, and robot left on de planet," Gen. Monahan replies as he shanks his next virtual golf ball.

A cybernetic waitress delivers SinWater; the men huddle around her and grab a drink.

"Mr. President?" Gen. Lawson says.

"You're up, Quint," Terry replies.

The four men hold up their glasses.

"To a greater Union," Gen. Monahan toasts.

They clink glasses and drink.

"Speaking of children," Terry begins. "Anything on our missing Framers?"

The generals look at each other in uncomfortable silence.

"C'mon! We're under martial fuckin' law!" Terry yells.

"You wanted de TEDs on de DL, yeah?" Gen. Monahan replies.

"Quint's right," Gen. Lawson says. "Last thing we need is NorPac second-guessing the merger after seein' blood on our streets."

"And last thing I need are three supposedly comatose Framers turning up on the D-Stream alive," Terry snaps. "Any ideas what they could possibly want with them?"

"Not sure about Titts and Igloo, but Contreras? Doze fuckers breed like rats," Gen. Tegashito jokes. "Maybe they're lookin' to bypass the lotto."

The men laugh. Terry looks over at the Old Nation's former headquarters in the distance.

"Keep the TEDs on a short leash," Terry says. "At least until we seal this fuckin' deal."

Rachaville

Henn leads Sev and his men through the massive crowd of citizens, including a substantial population of rachas, Union slang for people who live, work, and play with little to no sunlight, going about their daily routine. Like Henn, most locals have pale or much-lighter skin tones, thinner hair, and toned frames. Henn stops as the men look ahead in amazement.

"Boss, you recall dis place?" Chino asks.

"Seems more crowded."

"Like dey got de whole Union up in did bitch," Angel quips.

Swayzee turns to Vitchenko and asks, "When last you come here?"

"Bin-a-min," Vitchenko says as he grins at Henn.

Grinning, Henn turns to the men.

"Welcome to Subclarita, boys," Henn proudly exclaims.

Sounds and bright lights pierce up from an overpopulated megasubcity just northwest of the Los Angeles Bloc, partially swallowed hundreds of feet deep within an enormous man-made crater. The tips of Subclarita's superstructures—some hundreds of stories tall—peek above the earth as if desperate for sunlight and fresh air; solfils soak in as much renewable energy as possible. Lorian ships in the upper atmosphere dart across the upper atmosphere, briefly casting shadows over Subclarita and the surrounding area.

"Dis life ain't me," Swayzee says. "For real."

"Least *you* have a choice, grounda," Henn counters.

Henn walks toward the megasubcity. Vitchenko follows with the others close behind. Sev and Chino bring up the rear.

"We used to fly to de stars," Sev says. "Now we dig to de core."

Chino peeks down into the crater and asks, "How far down?"

Sev peeks down into the crater and deadpans, "Couple hundred maybe. Give or grab."

"Tink we betta grab," Chino quips.

They proceed down a path hundreds of feet belowground where scanners accept their false identities, granting them all access into the megasubcity. The further into Subclarita they venture, the less natural light and more brighter eyes they encounter. Everyone brightens their retinal displays to help navigate the dark maze of buildings that hinder sunlight, but not the foot traffic.

Minutes later, Henn leads the men down a less-populated alley.

"Dis place gives me de fuzzies," Swayzee says.

Glowing eyes from busy Rachas going about their business pierce the dimly lit walkways when faint sirens and chatter from patrolling Subtroopers, nicknamed Blarts, echo around them.

Ten minutes later, Henn leads the group to a dead end.

"Maybe next pad we get a view, yeah?" Swayzee jokes.

Angel grips his pistol as Henn opens a secret door and enters.

Sev turns to Vitchenko who nods for them to continue. Once inside, they hear the gateway close behind them. Suddenly, scanners blanket their bodies.

A wall slowly opens enough for them to pass through no more than two at a time.

"Boss, I tink we gonna need a raise," Chino says.

"I'll bring it up wit' De Man," Sev sarcastically replies.

They enter the dark room. The lights activate, revealing display screens, weapons, and other tech at their disposal. It's much nicer than the previous crash pad.

"Someone need a raise?" Gwenda New Zealand, now much older and with a bionic arm, asks.

Everyone turns to their right to see Gwenda aiming a gun right at them. Chino's eyes widen.

"Gweny?" Chino asks.

Gwenda's eyes widen. She holsters her sidearm.

"Chee?" Gwenda replies. "What de fuck?"

"She don't let me call her Gweny," Henn laments.

Gwenda and Chino embrace. Swayzee turns to Henn.

"She ain't no racha," Swayzee whispers to Angel.

"No shit," Angel whispers back.

"You fuck dis guy?" Henn asks.

"Chee's a family friend," Gwenda answers.

The others turn to Sev, who simply shrugs.

Vitchenko turns to Henn and says, "I gotta take a shit."

"T-M-I," Henn says as she points him to the bathstall.

Vitchenko disappears into the bathstall while Chino walks Gwenda over to Sev.

"Boss, Gwenda New Zealand," Chino says, providing introductions. "Gwenda, Major Contreras."

Sev and Gwenda first bump.

"New Zealand. Like de stories, yeah?" Sev asks.

"Contreras. Like de Fray-mahs, yeah?" Gwenda replies.

Sev nods with a slight chuckle and asks, "You got jizz on my pop?"

"Someone but can't identify," Gwenda replies.

"Still freelancin'?" Chino asks.

"Still Hive-in'?" Gwenda asks.

Chino smiles. Gwenda grins back.

Sev feigns a cough and interjects, "Finsig later, yeah?"

"Not good to fuck wit' De Children in dis Sec, Hiver," Gwenda replies.

"Dey fuck wit' my pop, I fuck wit' dem," Sev counters.

"Identify, Hiver," Gwenda asks Sev as Chino clears his throat.

"Gweny, recall what I said," Chino asks. "'Bout de one who found me near dead?"

"Him? He wasn't no Outy den," Gwenda says, pointing to Sev. "He was a pup!"

"His pop, de Fray-mah," Chino confirms, "was dat man."

Gwenda turns to Sev. She turns back to Chino and sighs.

"For real?" Gwenda replies.

Vitchenko returns from the bathstall.

"For real, for real," Chino answers. "I can show you de vid."

Chino places his index finger close to his implant.

"No need. I vouch for you," Gwenda replies. "Always."

"I pay you what I can," Sev asks.

"Pretty please?" Vitchenko begs.

"You got anudda prob," Gwenda says.

"What?" Sev asks.

Gwenda activates a virtual 3D rendering of the Sidekick Hotel sprinkled with color-coded symbols.

"I retrace your bullshit profiles dis mornin'," Gwenda says.

"We're fucked," Vitchenko says.

"We?" Henn replies.

Swayzee points to a cluster of similar symbols.

"TEDs," Swayzee says.

"No bueno," Angel deadpans.

"Shit, dey on to us so soon," Chino says.

Vitchenko calls out, "Guys."

Sev walks over to Vitchenko pointing at a closed-circuit video clip.

Wishbone converses with a few TEDs beside a personnel transport labeled TERROR ELIMINATION DEPARTMENT

Sev studies the video clip.

"Angel—"

"Already switch to backup profiles," Angel triumphantly replies.

"Less time to find Pop now," Sev says.

"Dis where Kah-Lee have de man," Gwenda says.

Gwenda displays another 3D building. It's very tall. A tiny dot flashes within one of the penthouses.

"Chee?" Sev asks.

"Extraction Plan Barbie," Chino replies.

"Barbie?" Swayzee asks.

Vitchenko whispers into Swayzee's ear.

"Dey 'bout tree days behind us. Means we got two," Sev says. "Angel, give Chee a hand."

"Right across the face, sir," Angel jokes.

"Use it and lose it, bro," Chino replies.

"Chenko?" Sev asks.

"Henn and I grab de pidge oh nine hundred."

"We gonna be real fuckin' tight," Sev says.

Swayzee raises his hand and asks, "Anyone here tink dis shit just a liddle too cray?"

"Yeah!" everyone else shouts in unison.

Sev turns to Swayzee and says, "Sarge wants a view. Sarge gets a view, yeah?"

Swayzee nods and halfheartedly replies, "Yeah, boss."

Chino gives Angel instructions then shoos him away as Gwenda approaches.

"Not what I expected," Gwenda says.

"Wish we had more time," Chino replies. "Lots to say."

Chino grabs her cybernetic hand and caresses it.

"Den we talk on de way," Gwenda replies.

Gwenda gently kisses Chino on the lips then hugs him. She looks over to see Henn teasing her by pantomiming a blowjob. Gwenda chuckles.

"What?" Chino asks.

"Nuttin'," Gwenda answers with a sly grin.

The TEDs

A sleek black tubecar pulls into a secret, heavily guarded station. Inside, Hector sits with a black hood covering his head.

"We there yet?" Hector sarcastically asks.

"Maybe the last stop should be right up your ass," Manny snaps.

The tubecar doors open. Manny removes Hector's hood. Hector removes his earplugs.

"I'm sorry, you say somethin'?" Hector sarcastically asks with a smile, knowing he can't hear anything.

"After you," Manny replies with a smile.

Manny shakes his head as he and Hector exit the tubecar. They weave through a gauntlet of Kah-Lee soldiers walking around. None of the men or women appear to have traditional Union implants, if any at all.

"Of course, I recall octopuses. I'm old, not senile," Hector replies.

"Picture a sleeper cell as one of those tiny suctions on its tentacles. Two agents within each cell are given a unique code that allows them to communicate with their respective mirrors on opposite sides of the cell," Manny explains.

"And if one or both are compromised?" Hector inquires.

"No one in the cell knows which two agents have these codes. And the ones with a code do not know who has the other. Any attempts to discover who has what code will bring repercussions."

"Needles," Hector responds.

Manny shakes his head.

"There's usually nothing left to recycle," Manny says.

"And you leave the others out in the cold until things cool off," Hector deduces.

"You always were a good student," Manny replies.

"Top of the fuckin' class—I recall."

"I think you left your modesty back at the station."

Hector looks around.

"Hell of an operation you got here," Hector says.

"Wasn't easy," Manny replies. "But as usual, your father owns most of the credit."

Hector and Manny walk past a large room where a group of Kah-Lee soldiers train in hand combat. Hector's attention turns to a corner where Invoice supervises a focused Jolly training shirtless. Strange scars crisscross down Jolly's lanky spine as he spars with a hologram of another teenaged stray projected from Jolly's small alien device. Jolly wipes his brow, briefly exposing a ring of small circular burn marks around his scalp just at the hairline.

"Another day," Hector replies, waving and waiting for Manny to assist with their names.

"Jolly and Invoice," Manny quickly whispers.

"Jolly," Hector says and adds, "and Invoice!"

"Nudder day, mang," Invoice replies.

Invoice feigns a cough to get Jolly's attention.

Jolly turns to Hector.

"Nuther day... Fray-mer," Jolly says before turning back to sparring.

Hector and Manny continue walking down the corridor. Invoice turns back to Jolly's training.

"What kinda sparrin' program is that?" Hector asks.

"Some kinda stray Xenocube," Manny replies with a shrug.

Hector stops and turns.

"Are you insane?" Hector whispers.

"You think if we just stick our bodies in the Earth, they won't find us?"

"So let's make it easier for them?"

"Where you gonna go?" Manny asks. "Zimbabwe?"

"Point taken," Hector concedes.

"Besides, the Xenos aren't our immediate threat," Manny replies.

"Really?" Hector says.

Manny stops and turns to Hector.

"And that hologram?" Manny replies. "It's Jolly's brother."

Hector looks over at Jolly sparring in the distance. He looks back at Manny.

"Dead?" Hector asks.

"Or the Trifect. Or Mexiland. Needles. Off world," Manny answers. "Who the fuck knows?"

Manny continues down the hall. Hector follows.

"How many strays?" Hector asks.

"A few dozen scattered across the Union for their own protection," Manny answers. "Mostly in the subcolonies where they can at least pass for rachas."

"But the stray laws have been rescinded for years," Hector says.

"And how many strays have you seen walkin' around?"

"I don't get out much," Hector replies.

"Really?" Manny counters.

"But I've met a few strays in my time. Very intelligent... extremely dangerous."

"True," Manny says. "Some like Jolly were apparently bred for combat."

"Yeah," Hector asks. "Sounds about right."

"Seems his owner took some pity."

"Last time I met a Xeno with a sweet spot, it damn near killed me," Hector sarcastically responds.

Hector and Manny approach a tunnel archway. Hector looks up at a partially destroyed twenty-first century sign:

WELCOME TO CALI

They walk under the archway into a cavernous compound. Smiling, Manny leads Hector inside his guarded private office. Upon entering, lights flicker on and soft electronic music plays. Hector smiles at the familiar tune.

"You've played this before," Hector deduces. "But it was different."

"Moira," Manny responds with a grin. "My inung and amang would play her all the time when I was a boy."

"No shit," Hector sarcastically mumbles.

"But I lost the music file during my escape," Manny laments. "It was the only thing left I have of them."

Manny walks over to his desk, opens a drawer, and pulls out two small containers of water.

Hector sympathetically nods before replying, "The shit kids listen to these days, huh?"

"Not just these days," Manny replies.

"Now, I know you're not talkin' about old hip-hip."

Sarcastically laughing, Manny tosses a water container to Hector and replies, "This'll go down much better. For real."

"Yeah?" Hector sarcastically responds. "Well, I got somethin' that'll go down much better for you…"

As Hector takes a sip of water, a large, living ant farm embedded in the wall behind Manny's desk draws his attention, along with the former Philippine national flag hanging above it.

"Ready to see what you saw back on the LBI?" Manny says as he walks behind his desk. Hector follows but stops to study the ant farm. While watching the overly populated insect society harmoniously cooperate, Hector sees something on the glass reflection. He turns toward Manny's desk and spots a photo of a fading portrait: Gen. Contreras and Manny standing in front of the rusted, decommissioned P413 Chinook.

"From the looks of things, a typical Tuesday afternoon," Hector deadpans.

Manny activates his electronic console and pulls out his modified zoomers. He wirelessly transfers the zoomers' data onto his desk console. A virtual rendering of what Hector saw earlier appears above Manny's desk: Lorian airships hovering high above the Union coastline. The images even show a few Lorian silhouettes through the airship's windows. The rendering zooms out to reveal four more airships in the upper atmosphere hovering inland.

"From what we can tell, these ships have minimal defensive artillery. And the Xenos inside them don't appear to be heavily armed or dressed for battle," Manny explains.

"Well I feel a whole lot better—not," Hector sarcastically counters.

"And these exact same ships appear every few days or so virtually invisible to most radar. For the time being, anyway."

Hector reviews the rendering.

"The further inland, the higher the altitude," Hector says.

"Good eye," Manny replies.

Hector turns to Manny and says, "Wait, these are... Xeno *tourists?*"

Manny nods and replies, "And we're the main attraction."

A gentle bell rings. Manny's office door turns transparent to reveal Bic standing between the two posted guards. Manny opens the door for Bic to enter.

"Sir, you gotta see dis," Bic says. "You too, Fray-mah."

Manny allows Bic to take the console. Bic activates a virtual map of all five sectors in the Union. He zooms in on Sector Four, then zooms in closer.

"Looks like Ontario Bloc," Hector says.

"Not bad for a hermit," Bic sarcastically replies.

The rendering zooms in on a large residential building surrounded by various colored symbols.

"TEDs," Manny says.

"Seventy-two hours ago," Bic explains.

"Kills?" Manny asks.

"Five," Bic answers. "So far we know."

"Five? Must be a training exercise," Hector sarcastically responds.

"Dis crash pad been dormant for mons," Bic says.

Bic pulls up a video clip. The recording shows troopers cordoning off the street while heavily armed TEDs exit the building after their raid.

"Great," Hector says. "Can this day get any fuckin' better?"

"Better hope, Fray-mah," Bic replies.

The video further captures one of the TEDs interrogating a group of residents outside when Crayton enters the frame. He holds out a device that projects the holographic profiles of Sev, Chino, Angel, Vitchenko, and Swayzee.

"No, no, no, no, no," Hector responds.

"Yes, yes, yes, yes, yes," Bic replies.

"Fuck," Hector says.

Manny points at Crayton.

"He the tween who killed that Xeno?" Manny asks.

Bic pulls up Crayton's 3D profile. Hector's eyes widen.

"Cray-Cray," Hector says.

"Gotta be a little cray-cray to bag a Xeno, right Éxi?" Manny says.

"Col. Crayton Stak," Bic explains. "Dat's a bad mudderfucka right dare."

"I wasn't impressed," Hector deadpans.

Bic accepts a personal incoming message on his comchat.

"Manny, we gotta find my boy before they do," Hector barks.

"Give me one reason—" Manny begins.

"Sir, he did it," Bic interrupts. "Tegashito did it."

Manny turns to Bic.

"Vanguard?" Manny asks.

Bic nods then replies, "We gotta take out dat bunker."

Hector turns to Bic.

"What bunker?" Hector asks.

"Sugar Bunker," Manny answers.

Hector pauses for a brief moment.

"The armory?" Hector asks.

"Ain't Poppa's armory no more, Fray-mah," Bic replies. "Dey testin' Xenos."

"Well that's cool and all," Hector counters, "but my fuckin' boy's in trouble."

"As I was saying," Manny interrupts. "Give me one good reason why we should help you."

"We negotiating now?" Hector asks.

"Think of it as a limited partnership," Manny says.

"I thought we were family," Hector says.

"Families help each other," Manny replies.

Hector pauses for a moment.

"Fine. I'll scratch your fuckin' back—when my boy's safe," Hector replies.

"Bic?" Manny calls out.

"I'll get Invoice on it," Bic replies.

"I'm goin' with," Hector says.

"No can do, Éxi," Manny responds.

"I need you wit' me in Sugar Bunker," Bic adds.

"Bullshit," Hector replies.

"You know your way around," Manny says.

"You need me to set charges?" Hector asks.

"I'll take care of de charges," Bic answers.

"Coltraine will be there with P-Doc and Tegashito," Manny replies. "Along with a means to control these new soldiers. Maybe you can talk some sense into her."

"And if I can't?

"Den your boy's dead anyway," Bic answers.

Manny extends his fist.

"Time to jump off the fence," Manny asks.

"How the fuck we gonna break into a military installation?" Hector asks.

"Your father took care of that a long time ago," Manny replies, still holding up his fist.

Hector sighs and turns to Bic.

"Invoice brings my boy back alive," Hector orders, "and fully functional!"

"I vouch," Bic agrees.

"And I vouch for my fuckin' arm," Manny adds.

Hector finally fist-bumps Manny; Bic exits the office and shuts the door. Manny opens a drawer and pulls out a small flask. He takes a swig and hands Hector the flask.

"Not how I thought my life would turn out either," Manny says.

Hector takes a swig and hands the flask back to Manny.

"Bic was right. Framers have way more value than I realized," Hector laments.

"Only thing more valuable than a good Framer is a dead one," Manny deadpans.

Hector stares at Sev's holographic profile. Manny takes another swig and hands Hector the flask again.

"Union fuckin' strong," Hector quips before taking another swig.

The Red Woods

Giant internal border gates to the Northwest Pacific Federation's heavily guarded Oregonia Province slowly open. A caravan of tactical armored commuters called *Tomcats* exits. *Tomcat Alpha*, the prime minister's executive vehicle, rolls in the middle of the pack. Above them, a swarm of *sparrows*, unmanned aerial assault drones, hover above like a small rain cloud. As the Tomcat caravan proceeds to an external border gate, NorPac residents outside the main territory cheer. Civilian vehicles slide to the right as the caravan passes.

An hour from the external border gate, the Tomcat caravan barrels a few miles down a private highway before exiting into a dense forest. All's relatively quiet...until a projectile hurtles toward the Tomcat caravan.

A sparrow immediately fires a countermeasure that successfully eliminates the foreign object. It then leads a small group of sparrows toward the object's calculated point of origin. At the targeted destination, the sparrows' scanners all fail to detect anything when an array of laser bullets takes out one of the sparrows. The remaining three sparrows manage to kill a few of the mysterious attackers before darting back to the Tomcat caravan.

After confirming the coast is clear, a gang of humans and robots known as the *Islanders* deactivate their camouflage tech. The fearsome group consists of thick, tan, tattooed cybernetic scavengers who quickly round up both the sparrow wreckage and their fallen. They load everything on their getaway stealth scooters and disappear into the woods well before the Union Border Patrol arrives.

Thirty minutes after the failed ambush, the Tomcat caravan rumbles through a dirt path in the woods until it arrives at the base of a mountain. Suddenly, a concealed entrance opens, swallowing the vehicles whole before closing.

One thousand feet below the mountain's base, NorPac Prime Minister Archon Devore and his elite personal guards known as *custodians* enter a grand room where Terry, Corin, and their PGs greet them. One of the robotic custodians carries with it a container.

Archon studies a nervous Corin as she silently exits the room and closes the door.

"Rough trip?" Terry asks.

"Fuckin' Islanders," Archon replies.

"Could've taken a tubecar," Terry says.

"I prefer the open air," Archon responds.

"Or one of your ships?" Terry asks.

"Seasick," Archon answers. "Besides, I enjoy the woods."

"You don't trust me," Terry deduces.

"We can't trust anyone anymore," Archon replies. "Isn't that how we both got here?"

The custodian carrying the container gently places it on the ground and opens it.

Terry smiles.

"Fuckin' oxy!" Terry shouts.

Archon smiles.

"You didn't think I'd forget, did you?" Archon says.

"Never had a doubt," Terry says.

"Bullshit!" Archon responds.

"You're right," Terry replies. "That alone would've been a fuckin' deal breaker."

They laugh as custodians remove bottles of NorPac Red from the container and carry them to a dinner table already set. Terry and Archon walk over to the table and sit.

"Hope you brought your appetite," Terry says.

"I could eat ten packs of vermin," Archon says.

Waiters place cooked steak medallions and a bottle of NorPac Red from the container.

"Can-Chee prime it is," Terry says. "Can't wait to bring those red fuckers into the fold."

Archon replies, "And delete those fuckin' scavengers out there."

Terry chuckles as waiters serve them.

"What are the odds two Xenos are havin' the same convo over humans right now?" Terry asks.

The men raise their glasses of wine.

"To the last men standing," Archon toasts.

"Last men standing," Terry toasts.

The men toast and drink. They dig into their beef.

"So martial law?" Archon inquires.

"I have a plan," Terry says.

"Does it include Kah-Lee sympathizers infiltrating my borders?"

Terry folds his arms and replies, "Look, I fucked up, all right?"

Archon slams his hands on the table like an erupting volcano and counters, "Fucked up? My father treated you like a son. The absolute least you could've done was show up to his funeral."

"Your father tried to convince my wife to go with you!"

"But she didn't. Did she? So get off your fuckin' high horse and stop actin' like you haven't been lickin' every piece of ass in your face!"

Terry sighs, unfolds his arms, and relaxes in his chair.

"You're right. I should've paid my respects. But he fuckin' disrespected me in my own home. Arch. At least give me that."

"That your fuckin' idea of an apology?"

"I'm sorry. Okay? Should I get on my fuckin' knees?"

"Wouldn't be the first time?" Archon retorts.

The men continue with their meal.

"Fuck you. We've both done a lot of shit we'd be ashamed of before Man Fall," Terry admits. "Even to each other."

"True. But you started it."

"Then I'm hopin'—fuckin' prayin'—we can finally end it and turn the page."

Archon holds up his wine and replies, "Anytin's possible. Asshole."

The men smile, toast, and drink once more. Terry sighs.

"Easier than I thought," Terry says.

"Never underestimate the power of greed, old friend," Archon replies.

They laugh.

"What's your fuckin' angle?" Terry asks.

"A secluded compound on the coast where I can enjoy my last days drinkin' and fuckin' in peace," Archon answers.

"And that's different from your current situation how?" Terry sarcastically asks.

"Without the bullshit responsibilities," Archon replies.

Terry pauses, nods in agreement, and then sighs.

"Can't tell you how many times I just felt like…fuck it," Terry says.

"Burn it all down and call it a fuckin' day," Archon concludes.

Terry looks at the window display showing a beautiful lakeside sunset.

"Think we'll be remembered, Arch?" Terry asks.

Archon looks at the display, then back at Terry.

"You mean while they're sitting on a fuckin' rack waitin' to be flayed?" Archon replies. "Or being dragged around by a metal ring bolted to their fuckin' heads?"

"Always the optimist," Terry deadpans.

"Misery loves company."

"Seems like yesterday the three of us were giving our parents headaches in Mesquite."

"You were cryin' like a little bitch when we found out you were moving to Canada." Terry chuckles.

"Yeah, well, it all worked out. Didn't it?"

"Speaking of which, Jax sends her love," Terry says.

"She always had plenty to go around," Archon replies.

They chuckle, toast, and drink some more.

"And *I'm* the asshole," Terry playfully responds.

Hostile Takeover

The next day, Capt. Theroux drives Terry through the Sugar Bunker corridors in a mini while PGs Kindle Wilis and his robotic partner DAF47 sit in back.

"Permission to speak, sir," Capt. Theroux asks.

"Spit it out."

"What's the prime minister like, sir?"

"A spoiled little brat. Just like he was growing up."

"Yes, sir."

Capt. Theroux's mini drives through two tunnel checkpoints that lead into an enormous warehouse packed with fetus-containing tubes filled with liquid.

"Captain, I thought we were taking the shorter route," Terry says.

"Mr. President, Gen. Tegashito transmitted new instructions," Capt. Theroux replies with a smile.

The minis cruise between two rows of the tubes as lab techs carefully inspect each one. Although the fetuses are in various stages of life, they have minuscule blinking devices embedded in their transparent brain stems. This time, however, 99 percent of the tube consoles display a *solid green light* with a few solid red and the rest flashing yellows, a clear indication of overwhelming success. Terry's eyes widen.

"Son of a bitch," Terry says.

"The general thought you might like, sir," Capt. Theroux says.

"Oh, I fuckin' like."

"Oxy, sir."

Capt. Theroux's mini pulls in to a designated spot for Terry and his PGs to disembark, before driving off. Terry and his PGs continue to a gate where Jaxine, Gen. Tegashito, PG Hemingway, and PG Jericho-19 greet them with smiles.

"Hope you enjoyed the scenic route, Mr. President," Gen. Tegashito greets.

Terry smiles and replies, "Shima, you motherfucker."

Terry turns to Jaxine who says, "Surprise."

"Get over here, you," Terry replies as he grabs Jaxine for a hug.

Jaxine, Terry, and Gen. Tegashito excitedly embrace each other then proceed to hug their four PGs, who in turn hug each other.

"Okay, okay," Terry playfully says. "Enough with the fuckin' orgy."

Moments later, Gen. Tegashito leads Jaxine and Terry into the control room. He presses a button on the wall that lowers the entire room down a few levels. Gen. Tegashito then walks over to the large window display that lights up to reveal a furnished entertainment room on the other side. Gen. Tegashito presses a button on the wall panel. Nothing happens for the first minute, which is confirmed with awkward silence.

"Shima, if you discovered how to graft cloaking tech to skin, I will blow you right now," Terry says.

Laughing, Jaxine replies, "Get in line."

Suddenly, the door to the entertainment room opens. Five Tween Defense Club soldiers enter the room and line up at attention facing them.

Gen. Tegashito activates the intercom.

"This is General Tegashito speaking."

The soldiers salute at their reflections.

"Sir!" they yell.

"At ease," Gen. Tegashito orders. "Today's your lucky day. Until further notice, I want you to simply relax and make yourselves comfortable. Understood?"

"Yes, sir!" the soldiers shout.

"Union strong!" Terry shouts.

"Union strong!" the soldiers reply.

Gen. Tegashito turns off the intercom. He—along with Jaxine and Terry—watches as two of the soldiers play video games, two play cards, and the fifth decides to take a nap.

A small square on one of the control room's walls lights up. Jaxine presses the square, which releases a hot cup of tea that she hands to Terry.

"Kettle tea?" Jaxine says.

"Thank you, my dear," Terry replies.

Gen. Tegashito walks over to another wall in the room. He uses a retinal scan to open a compartment then pulls out a remote and a small *VImplant*. Gen. Tegashito walks back over to Jaxine and Terry.

"Although these bad boys are smaller than our traditional implants, I can't get them to stop glowing through the skin," Gen. Tegashito says. "Damn Xenotech."

Gen. Tegashito hands Terry the implant then uses the remote to successfully link with the VImplants attached to the soldiers' neural networks.

Jaxine and Terry study the soldiers in the adjacent room while Gen. Tegashito remotely transmits his commands.

In the entertainment room, the napping soldier suddenly pops up, heads over to the window, and stands at attention. The other soldiers continue what they're doing when, suddenly, one of the soldiers playing video games inexplicably jumps up and joins the napping soldier at attention.

Confused, the three remaining soldiers slowly decide to join the others at attention. A few seconds later they sit at the table and proceed to play cards. They all start singing the *Sin Vegas Union Anthem* in unison. While singing, they turn and look to their mirror—directly at Jaxine, Terry, and Gen. Tegashito.

Eyes beaming with joy, Terry turns to Gen. Tegashito.

"No exploding heads?" Terry asks.

"None yet, sir," Gen. Tegashito explains. "And we even managed to dim the blinking. You'd have to be pretty close to notice now."

"How?" Terry asks.

"The tech in Fresno I told you about. Apparently, he found a way to synthetically replicate the chemical compound found in both the Xeno's complex vascular system and their zeezee implants," Gen. Tegashito answers. "By harvesting this compound through hybrid stem cells, we've finally been able to manufacture biocircuitry strong enough to keep the brain from overloading."

"So no exploding heads?" Terry inquires.

"At least long enough to keep their heads on during battle," Jaxine adds.

"But they still need to be battle-tested to confirm limitations," Gen. Tegashito answers.

"And where is this fine, upstanding citizen so I can show my deepest deep gratitude?" Terry asks.

Gen. Tegashito clears his throat.

"Needles, sir," Gen. Tegashito replies.

"It appears he su-eed in his unit," Jaxine replies.

"No signs of foul play," Gen. Tegashito adds.

Terry frowns.

"When did this happen?"

"About fifteen months ago," Gen. Tegashito replies.

"So why the fuck am I hearing about this now?!"

"It took ten months just to crack his encrypted software," Gen. Tegashito replies.

"Assume I go along with this...bullshit. Anyone else know about this?" Terry asks.

"No signs of identity or digital theft," Gen. Tegashito answers.

"As far as we know," Jaxine adds.

"Given recent developments, I'd have to agree both of you know very little!" Terry hisses.

Suddenly, a commotion turns their attention to the soldiers now fighting each other. The combat turns more acrobatic and brutal as they use firsts and furniture on each other. They fight as if they do not recognize each other while Jaxine, Terry, and Gen. Tegashito safely observe the bloody brawl.

"How many?" Terry asks.

"About a hundred fifty Gen Ones awaiting orders."

"And they won't even know it!" Jaxine adds.

"And how many can that thing control?" Terry asks.

"Guesstimates are currently at around sixty, give or take. But once we figure out a way to sync this with ThinkLink, we could theoretically control a human being from cradle to Needles," Gen. Tegashito answers.

"A superior race capable of beatin' the Xenos," Terry says.

"Without fear or hesitation," Jaxine adds.

"An entire population under a single consciousness," Gen. Tegashito replies.

Tears welling up, Jaxine stares at the soldiers.

"What do you think, Terry?" Jaxine asks.

Terry walks closer to the window to study the carnage. The entertainment room is totally destroyed. All five bloodied soldiers lay lifeless on the floor.

"Time frame for an initial rollout?" Terry asks.

"Actually, Mr. President…we've already begun," Gen. Tegashito replies.

"We have?" Terry replies.

Suddenly, Gen. Tegashito stabs Terry in the back of the neck with a needle and injects him. He catches Terry and carries him over to the couch and lays him down.

"Ready?" Jaxine asks.

Gen. Tegashito stands, fixes himself, then nods.

Jaxine opens the door. PGs Kindle Wilis and DAF47 enter, followed by PGs Hemingway and Jericho-19. Jaxine shuts the door; PG Hemingway knocks out PG Wilis while PG Jericho-19 short-circuits PG DAF47.

"Big sorries, Daff," PG Jericho-19 apologizes to PG DAF47.

Gen. Tegashito presses the wall button to lower the control room one level down where they see a surgical room being prepped by a team of loyal staff.

"Time?" Jaxine asks.

"Plenty before the opening ceremony."

"This had better work."

"Trust me, my queen," Gen. Tegashito replies. "This plan will work!"

The PGs deliver Terry into the surgical room through a door that opens beside the window.

PG Hemingway turns to the control room and mumbles to his mechanical partner, "Tink we can reprogram him to return my socreds from losin' dat bet?"

"No shit,' PG Jericho replies.

Gen. Tegashito actives his comchat as he walks toward Jaxine.

"Captain, initiate Privacy Mode Cabbage Patch," Gen. Tegashito orders. "Four hours."

"Copy dat, sir," Capt. Theroux affirms via comchat.

Jaxine and Gen. Tegashito gaze at each other. Jaxine moves to within an inch of him.

"You're married," Gen. Tegashito responds.

"Like the Old Nation, marriage is dead," Jaxine retorts as she grabs his left hand with her right.

Jaxine's hands then slide up to Gen. Tegashito's chest. He pulls her closer; they passionately kiss.

"Union strong," Gen. Tegashito says as he kisses her neck.

"Ooh…feels bloody strong to me," Jaxine sensually replies.

In the heat of passion, Jaxine silently pulls out a needle and injects Gen. Tegashito with it, instantly knocking him out. She then shoves Gen. Tegashito into the waiting arms of PG Jericho-19.

"And thanks for the plan," Jaxine taunts an unconscious Gen. Tegashito.

The Merger

One week later, hundreds of thousands of Union and NorPac supporters cheer as the NorPac Tomcat convoy, this time sans sparrows, rumbles through the Sanjose Bloc and into the massive Veterans Arena. A trooper phalanx grants the motorcade safe passage to its respective VIP parking area while SkyHawks and aerial drones blanket the partially sunny sky.

Cybernetic and robotic troopers usher the NorPac delegation, led by Prime Minister Archon Devore, Subprime Minister Alexi Goatee, and Governor-General Racene Gladigan, toward the Framers Outpost, a large VIP structure just outside the arena. Attendees, including Dyson and Corin, shower their guests with adoration as they enter the complex.

Inside, Terry, Jaxine, Gen. Tegashito, Gen. Lawson, the remaining board of directors, and a few high-ranking reps stand single file, greeting incoming guests with fist bumps. The foreign dignitaries take their designated seats after the gauntlet of salutations. Terry and Archon greet each other.

"The three of us, together again," Terry says. "Who would've thought?"

"Your wife, when we were driving our parents crazy back in Mesquite," Archon replies as he glances at Terry's neck. "Upgrade?"

Terry caresses the small incision on his neck with uncertainty.

"Gotta keep up with the Joneses," Jaxine interjects. "Right, honey?"

"Of course," Terry replies, then smiles. "My queen."

"Oh-kay," Archon sarcastically replies as he moves on to Jaxine.

Jaxine and Archon both air-kiss each other's cheeks.

"Our fathers would be proud," Jaxine says.

"The Three Stooges reunited. Congratulations, Jax."

"Couldn't have done it without you, Arch."

Archon continues down the line. Jaxine greets the rest of the delegation when Terry leans over to her.

"When did I get an upgrade?" Terry whispers.

Jaxine slyly reaches into her pocket and presses a button on the remote. The eyes of all the corrupted officials, including Terry's, lightly flicker.

Jaxine and Terry continue greeting the delegation.

"Last week, remember?" Jaxine whispers back.

"Oh yeah," Terry whispers. "Wish we could store our memories."

Gen. Lawson fist-bumps the delegates as they pass right to left when a beautiful female dignitary fist-bumps him next. He quickly checks for the next approaching delegate, an elderly man two hosts away. Seeking an opportunity to catch a glimpse of the previous delegate's backside, Gen. Lawson turns back left to see Gen. Tegashito doing likewise. However, Gen. Lawson's grin melts away when he spots the new VImplant blinking through Gen. Tegashito's neck, replacing his normal implant.

Gen. Tegashito turns back and exchanges glances with Gen. Lawson. He smiles, and Gen. Lawson reciprocates.

The elderly delegate finally arrives before Gen. Lawson, and they fist-bump. As Gen. Lawson turns to greet the next delegate, he spies the back of Zona-Sec Director Yindora Zu's neck as she prepares to get her next delegate. Surprisingly, Dir. Zu doesn't appear to have a VImplant. However, Gen. Lawson's retinals scan the redness below both Dir. Ferouk's and Interim Dir. Lampost Cooper's ears to determine they have VImplants as well. Using his retinal display, Gen. Lawson transmits an encrypted *9-1-1* text to Maj. Hickson.

I Know a Guy

Hector, Manny, Bic, Jolly, and a handful of Kah-Lee officers huddle around a holographic rendering of the Sugar Bunker. Muted display screens behind them broadcast a D-Stream transmission of the Union-NorPac merger signing ceremony. Hector spots an ecstatic Jaxine proudly watching Terry and Archon place their finsigs on the official merger e-tab. With the prints of two fingers, the formerly autonomous nations are now one.

Manny catches Hector staring at the screen.

"General?" Manny says.

Jolted, Hector turns to Manny.

"My bad," Hector replies.

"Long time since anyone call you that?"

"Longer time since I saw her genuinely happy," Hector answers, pointing at the screen.

Bic looks up at Jaxine on the display and asks, "You gonna vouch for dat bitch, Fray-mah?"

"No. But at least I can see her," Hector counters. "Am I gonna see this person you're about to vouch with *my* life?"

"Gonna be tough to do now," Bic says.

"Oh yeah?" Hector asks.

Manny leans over to Hector and replies, "*She* was the suicide in P-Bloc."

"Oh," Hector says. "I didn't know."

"Course you wouldn't," Bic snaps.

"But we'll mourn her right," Manny interjects.

Hector and Bic turn their attention back to the Sugar Bunker's virtual schematics.

"You sure we got enough time?" Hector asks.

"More than enough," Manny answers. "I hope."

"You truly do inspire," Hector deadpans.

Suddenly, both Manny and Bic receive separate, encrypted transmissions via their respective retinal displays.

"Fuck," Bic cheers.

"Fuck," Manny barks.

"So what's with the fuckin' mixed signals?" Hector asks.

"Invoice might have some jizz on your boy," Bic says.

"And that's a good thing, right?" Hector replies.

"He thinks he found your son. He's movin' to intercept," Bic adds.

"Rico Suave's underground," Manny says.

"And who the fuck's Rico?" Hector asks.

"High-level asset," Bic answers.

"Our highest," Manny adds. "With him MIA, that cuts the Hive's response time to about five, ten mins tops," Bic says. "If we're lucky."

"You'd be lucky to get three charges set," Hector says.

"So who we gonna find wit' dat kinda Defense cred last min?" Bic asks.

"And someone we can vet real time," Manny adds.

Bic checks his retinal display.

"We gonna need a—" Bic says.

"I know a guy," Hector interjects. "But it won't come cheap."

Au Revoir

The sun sets as Henn walks into an empty, private alley. Confirming the coast clear, she uses her retinal display to locate a secret door and knocks on it. The door opens, and she hops inside. Sev quickly peeks out before closing the door.

Seconds later, an aerial drone buzzes overhead, quickly scanning the building. Its scanners show nothing out of the ordinary as it continues over the neighborhood.

Inside the hollowed-out building, Sev walks Henn past a parked SkyHawk.

"Cuttin' it close," Sev says, looking up at the patrol drones scanning a tall building a few blocks away.

"Traffic's a bitch," Henn says to Sev. "But they're in position."

"Good," Sev replies. "Could really use you on de team."

"No one uses me," Henn counters.

Sev nods as he escorts her to Angel, who's sitting at a console. He and Henn watch Angel remotely operate a tiny *bug drone* flying up the side of a megascraper a few blocks away.

The drone lands on the outside of a penthouse living-area window. It scans the interior before flying to the other penthouse windows and scanning the interior again. Its infrared scanners reveal the level's light Kah-Lee security team protecting an unarmed individual watching the stream in the master bedroom.

"We can take deez fuckers," Angel says.

Henn turns to Sev.

"Den let's take 'em," Sev orders.

Angel nods. Using his scanner, Angel digitally paints the unarmed individual's silhouette blue, labeling it a friendly. He then transmits the data to his teammates in the field.

"Heisman blue," Angel says into his comchat. "Repeat, Heisman blue."

"Got it," Chino replies via comchat.

"Recall, try no kills in case we need intel," Sev orders.

"Vid archive uploaded," Angel confirms into his comchat.

A few blocks away in the megascraper's lobby, Vitchenko and Swayzee—each wearing backpacks—join a lift with residents. They exit with the last resident and find the stairwell. Angel remotely activates a video loop of the stairwell sec cams taken a couple of weeks prior. Swayzee uses a wireless access code to override the security locks. The two men then take the stairs twenty flights up to the roof. Swayzee again overrides the security lock, so they can access the building's rooftop.

Minutes later, Chino and Gwenda enter from outside into the same lobby area, arm in arm. Appearing intoxicated, Gwenda relies on Chino for support. They enter another lift with a few residents.

"Honey, I tink it's comin' up!" Gwenda shouts.

Disgusted, the residents quickly exit the lift, leaving Chino and Gwenda alone as the lift door closes. Chino presses *level 96*. The walls transform into digital ads as the lift rises.

"So sorry about Nix," Chino says. "I really tried callin'—"

Gwenda kisses Chino. The two passionately make out until their retinal displays warn of their approach to level 96. They briefly smile before composing themselves two floors before the lift stops. Gwenda stumbles out as the doors open. Chino runs out and grabs her.

In the corridor, an armed cybernetic Kah-Lee sentry watches porn on his retinal display when the lift light and soft bell catches his attention. He looks up to see Chino grab Gwenda as she stumbles out of the lift.

The lift door closes as the Kah-Lee sentry cautiously walks over to them, unaware that Angel has successfully hacked level 96's security system.

"Identify," the sentry says.

"My bad, bro. My roomie had a liddle too much—"

"Dis a private level, bro," the sentry says. "Identify."

Gwenda answers with a few dry heaves before taking a knee; Chino supports her. On guard, the sentry keeps his focus on Chino.

"One more time. Identify—" the sentry orders.

Suddenly, the sentry convulses as nearly one thousand volts from Gwenda's concealed stunner courses through his body as he hits the ground. Gwenda retracts the stunner cable back into her sleeve.

"All good," Chino says into his comchat.

"In position," Swayzee replies via comchat.

Vitchenko and Swayzee shield themselves under one of the many elevated solar panels on the building's roof. Settling on a safe spot, Vitchenko empties both men's backpacks, while Swayzee keeps an eye out for trouble. As darkness falls, Swayzee sees a small group of pidges speeding around a neighboring structure a few yards away, when a gunshot rings out. Suddenly, one of the pidges hurtles downward while the others frantically continue on their perilous journey. Vitchenko expands both emptied backpacks then connects them with the help of a mini 3D printer called an instaprint to create key parts, assembling everything into a camouflaged *wallcrawler*.

After constructing the wallcrawler, Vitchenko and Swayzee enter it. Swayzee activates the wallcrawler and lowers them down to level 96, stopping beside a window to a room currently occupied by an armed Kah-Lee sentry who exits the room.

Swayzee pilots the wallcrawler over the window, where it expands to cover the glass. Vitchenko then pressurizes the wallcrawler canopy around them. He switches the display to show the feed from Angel's bug drone now camped outside the master bedroom window. The wallcrawler also determines both the position of the penthouse occupants and whether each individual is armed. Vitchenko uses a silent laser suction drill to cut a hole in the window. The wallcrawler's suction arms quietly remove the glass, allowing Vitchenko and Swayzee—weapons drawn—to enter the room undetected.

The bug drone scans the master bedroom, which appears empty. However, its scanners indicate that someone now occupies the bathstall.

Back in the building hideout, Angel tracks the Kah-Lee penthouse sentry returning to the breached room.

"Company, Chenko," Angel warns via comchat.

Inside the breached room, Vitchenko and Swayzee hide. The sentry opens the door and enters the room. He looks out the window to gaze at the peaceful evening skyline, when his retinal scanner detects window glass particles on the floor. As the sentry walks closer to inspect, Vitchenko quietly closes the door.

The sentry turns to Vitchenko when Swayzee grabs him from behind, covers the sentry's mouth, and injects the sentry. Swayzee lowers the unconscious sentry to the ground and drags him off to a corner. Vitchenko turns back to the door.

"We clear?" Vitchenko whispers into his comchat. "Angel?"

"Boss, come in," Chino calls over the comchat. "Chenko?"

"Yeah," Vitchenko whispers.

"We got no outside chat. Suggestions?"

"Goin' in de hall," Vitchenko replies as he takes few quick breaths.

He slowly opens the door just as a smiling Kah-Lee sentry walks by. The sentry turns and stares at Vitchenko in total shock. Vitchenko quickly snatches the sentry into the room; Swayzee hurries in behind him and quietly shuts the door, then sighs.

"Fuckin' close, bro," Swayzee whispers.

Laser bullets pound on the metal door. A few eventually tear into the room.

"Breach!" another Kah-Lee sentry yells as heavy footsteps patter through the halls.

The front door opens, and a sentry quickly succumbs to Gwenda's stunner. Guns blazin', Chino and Gwenda charge into the room.

"Long coms jammed!" a Kah-Lee sentry yells.

Vitchenko and Swayzee exit the room and help Chino and Gwenda subdue the remaining sentries without fatal casualties. Gwenda turns to Chino.

"If dey not de jammers, den who?" Gwenda asks.

"Who you tink?" Chino answers.

"Shit," Gwenda mumbles. "Wit' you one day and already got heat on me!"

"My curse wit' de ladies, yeah?" Chino sarcastically replies.

After clearing the living area, Gwenda and Swayzee secure the penthouse entrance while Chino and Vitchenko head to the locked master bedroom. Chino hacks the lock while Vitchenko uses his retinal display to see inside the dark room via the bug drone outside. He hands Chino a stun grenade.

Outside, the bug drone warns that the blue friendly in the bathstall is aiming a weapon at the master bedroom door. As the blue friendly exits the bathstall, the bug drone self-destructs. The sparks distract the blue friendly's attention toward the window.

Suddenly, a series of faint beeps draw the blue friendly's attention. He turns just as Chino's stun grenade ignites, freezing the target in place.

The lights flicker on. Still frozen, Framer Topaz Titts snaps out of his trance to find Vitchenko holding him at gunpoint.

"I did what I did for de Union," Topaz says. "For all of us!"

Chino uses his retinal scan to confirm Topaz's profile.

"At ease, Fray-mah," Chino replies.

"Where's Fray-mah Contreras?" Vitchenko asks.

"Hec?" Topaz asks. "We got him?"

Chino and Vitchenko look at each other.

"You playin' wit' De Children?" Chino asks.

Topaz's eyeballs wander.

"Lemme explain," Topaz sighs.

Vitchenko vice grips Topaz neck and barks, "Treason."

"Protection," Topaz exhales.

Chino grabs Vitchenko's arm to calm him down; Vitchenko releases his grip.

"From who?" Chino asks.

As they question the Framer, alarms blare and lights flicker. Chino checks his retinal display.

"De fuck?" Chino says.

Topaz's eyes widen.

"Aww shit," Topaz says. "Aww shit."

"We gotta bounce. Now," Gwenda barks.

The lights shut off. Emergency lights activate.

"*Residents, this is de T-E-D. For your safety, please remain in your units until further instructions,*" Wishbone orders over the intercom. "*Failure to comply may result in termination.*"

Chino turns to Vitchenko and says, "Did he say... 'may?'"

"We'll buy time," Vitchenko says. "Sway, wit' me."

Vitchenko and Swayzee sprint out of the penthouse.

Gwenda turns to Chino.

"Where de fuck are—" Gwenda asks.

"Dey'll come," Chino replies.

Vitchenko and Swayzee run toward the lifts; the lifts slowly rise in a coordinated fashion from the ground level.

"Upcoming!" Vitchenko says.

Vitchenko pulls Swayzee back a few feet behind an archway.

"What you gonna do?" Swayzee asks.

"Sway," Chino calls out via comchat. "Need a hand in here."

"I'll roll de carpet," Vitchenko replies. "Go help Chee."

"Be right back," Swayzee replies as he runs back into the penthouse.

Vitchenko opens his pouch, pulls out his clearcurt discs, and places them around the archway. He then uses his retinal display to activate the discs; a transparent forcefield falls down, forming an invisible barrier.

Seconds later Chino, Gwenda, and Swayzee drag the unconscious sentries and lock them in the master bedroom. They then grab whatever they can to construct barricades in the living area and corridor.

Vitchenko then runs inside the penthouse. He places the remaining discs along the ceiling by the door and turns to leave when Chino stops him.

"Don't be a hero. Fall back if it gets too hot, yeah?" Chino says.

"If dey don't—" Vitchenko asks.

"Dey'll come," Chino replies.

"Okay, Cap," Vitchenko says as he runs back out the front door.

"Right behind you," Swayzee chimes in, trailing behind the giant.

Swayzee runs out after Vitchenko while Chino and Gwenda prepare more defenses. Topaz tries to activate the room's security system from the control panel.

"De TEDs override security," Topaz warns.

Gwenda runs over to the panel.

"Move," Gwenda barks.

She shoves Topaz aside and stares at the control panel.

"You gotta *black code*?" Topaz asks.

"Sometin' like dat," Gwenda says.

Gwenda punches the control panel as Chino arrives.

"How dey find us so fast?" Topaz asks.

"Lotta snitches in dis sec," Gwenda answers.

Chino grabs Gwenda.

"Take Fray-mah in de crawla while you got time!" Chino orders.

"You?" Gwenda replies.

"Dey'll come," Chino says. "You go!"

Chino and Gwenda lock lips.

"Uh...nudda day, lovers?" Topaz cries out.

Back in the alley, a larger secret door that encompasses the smaller alley door opens. Henn drives the SkyHawk into the alley and prepares for liftoff while Sec copilots and Angel mans the guns.

Back inside the megascraper, Vitchenko and Swayzee crouch behind barricades.

"How many you know make it chroo a *TED Chat*?" Swayzee asks.

"Alive?" Vitchenko responds.

"We all in de same club, yeah?" Swayzee replies.

The lift opens. TED officers pour out and form a protective barrier in front of Crayton and Wishbone, who exit last.

"In violation of Union Statute 222.456.103.54976-A, we find you guilty of treason," Crayton says.

Vitchenko turns to Swayzee and asks, "Answer your question, Sarge?"

"Treason?" Swayzee snaps back at Crayton. "Colonel, we on otto-rized leave!"

"Terrorist crash pads ain't classified as tourist spots, asshole," Wishbone counters.

"Where's minor Contreras?" Crayton barks.

"De Major's takin' a dump, sir," Vitchenko replies. "We can tell him you stop by—"

Swayzee tries to peek above the barricade when Wishbone fires a laser bullet at him. However, the laser bullet hits Vitchenko's clearcurt and bounces back, hitting the head of a TED officer, who falls to the ground. Crayton turns to Wishbone.

"My bad," Wishbone sheepishly apologizes.

The remaining TEDs unemotionally cast aside their fallen comrade and close ranks.

Swayzee turns to Vitchenko.

"How long you tink dat last?" Swayzee whispers.

Vitchenko shrugs then whispers back, "Gonna find out."

A TED robot charges the clearcurt, getting instantly vaporized. Wishbone takes out another weapon and fires up into the archway. After a few moments, the weapon pierces the structure, rendering the discs—and clearcurt—moot; a firefight ensues.

Inside the penthouse, Gwenda and Topaz reach the door to the breached room just as a small aerial drone fires at the wallcrawler, destroying it. The damage sends wallcrawler debris crashing to the ground, likely killing unfortunate citizens below.

A faint voice crackles over the team's comchats.

As the aerial drone prepares to fire on Gwenda and Topaz, it explodes.

Henn's SkyHawk appears from the smoke. Angel stands by the open side doors.

"Choo-choo! Train pullin' out," Sev greets via comchat. "Pops taught me dat!"

Gwenda and Angel help Topaz into the SkyHawk. Chino runs up to Gwenda.

"Dey made it!" Gwenda yells.

"Told you," Chino replies. "Now up you go!"

Chino helps Gwenda into the SkyHawk as Angel secures Topaz to a chair.

Gwenda secures herself in her chair.

"Man down!" Vitchenko shouts via comchat.

Without hesitation, Chino hand-signals Angel their agreed upon *fallen evac code.*

Angel hesitates for a split second before using his retinals to override the seat locks. He then grabs three *powerchutes* and tosses them to Chino. They nod at each other. Watching this unfold, Gwenda tries in vain to remove her seat restraints.

"What de fuck! Angel!" Gwenda shouts. "Chee!"

"Sorry, sis," Angel replies. "For real."

Angel ducks, so Chino can blow Gwenda a kiss before Angel shuts the door.

"Boss," Angel screams. "FEC Jango!"

Sev and Henn turn to see Chino holding the FEC sign, then a quick salute before running with the powerchutes toward Vitchenko and Swayzee.

"Chee," Sev cries out.

"Get Pop," Chino replies via comchat. "Save Gwen."

Crying, Gwenda tries in vain to free herself as she catches one last glimpse of Chino before yelling, "Chee!"

Sev turns to Henn. "Go, or we all die for real!"

"Eve—" Henn exhales.

"Gotta split up, Henn," Vitchenko says via comchat. "We meet later, okay?"

"Dey got chutes," Sev warns Henn. "We don't."

Sev points to another aerial drone heading toward them.

"Go!" Angel screams.

"You betta make it, Chenko!" Henn yells.

"Henn, no!" Gwenda screams. "Please!"

Henn reluctantly pilots the SkyHawk away as the new aerial drone fires on them.

"Angel!" Sev shouts via comchat.

"Got it," Angel replies.

A pidge farmer spots the SkyHawk navigating the maze of superstructures with two aerial drones in hot pursuit. The aerial drone's laser bullets miss the SkyHawk, pelting the megascraper.

Angel fires back and hits the aerial drone pursuing them. The damaged aerial drone sideswipes the pidge farmer's rooftop and crashes to the ground.

Back inside the penthouse, Chino runs into the living area where Vitchenko and a mortally wounded Swayzee have fallen back. Chino pulls Swayzee away from the door and Vitchenko's activated clearcurt.

"Dey came," Vitchenko confirms.

"Dey came," Chino concurs.

"Dat's what she said," Swayzee replies with a smile and a final breath.

Laser bullets hammer the front wall, eventually piercing it. However, they hit the clearcurt and bounce back, killing a few more TEDs. The firing stops.

"Dis ain't gonna hold long," Vitchenko says.

Chino hands Vitchenko a powerchute.

"Den what we waitin' for—"

Suddenly, the floor caves in beneath them, and the three men crash into the penthouse below. The dust settles, revealing Crayton and four TEDs surrounding them as frightened residents look on from their hallway. Both injured, Chino and Vitchenko turn to each other.

"Killa ride, bro," Chino mumbles.

"On de udder side, bro," Vitchenko mumbles.

Chino and Vitchenko draw their weapons and fire; Crayton and the TEDs beat them to the draw. Wishbone arrives when the dust settles.

"Sir, we got live Kah-Lees in de masta upstairs," Wishbone says.

"Prep dem for TED Chats," Crayton orders.

Wishbone checks his retinal scan.

"Aside from deez bitches, only one udder DNA match," Wishbone says. "Fray-mah Topaz Titts. But he not here."

Crayton turns to Wishbone and asks, "Den where is he?"

Gweny and Henn

Heavily damaged, Sev's SkyHawk crashes to the ground. Minutes later, troopers converge on Henn's downed SkyHawk in an *Unprotected Zone* about thirty blocks from the penthouse. Inside, Sev, Angel, and Topaz remain unconscious. Troopers close in on the SkyHawk when they're ambushed by Gwenda and Henn, who easily take them all out.

"Old times, yeah?" Henn says.

"Whateva," Gwenda replies as she walks away.

"What about dem?" Henn asks, pointing at the SkyHawk.

"Dey leave Chino," Gwenda replies. "I leave dem."

"You know Chino made de call, yeah?" Henn counters. "So did Chenko."

"Den you stay," Gwenda says.

"Since when you pass on revenge?" Henn answers.

Before Gwenda could respond, the two hear movement from the SkyHawk. Gwenda pulls out her weapon and aims.

Blocking her view, Henn heads back inside the craft to investigate. She sees Topaz trying to stand and helps him up.

"Praise de Union," a groggy Topaz preaches. "I'm still alive."

"Night's long, grounda," Henn replies.

Henn looks over to see Sev and Angel rise as well. They all exit the SkyHawk. Topaz studies Sev.

"Pause a sec," Topaz says. "You Hec's boy?"

"In de flesh, Fray-mah," Sev replies. "Where is he?"

"Safe, I hope," Topaz replies. "For real."

"Close one, yeah?" Angel says.

"All good?" Sev asks.

"Yeah," Angel, Henn and Topaz answer.

"No," Gwenda answers.

They look over to see Gwenda with her hands up. They're surrounded by another group of cybernetic and robotic troopers with guns trained on them. They raise their hands.

"Identify," the robotic troopers order in unison.

Topaz coughs.

"I am Framer Topaz Seymour Bartholomew Titts. Scan to verify!"

The troopers cautiously move in when something diverts their attention. Laser bullets pierce the troopers, turning them into bloody scraps of bone and metal.

Moments later, a group of Kah-Lee soldiers led by Invoice appears from the shadows and converges on Sev and the others.

"Major Contreras," Invoice says. "Someone wants to chat."

"De Man?" Sev rhetorically asks.

"De pop," Invoice replies.

Sev and his team glance at each other in bewilderment.

Family Reunion

A tubecar pulls into a station and stops. All wearing hoods and earplugs, Sev, Angel, Gwenda, Henn, and Topaz exit the car in cuffs. Invoice and a couple of Kah-Lee soldiers remove their hoods and cuffs on the platform; the guests remove their own earplugs. Hector greets Sev with a bear hug and kiss on the cheek.

"Pop!" Sev says with a smile.

"Sight for sore eyes," Hector says.

"What dey do to your eyes?" Sev sarcastically asks, then admits, "I kid!"

"Heard you were lookin' for me," Hector says.

"Wish word traveled faster," Sev replies as he pulls Zerina's chip from a pocket and hands it to Hector.

Hector nods and places the chip in his pocket. He then turns to Angel and hugs him.

"You okay, son?" Hector asks.

"Alive, sir," Angel replies. "Happy you are too."

"We heard from bystanders," Hector says. "Sorry about your friends. All good men."

Angel nods.

"De best," Angel replies. "Pard, sir. I need a bathstall."

"Dis way, mang," Invoice says.

Invoice and a Kah-Lee soldier escort Angel to a nearby bathstall.

"Pop, our new friends," Sev says.

"Thanks for bringing my—" Hector replies.

"Better be worth it, Fray-mah," Gwenda says as she's elbowed by Henn.

"No prob," Henn responds.

"Hec, you ol' piece o' shit," Topaz shouts.

237

Topaz walks over to Hector and Sev. He and Hector embrace.

"Tope?" Hector replies. "What the fuck?"

"Last I saw your boy he was a pup," Topaz replies. "Look just like your old man!"

Bic intentionally coughs.

"Fray-mah Titts?" Bic interrupts.

"Miss you too, Bic," Topaz replies.

"We don't have time," Bic warns. "Tegashito's coup just began."

Gwenda and Henn turn to each other and laugh.

"Sounds like a fuckin' Hiver prob," Gwenda says.

"So just transmit our overtime creds den we bounce," Henn adds.

"You know…zeezees don't spend socreds, yeah?" Bic counters.

"Nye-dah can two dead bitches, yeah?" Gwenda and Henn reply in unison.

Hector walks over to Gwenda and Henn.

"You'll get your pay," Hector says. "But my friend speaks truth—as do you. It's not your problem today. But it will be tomorrow. If the Hive goes down like this, no one will be safe. No one."

Gwenda and Henn turn to each other.

"We'll double your overtime rate," Manny adds.

Gwenda walks over to Hector.

"My mum and dad…dey kill and die for you, yeah?" Gwenda responds. "And Pop."

Gwenda taps Hector on his shoulder then walks away. After an awkward silence, Hector turns and asks, "So…is that a *yes?*"

Sev looks at Henn, who barely nods.

Inside Job

Hundreds of feet belowground, a modified tubecar pulls into an apparently abandoned station and parks behind an older-model tubecar covered in dust. The doors open; Hector, Bic, and a contingent of Kah-Lee soldiers exit. Bic directs two of the soldiers to inspect the older tubecar while the others secure the station. He looks around.

"My unk helped build dis for your pop," Bic says. "Taught he was cray-cray—we all did. But not my unk."

"Seems we have somethin' in common after all," Hector counters.

"Took nine munts to build. Right under de Hive's nose!" Bic says.

Kah-Lee soldiers exit the older tubecar and give it the *all-clear* sign before rejoining the others awaiting instructions.

Bic walks over to a wall and reveals a hidden panel. He enters an access code. A section of the station floor opens to stairs leading down into a small armory. Kah-Lee soldiers enter the armory to collect weapons.

"That old tech still work?" Hector asks.

Kah-Lee soldiers inspect the weapons, which appear to be functional.

"Only if dey kill," Bic answers.

Hector clears a table and pulls out a small projector that activates a virtual map of Sugar Bunker.

"No sign of detection," Hector says. "A little sunshine on an otherwise fucked-up day."

"Tunnel One shows up at 15:25. Seven-five mins to set charges and get back,"

239

"Sev in position?" Hector asks.

"Should be dare any min," Bic answers. "Don't worry, Fray-mah. We know what your boy can do. He'll be fine."

"Ain't worried about them gettin' in," Hector replies.

"Worry about doze charges," Bic counters back. "Sink timers!"

Everyone synchronizes their timers.

"And break a leg," Hector replies.

Everyone appears puzzled.

"Why do dat?" Bic asks.

"It means good luck," Hector explains. "My mother used to say it."

"Sound more bad den good, yeah?" Bic asks.

"Old Nation shit," Hector replies. "What can I say?"

"Nudda day, Fray-mah," Bic says with a smile.

"Hope so, Bic," Hector replies. "Hope fuckin' so."

The Black Code

Four heavily armored DCs make their way to the Hive. Inside the first Dick, Sev, Angel, Gwenda, and Kaleb Akintola, an olive-skinned Defense Club trooper, all don concealed camoneks under their high-ranking Defense Club skins. Kaleb stares outside.

"So where you from, Troopa?" Angel asks.

"Fresno, born and raised," Kaleb replies, still looking outside. "Servin' dare all my life."

"Gotta name?" Gwenda asks.

Kaleb turns to Gwenda.

"Trooper Kaleb Akintola, ma'am," Kaleb answers before looking back outside.

"I heard you took out de tween researcher?" Sev says. "Pretty slick makin' it a *su-ee.*"

"But he booby-trapped de files," Kaleb replies. "Now we here."

"You still bought us time, Troopa," Sev counters.

"Time will tell, sir," Kaleb responds.

Gwenda looks out at the hazy skyline. Her thoughts drift back to when, *as a young girl, she woke from surgery to see Chino's face for the very first time.*

"Chee was our bruh-dah," Angel says. "Now we yours."

Gwenda turns to him and sarcastically asks, "Dat mean you gonna leave your sista too?"

Angel nods and replies, "Only if you say de magic words."

Sev turns to Gwenda.

"Gwen, Chee didn't stay for us," Sev says.

"Coulda fooled me," Gwenda responds.

"Den you are de fool," Angel counters. "'Cause he stay for de one dat got away. For real."

Tears well in Gwenda's eyes when everyone's implant timers vibrate.

"Angel," Sev orders.

"Black code one on de way," Angel says.

Angel transmits a black code to the private-access gate ahead. Kaleb silently looks outside while the other three huddle.

"For Chino," Gwenda says.

"For Chenko and Sway," Sev adds says.

"For Murf, Klondike, and Ray-fee," Angel concludes.

Caught off guard, Kaleb turns to see the three silently staring at him.

"For all we may leave behind," Kaleb replies.

"Not much for words, huh?" Angel quips.

"You should take a lesson," Gwenda replies to Angel with a grin.

The three nod as their caravan pulls up to a private access gate.

Outside, CGs scan the vehicles for identification. The ranking CG uploads Angel's transmitted black code. The following pops up on the CG's display:

PROTOCOL 6TR4 PRIORITY AUTHORIZATION

The ranking CG authorizes the DCs to enter.

"How much for a BC?" Gwenda playfully whispers.

"Your life," Angel whispers back.

"Ain't dis my cred?"

Sev chuckles then adds, "Nice try, sis,"

"Heisman yellow," Angel orders through his comchat. "Recall, Heisman yellow."

Everyone in the DCs sets their digital signatures to a yellow-hued retinal bandwidth.

The DCs park in a garage structure.

Gwenda says to Sev, "You sure he gonna be inside?"

"Dat's what De Man said," Sev replies.

A series of notifications simultaneously pop up on everyone's retinal screens or communicators. Gwenda nods.

Sev, Angel, Gwenda, Kaleb, and a group of human and robotic soldiers loyal to Gen. Lawson exit their vehicles. Sev leads the group inside.

Down another hallway, an unsuspecting Crayton and Wishbone enter the commissary. Walking past an empty Needles recbin, they sit and place their order on the table console.

"Our last Kah-Lee guest didn't make it," Wishbone reports.

"Less paperwork for us," Crayton deadpans.

"Fuckers can cover tracks," Wishbone says.

"We're gettin' close," Crayton replies. "I can feel it."

The Board

Gen. Lawson, Maj. Hickson, and an entourage of loyal Outer Defense Club officers enter the Hive through a secret passage that leads them into Gen. Monahan's private office. Gen. Monahan exits his luxurious bathstall to find himself in Maj. Hickson's chokehold. Gen. Lawson and Maj. Hickson lock eyes as Gen. Monahan passes out. Maj. Hickson then hands Gen. Monahan off to fellow soldiers who gently place him on his couch.

"You look like you enjoyed that a little too much, Major," Gen. Lawson quips.

Grinning, Maj. Hickson replies, "Not at all, sir."

Maj. Hickson pulls out an injector gun and hands it to Gen. Lawson, who walks over and injects Gen. Monahan to keep him knocked out. Everyone moves quietly as Gen. Lawson activates the wall display. Using Gen. Monahan's private codes, Gen. Lawson accesses the Hive's closed-circuit cameras and locates Sev's team in yellow hue, making their way to the communications room. Maj. Hickson checks his retinal display.

"Sev's black codes worked, sir," Maj. Hickson says.

"They should," Gen. Lawson replies. "They're Monahan's."

"Fuckin' Hawkin', sir."

"Don't get cocky, soldier. Plenty of Powerball left," Gen. Lawson counters.

Maj. Hickson nods and heads to the office console. He switches a camera feed to the Man Cave. The five sector directors are unconscious and confined to their chairs with corrupted GCs posted outside the room.

"Got 'em," Maj. Hickson says.

"Let's go," Gen. Lawson orders.

Three of the general's soldiers remain inside his office: one with eyes on the cameras, one on the door, and the third on a sleeping Gen. Monahan.

Gen. Lawson, Maj. Hickson, and the rest of the men venture back into the secret passage where they encounter a larger group of loyal soldiers awaiting instructions.

"A-Group, with me to the Board Room. B-Group, follow Uthman to the Security Wing. C-Group, with Hicks to the armory," Gen. Lawson orders.

"Recall, yellows are friendlies," Maj. Hickson reminds everyone.

The men reconfirm their retinal-display settings.

"Vamonos," Lt. Uthman orders his group.

Minutes later, Gen. Lawson and A-Group access a secret door that leads them into a large, private bathstall near the Man Cave. Gen. Lawson leads the men out of the bathstall and into the hallway. They approach the Man Cave guarded by two robotic CGs. The CGs salute but refuse to stand aside.

"General," CG-916 says. "We received no notification of your presence."

"You received Gen. Monahan's code, correct?" Gen. Lawson asks.

"Affirmative, General," GC-808 answers. "However, we have no record of your arrival."

Suddenly, the robotic CGs collapse.

"Nor anything else," Gen. Lawson deadpans.

Gen. Lawson opens the Man Cave doors. He and his loyal soldiers enter with the two disabled CGs. Two of the general's loyal *clonebots* seamlessly replace CGs 916 and 808 and close the door. Seconds later, a few CGs double-time down the hall past them. Once the coast is clear, the two clonebots nonchalantly fist-bump each other.

Inside the Man Cave, Gen. Lawson and his men spot the unconscious directors resting peacefully in their respective chairs. He and three loyalists quietly sneak behind the sleeping directors and pull out injector guns. They inject Directors Lampost Cooper, Yindora

Zu, and Wynten Mones. Gen. Lawson prepares to inject Dir. Ferouk when Dir. Ferouk wakes up.

"Derek?" Dir. Ferouk asks.

"Another day, Meta," Gen. Lawson replies.

"Help—" Dir. Ferouk begins to shout as Gen. Lawson punches him in the face, knocking him out cold.

Gen. Lawson then injects Dir. Ferouk as a precaution.

"Another night, Meta," Gen. Lawson quips, gently tapping Dir. Ferouk's cheek.

Gen. Lawson and the three loyal officers each take out a small device that punctures through the directors' necks, disabling the VImplants. The general and his men spray the wounds with Nanorem. Gen. Lawson activates his comchat.

"Man Cave secure," Gen. Lawson says.

"Armory secure," Maj. Hickson replies via comchat.

"Security Wing secure," Lt. Uthman replies via comchat. "Friendlies approaching Coms."

"Commence Phase Two," Gen. Lawson directs into his comchat.

Failure to Communicate

Sev, Angel, and Gwenda lead their team down a hallway toward the communications room. Along the way, their retinal scans show certain Defense Club soldiers and personnel highlighted in a yellow hue to signify their allegiance to Gen. Lawson. In turn, those friendly soldiers also see Sev, Angel, Gwenda, and their team in the same yellow hue. They assist in allowing Sev's group safe passage by distracting anyone who attempts to approach the group or appear skeptical.

Angel and some of his team peel off from the main group to assist sympathizers with securing access points to the communications room. He transmits a second black code to the CGs posted at the communications-room door just as Sev, Gwenda and a few other soldiers arrive. Sans hesitation, the CGs open the main doors to the communications-room.

Sev, Gwenda, and the others enter to find Sergeant Springsteen Chakote and his staff at attention. They form a row in front of Sev and Gwenda while Kaleb and a few comrades commandeer the unmanned control panels. Gwenda looks around the room. She makes eye contact with Defense *Grunt* Linkin Geferson, highlighted in a yellow hue, who gently nods.

"Sir, I don't recall a surprise inspection," Sgt. Chakote says.

"Would it be one if you did, Sergeant?" Sev snaps back.

"No, sir."

"Damn right, Sergeant," Sev replies, pacing the row. "Now I know tings have been uh…fucked up de past few weeks. So as reward for your dedication, *if* you pass dis inspection, I will immediately transmit authorization codes grantin' each of you one week leave wit' two water creds each. How you like dem Powerballs, yeah?"

"Union strong," the smiling staff chant in unison.

Initially excited, Sgt. Chakote turns skeptic when his retinal scan picks up an anomaly while looking at Kaleb whose phony profile flickers.

"Zeezee," Sgt. Chakote blurts out as Gwenda hits him with her stunner.

Sev, Angel, and Geferson knock out the other staffers.

Geferson runs over to a display to see the camera feed outside the door. He opens the door to allow Sev's men to carry the unconscious CGs inside. Gwenda directs Sev's men to drop the GCs next to an unconscious Sgt. Chakote and staff when she turns to the door.

"Company," Gwenda calls out.

Sev turns to see Maj. Hickson and C-Group, all in yellow hue, enter.

"Hec," Maj. Hickson playfully greets.

"Hick," Sev playfully replies.

The two embrace. Grunt Geferson relieves Kaleb from his duties.

"Coms secured, sir," Maj. Hickson confirms in his comchat.

"Monahan?" Sev asks.

"Takin' a power nap," Maj. Hickson answers.

Angel hurries inside.

"Boss," Angel says. "Cray-Cray and Wishbone in de commissary."

Sev looks over at Gwenda.

"I'm starvin'," Gwenda responds.

Sev turns to Maj. Hickson.

"We got dis," Maj. Hickson says. "You go."

Sev turns to Angel and says, "Let's get Cray-Cray."

"I gonna break a Wish." Angel adds.

Sev and Angel turn to see Gwenda heading toward the commissary. Sev, Angel, Kaleb, and their team chase after her.

Meanwhile, Gen. Monahan sits up on his office couch. Gently touching the Nanorem-covered wound left from his disabled VImplant, he flinches in pain.

Gen. Lawson hands Gen. Monahan a cup of SinWater. Gen. Monahan takes a few sips to dampen his dry throat.

"Tink you can pull dis off?" Gen. Monahan asks.

"I put our odds at about even now," Gen. Lawson says.

"Sooner or later dey'll need more food. More room," Gen. Monahan counters. "What den?"

"Not your problem anymore, Quint. You've been relieved from duty."

"Feel good to betray your friends? Family?"

"You have seniority on dat. So you tell me," Gen. Lawson replies.

"I *knew* you never let it go," Gen. Monahan deduces.

"He was my son."

"Fuckin' my wife! He made it personal, Dee, not me. And if Terry didn't vouch—"

A laser bullet drills through Gen. Monahan's brain, splattering blood behind the headless corpse as it falls back; his cup falls to the ground. Holstering his weapon, Gen. Lawson pours himself a cup of SinWater and raises it over the corpse.

"Nudda life, Quint," Gen. Lawson replies as he downs his drink.

Peekaboo

Crayton and Wishbone enjoy ratloaf, bug skewers, and fresh water in the commissary.

"De courier always pays de price," Wishbone asks.

"So den promotion our new price," Crayton whispers. "Or we start our own fuckin' coup, yeah?"

Wishbone nods.

"Hey, Sev's lease-mate," Wishbone says.

"Don't tink I taught of dat?" Crayton asks.

"Her advocate," Wishbone clarifies. "Maybe she got some jizz, yeah?"

Crayton smiles and nods. He activates his retinal display to locate Rusani Cutwater but receives an error message. Not only that, he discovers he's had no signal for the past five minutes. He tries to refresh his connection.

"What de fuck," Crayton says. "I got no signal."

Wishbone tries in vain to access his network.

"Me too," Wishbone replies. "But comchat still works."

They look around and notice everyone in the commissary unable to access wireless communications. Wishbone checks his retinal display:

ERROR—NO SIGNAL

"Come on," Crayton yells as he gets up to leave.

Wishbone grabs their trash, dumps it in the recbin, and follows Crayton out of the commissary. As they walk down a hallway, a group of cybernetic CGs run toward them.

Wishbone stops one of them while the others continue down the hall.

"What up wit' de network?" Wishbone asks.

"Don't know, sir. Maybe part of de inspection protocol?" the cybernetic CG answers.

"Inspection?" Crayton asks.

"I just upload de orders, sir."

"Share," Crayton orders.

The cybernetic CG transmits the black code to Crayton and Wishbone then takes off.

"Dis came from Coms," Wishbone says.

"Den let's communicate," Crayton replies.

Crayton and Wishbone head toward the communications room. Just as they turn a corner, they make eye contact with Sev, Angel, and Gwenda heading toward them.

Instinctively, Crayton draws his weapon and fires. He and Wishbone then run back in opposite directions.

"Cray-Cray's mine," Sev orders.

"Ladies first," Gwenda replies as she sprints past Sev.

Sev, Gwenda, and a couple of friendly soldiers chase after Crayton; Angel, Kaleb, and the remaining friendlies pursue Wishbone.

Alarms blare throughout the Hive as government loyalists attempt to wrestle control back from Gen. Lawson's men.

Sev, Angel, Gwenda, and Kaleb continue their dual pursuits of Crayton and Wishbone through various gun battles taking place in the Capitol; members of Sev's and Angel's respective groups are killed during the firefights.

During a skirmish, Kaleb takes a couple of laser bullets to the leg and shoulder. Friendly Robot CG-98347 tends to him.

"I'll live. Get his back," Kaleb orders the robot. "That's an order!"

"Sir," CG-98347 replies, then takes off.

Wishbone shoots his way into the motor pool with Angel and a robotic CG-98347 hot on his heels. Angel and CG-98347 search the garage and check the parked DCs. Suddenly, a DC speeds right toward Angel when CG-98347 shoves him out of the way. It tries to evade the DC but is clipped and crashes to the ground, disabled waist down from the impact.

The DC uncontrollably swerves and crashes into another parked dick. Wishbone stumbles out of the crashed DC and tries to flee, when Angel tackles him to the ground. They roll around the ground when Wishbone gets the upper hand and pummels Angel. CG-98347 aims for Wishbone, but the crashed DC blocks him from the robot's direct line of sight. CG-98347 calculates multiple laser bullet trajectories, but none will hit its mark. However, the robot spots a trajectory.

"Peekaboo. I see you," CG-98347 deadpans.

Wishbone tries to stab Angel with a blade. Angel desperately tries to keep the blade from inching lower, but he's slowly giving ground.

"De fallen await," Wishbone says.

CG-98347 forcefully slides its weapon across the floor. The gun ricochets off of the base of a nearby pillar then stops almost perfectly within Angel's reach. Holding Wishbone's knife-wielding hand, Angel uses his free hand to grab the robot's weapon and aims it at Wishbone's bloody face.

"I blow dem a kiss," Angel retorts.

Angel fires, blowing Wishbone's face clean off; blood and brain matter splatter on his face. Wishbone's headless body crumples onto the floor beside Angel. Looking up at the ceiling, Angel catches his breath while CG-98347 drags itself beside him.

"Tanks, uh…" Angel says.

"Carla Gene," CG-98347 says.

"Angel," he replies, fist-bumping CG-98347.

"I don't know about you, Angel," CG-98347 says. "But I could use a good reboot right about now."

"Me fuckin' too, Carla Gene," Angel responds. "Me fuckin' too."

Meanwhile, Crayton circles back toward the commissary while Sev, Gwenda and a cybernetic soldier chase after him. The cybernetic soldier instinctively sacrifices itself to save Gwenda from a barrage of laser bullets; it dies instantly.

Sev and Gwenda find themselves trapped by a group of Hive loyalists when the loyalists are riddled with silent laser bullets. The pair look behind the dead soldiers to see the Native and his larger, cybernetic bodyguard with the wolf tattoo lower their weapons.

The Native nods at Sev who nods back, then turns to see Gwenda sprinting toward the commissary. Sev chases after her, catching up to her waiting at the commissary door.

Gwenda points to Crayton standing unarmed in the commissary waiting for them.

"We have history," Sev says.

"Then do it," Gwenda counters before relenting.

Sev aims and fires his gun, but it's empty.

"Shit," Sev says.

"Aww. Maybe liddle Ocho not yours af-tah all, yeah?" Crayton jokes.

Gwenda aims at Crayton and fires, but her gun's empty too.

"Fuck," Gwenda says.

"Major, we settle dis like men, yeah?" Crayton asks.

"Scared of a treesome?" Gwenda asks.

"Careful, bitch," Crayton asks. "I can be rough."

"I'm always rough," Gwenda retorts.

All three whip out their *laserblades*.

Sev and Gwenda nod at each other before charging at Crayton. Gwenda fires her stunners, but Crayton disables them with his own countermeasures. Though Sev and Gwenda are both impressive fighters, it's clear that Crayton could easily take either individually. Crayton knocks down Gwenda and continues his fight with Sev. He's got Sev on the ropes when he taunts, "Two liddle pussies…sittin' in a—"

Suddenly, Gwenda puts Crayton in a sleeper hold.

"Sweet dreams," Gwenda says.

Crayton violently flips Gwenda to the ground, slips out of her chokehold, and looms over her.

"What a waste," Crayton says.

Crayton turns right—into Sev's punch and stumbles back. He regains his bearings and attacks Sev. After trading blows, Sev manages to break Crayton's arm and restrain him from behind. Crayton screams as Gwenda stabs him repeatedly in the body with her laser-blade. Sev finishes Crayton off by snapping his neck.

"What a waste," Gwenda says as she nods toward the Needles recbin attached to a commissary wall.

Sev and Gwenda load Crayton into the large recbin. Sev locks it then programs it for retrieval. Maj. Hickson arrives with a few soldiers and looks around.

"Where Cray-Cray?" Maj. Hickson asks, lightly panting.

Sev and Gwenda turn to each other and reply in unison, "Needles!"

Till Death Do Us Part!

Inside Sugar Bunker, Bic and his team—all disguised as SB personnel—enter through a ventilation room that leads to a concealed access point. He waits for everyone to go through before turning back to the access point.

"Bon chance," Bic whispers as he closes the access point behind them.

Bic and his team blend into the chaos then split up into smaller groups. He arrives at his destination and sets his charge in a server room.

Later, their PGs and a couple of Vanguardian escorts, Jaxine, Terry, and Gen. Tegashito walk down a down a hall en route to Tunnel One.

"Derek's ghost," Gen. Tegashito says.

"And you're a bloody fuckin' general," Jaxine snaps. "So unghost him and kill him!"

"Tell Quint to get off his fuckin' ass and help," Terry asks.

Gen. Tegashito activates his retinal display and tries to transmit.

"I can't," Gen. Tegashito replies.

"Can't get Quint?" Jaxine asks.

"Can't get a signal," Gen. Tegashito says.

Terry activates his retinal display and adds, "Neither can I."

Suddenly, alarms go off throughout Sugar Bunker.

Breathing heavily, Capt. Theroux catches up with them a few yards from Tunnel One.

"We're under—" Capt. Theroux screams.

A tremor rocks the base.

"Xenos?" Jaxine asks.

"Kah-Lee, ma'am," Capt. Theroux answers. "Air drones and SkyHawks!"

"SkyHawks?" Gen. Tegashito asks.

"Tunnel One's compromised," Capt. Theroux begs. "You should post up in the control room."

"Please, Your Highness," Gen. Tegashito replies.

Gen. Tegashito pulls Jaxine back with the others to the control room.

"Defense stations! Defense stations," the Sugar Bunker AI repeats as explosions, both heard and felt as they run through the halls, rock the base.

"Don't worry. Those missiles can't get to us," Gen. Tegashito says as he activates the main console.

"Great. So we'll be buried alive?" Jaxine replies.

"All units, execute Code Trivago," Gen. Tegashito orders. "Repeat. Code Trivago!"

"Sir, we're cockblocked from de Hive," Capt. Theroux says.

Terry runs over to the main console. He types in his personal access code. Grainy analog feeds from various closed-circuit sec cams show skirmishes taking place throughout the Union.

"Fuck," Terry says.

"Now that's a shitload of Children," Gen. Tegashito deadpans.

Jaxine watches the action unfolding.

"This is not fucking happening," Jaxine yells.

Gen. Tegashito enters launch codes to deploy the SB SkyHawks and unmanned aerial drones.

"Gerly, prepare for the ground assault," Gen. Tegashito orders. "Intercom channel 359."

Capt. Theroux turns to Jaxine, who nods.

"Sir," Capt. Theroux replies as he heads for the exit.

Outside, drones descend upon the base, firing at will. Siren wails trail off into the desert. SB SkyHawks and aerial drones race upward to intercept and a fierce aerial battle ensues. On the ground, Henn joins hundreds of Kah-Lee soldiers rushing the base. Though advanced, Henn's old school weapons appear crude with the exception of her torchblades. Her fearsome battle skills enable her and dozens of others to breach Sugar Bunker defenses and enter with extreme caution.

Back inside, Bic heads back toward the ventilation room when he sees Gen. Tegashito execute one of Bic's men. The general instructs his soldiers to seek out and eliminate any infiltrators they find. Taking out a laserblade, Bic creeps up behind an unsuspecting Gen. Tegashito. However, Gen. Tegashito turns and aims his gun. Bic knocks Gen. Tegashito's gun from his hand and tries to stab him. However, Gen. Tegashito knocks Bic's laserblade from his hand and stuns Bic with a solid right cross. As they retreat in opposite directions, both men pull out sidearms and fire laser bullets at each other.

Capt. Theroux arrives with a group of SB soldiers, providing cover for Gen. Tegashito to retreat.

"Fucked wit' de wrong soldier, Kah-Lee bitch!" Capt. Theroux yells.

Capt. Theroux and his men pin Bic down when his SB soldiers are shredded with laser bullets. Capt. Theroux takes a laser bullet and falls. Bic turns to see Henn instruct a group of Kah-Lee soldiers to assist him. She nods at Bic then chases after Gen. Tegashito. The Kah-Lee soldiers check the dead when Capt. Theroux opens fire, killing most of them. Still bleeding, Capt. Theroux runs out of ammo when Bic jumps him from behind and repeatedly stabs Capt. Theroux in the neck with his green Bic pen. Capt. Theroux falls; Bic wipes the blood from his pen puts it away. He checks his timer and wounds then keeps moving.

Meanwhile, Gen. Tegashito runs past a few SB soldiers guarding his personal DC parked in a secret garage annex. He hops in back.

"Go!" Gen. Tegashito shouts.

The driver peels out of the garage. Laser bullets take out the SB soldiers providing cover for the general as Henn sprints into the garage. She pulls out a magnegrenade, attaches it to her torchblade, and fires. The torchblade sinks into the DCs rear just as the magnegrenade detonates. The explosion flips the DC upside down. Henn runs toward the wreckage, but the explosion caves in the tunnel between her and Gen. Tegashito's DC. She's forced to head back toward the ventilation room.

Inside the control room, Jaxine watches the displays when she spots Terry at the main console.

"What are you doing?" Jaxine asks.

"Cutting a deal."

"What?"

"Are you fuckin' deaf and blind, woman? If we don't cut a deal now, they'll have us for dinner. Literally."

Suddenly, smoke emanates from the surgical wound where Terry's VImplant was recently embedded. Terry winces.

"My father always thought you were a pussy," Jaxine says. "Ever stop and ask yourself how a predictable, whiny little bitch like you got this far in life?"

"What the…" Terry exhales as his eyes lock onto the remote in her hand.

"I'll give you a hint. Me."

Blood trickles from Terry's neck; he tries to plug the wound. "Bitch."

"What was it you used to tell me? Don't hate the player. Hate the game."

"I'll…give…you…any…"

"No more deals for you, my love," Jaxine says with a shrug and then adds, "you've played your last hand. I'm the house now."

Terry falls to the ground, and a few small sparks set off. More blood pours out, forming a coagulated pool around him. Jaxine ignores her former husband and walks over to the table and places the remote down. She continues watching the attack unfold on various displays. She looks to her left to see Hector pointing a gun at her.

"You?" Jaxine asks, clutching her heart.

Hector glances over at Terry's corpse on the floor.

"Gonna ask you the same thing," Hector replies. "Looks like trouble in paradise."

"Irreconcilable differences," Jaxine replies.

Though Hector keeps a sharp eye on Jaxine, he initially fails to notice the remote on the table to her right.

"I don't think your boys out there can chew through metal fast enough to stop a laser bullet in your brain," Hector says.

"Hec, listen to me. We're gonna need more than a fighting chance against the Xenos when they come. And they will come."

"And you base this on?"

"Human nature."

"If your idea of human nature means turning our species into your personal fuckin' zeezees, tanks but no tanks," Hector replies.

"Oh, now you wanna play el presidente? Better thirty years late than never, I suppose," Jaxine says. "Okay, let's run this shit together."

Hector nods to Terry on the ground and replies, "That's what *he* said."

"Hec, please. Stop this madness while we still have—"

Suddenly, Gen. Lawson's face appears on all the SB displays.

"Citizens, this is Outer Defense General Derek Lawson. It's with deep sadness to inform you that both President Gee and Gen. Monahan were gravely wounded during an attempted coup led by traitorous forces loyal to both Tween Gen. Hiroshima Tegashito and Board Director Jaxine Coltraine. Your sector and bloc leaders will DM you over the coming days. But rest assured, this insurrection was successfully put down by the brave citizens of an institution that will ensure the continuation of our species for centuries to come. And though these past few months we have seen our confidence shaken, our resolve has not. In the meantime, should you see anything suspicious, immediately contact your local Defense Club branch. Union strong!"

Hector studies the defeat on Jaxine's face.

"You were saying?" Hector sarcastically asks.

"Open your fuckin' eyes, Hec," Jaxine replies. "We're literally digging our own bloody graves."

Hector lets the words sink in. He looks up at the displays. Gunfire crackles closer, momentarily distracting him long enough to see the remote on the table; Hector and Jaxine dive for the remote. Hector tosses the table, catapulting the remote as Jaxine dives at empty air. He grabs the remote when Jaxine screams, "Guards!"

Hector quickly fires at the door panel to lock out the Vanguardians, who bang and fire on the door in vain. Hector holds Jaxine at gunpoint.

"Their cities expand while ours overflow," Jaxine says. "Cannibalism's back on the table, Hec. We're running out of fuckin' time!"

"You're right, Jax. Our time's up," Hector replies. "Let the pups decide how to use theirs."

A tear runs down Jaxine's cheek. She lowers her head.

"Our fathers made the tough calls," Jaxine snaps. "Now they're revered!"

Jaxine uses her retinal display to link with the remote. She activates all the Vanguardians and Sugar Bunker personnel embedded with the VImplant.

"What happened to the daughter of Wolf's Creek?" Hector asks.

Jaxine looks up and answers, "She's a queen now. With a quarter billion mouths to feed."

Hector notices a faint twinkle in Jaxine's eye. He looks down at the remote to see it blinking.

"What the—" Hector says as more explosions rock the base.

The aftershocks throw Hector off-balance. Jaxine rushes Hector, knocks his gun away, and kicks him in the balls. Hector drops to the ground, grabbing his privates. Jaxine tries to snatch the remote, but Hector won't let go as they wrestle for it on the ground.

Throughout Sugar Bunker, hacked SB personnel involuntarily kill everyone—including their unhacked colleagues, then swarm back inside the in an effort to protect their queen. Controlled by his VImplant, Dyson chokes an uncorrupted Corin to death then joins a still living but maimed Gen. Tegashito along with hacked SB personnel heading toward the control room.

As Hector and Jaxine struggle for control of the remote, display screens above them show the soldiers alternating between continuing their involuntary objectives, aimlessly wandering or banging their heads against walls. Some even fight each other.

In another room, Henn and a few Kah-Lee soldiers hide as hordes of corrupted SB personnel pass between them and the ventilation room leading back down to the modified tubecar.

Back in the control room, Jaxine bites down hard on Hector's organic hand. He screams as she spits out his pinky.

"I'll enjoy killing that bitch roomie of yours," Jaxine yells. "Maybe even more than I did Zerina!"

"You...mother...fuckin'..." Hector barks.

Hector's eyes widen and swell with pure rage. Using his metal hand, he grabs Jaxine's wrist and tries crushes it, but he can't.

"Every woman has her secrets," Jaxine says as she reaches back and claws Hector's face with her organic hand, leaving a deep scratch on his face.

Jaxine elbows Hector's body with her cybernetic arm, breaking two of his ribs. Hector closes his eyes, briefly flashing back to that time when *Jaxine consoled him after Zerina's memorial.*

Game over, bitch, Hector thinks to himself through the pain.

Eyes still closed, Hector's cybernetic hand clutches Jaxine's neck and snaps it. Jaxine releases the remote as her limp body falls on top of it. He rolls her over to find the remote crushed. He looks up at the displays.

"Uh-oh," Hector mumbles.

He watches as the Vanguardians and other hacked SB personnel—including Gen. Tegashito and Dyson—fall where they stand as the VImplants bore holes in their spines and blood pours from their mouths, eyes, and nostrils.

Coast now clear, Henn and the few remaining Kah-Lee soldiers exit the office, carefully stepping across the sea of corpses and make their way back to the ventilation room as a surviving SB soldier spots them and takes aim. Clutching a gaping wound in his chest, Bic fires a laser bullet into the back of the SB soldier's head. Exhausted, he leans back onto a nearby wall, slides down to the ground in a seated position, and looks up as he takes his final breaths; blood trickles from his mouth.

"Unk... Mom..." Bic says as he sheds a tear. "See you soon."

Henn nods in gratitude then leads the others back through the concealed door to the modified tubecar.

Outside, Kah-Lee soldiers shoot down the remaining SB aerial drones then retreat as fast and far from Sugar Bunker as they can.

At an undisclosed location, Manny's timer counts down to zero. Taking a deep breath, he remotely activates the charges planted throughout Sugar Bunker while Invoice, Jolly, and dozens of Kah-Lee protect him.

Back at Sugar Bunker, Hector makes his way to the ventilation room. However, it's completely blocked with debris. He follows the base signs to the nearest manned drone bay and heads for it. Along the way, he grabs a few access cards from dead SB officers.

Inside the drone bay, Hector finds a SkyHawk in need of some repair. He hops in and discovers it's operational but has no steering handles. He spots the virtual autopilot button and presses it.

Otto, wearing a space uniform taken from *Battlestar Galactica*, appears.

"Howdy, buckaroo! Name's—"

"Otto, get us the fuck outta here!"

"Okay, okay. Don't get your san-eez in a bunch. Identify, s'il vous plais."

"Excuse me?"

"I don't know you from Ed Sherman," Otto replies. "So if you wanna go, I need to know."

Hector picks one of the pilfered access cards and sticks it into the console. Otto flickers then starts up the SkyHawk.

"Ticktock, Otto!"

"Saddle up, Captain," Otto says then stares at the console "Uh-oh."

"Uh-oh what?"

"I'm afraid my program's not fully functional."

"Mine won't be either if we don't get take the fuck off!"

"Sorry, Cap," Otto responds. "But without more memory, I can't fly this bird."

Hector pauses, then pulls out Zerina's chip from his pocket. He runs over to the console, kisses the chip, inserts it into a control slot, and then presses a button above the slot. Suddenly, Otto transforms into a hologram of Zerina in her twenties. She spots Hector and smiles.

"Hec?"

"Hey, baby. I'm in rush. Can you fly this thing?"

Zerina's eyes flicker. "I think so. What's wrong?"

"Tell you later. We gotta move now."

They lock eyes; Zerina nods. The SkyHawk ignites and takes off down the runway. As it launches from the base, a returning SB drone heading straight for them pops up on the windshield display.

"No auto-gun package installed," Zerina warns. "Hope you can shoot."

"So do I," Hector replies as he mans the guns.

Hector opens fire on the SB aerial drone, blowing it up. He secures himself in his seat and checks his expired timer. Hector closes his eyes.

Sunrise appears as Zerina pilots the SkyHawk away from Sugar Bunker. The charges detonate, brightening the hazy dawn sky. The chain reaction causes an explosion seen from both the Pacific Ocean to the west, as well as the Trifect a great distance east.

"Couldn't shave your balls that close," Zerina quips. "Otto told me to say that."

"I'll give him that one."

The shockwave catapults them upward at a ridiculous rate of speed. Sparks fly inside the cockpit as they ascend through the demarcation line; oxygen masks drop. Hector grabs one and puts it on while Zerina seals the SkyHawk from environmental contaminants. The SkyHawk exits the demarcation line and enters Earth's lower atmosphere. The SkyHawk's windshield display digitally tracks the heavy Lorian ship traffic speeding through space and between Earth and the moon. Hector and Zerina stare at the windshield with blank expressions.

"I think I just wet myself," Zerina quips.

"Me," Hector deadpans, *"two."*

Alarms blare as the SkyHawk descends back toward Earth on the east side of the demarcation line. It careens toward the earth.

"Strap in, baby," Zerina says. "I got you!"

"Now I *know* that's you!"

Smiling, Zerina watches Hector strap into the pilot's chair then says, "Good to see you again, my love. Wish we had more time."

They lock eyes as the SkyHawk glides over another field of unsalvageable alien and human metal.

"What are you talkin' about?" Hector replies. "We got all the time in the—"

The SkyHawk crashes many, many miles east of the demarcation line, tearing it apart.

Sometime later…

"Baby, wake up. Hec!"

A bloodied and bruised Hector wakes to find himself confined to the sideways-facing pilot's chair and Zerina in his face. There's open desert air and smoke billowing around them.

"Am I?" Hector asks.

"Not yet. But you will be if you don't move."

She releases his restraints, but Hector doesn't move. Wincing, he looks down to find a metal rod keeping him attached to the pilot's chair and removes his oxygen mask. Zerina helplessly watches as Hector pulls himself from the rod and crashes to the floor. A compartment on the console pops open; a first-aid kit falls out. Hector slowly makes his way to the console and pulls himself up. He grabs the first-aid kit then turns to the console.

"Love, it was enough to re-cog-nize," Hector sings.

Zerina scans Hector's failing vitals as he reaches for her chip.

"To see, I was the rea-son you feel sick inside," Zerina sings back. "Love, it cut a hole in-to your eyes."

"You couldn't…see you were the car I crashed…burning side," Hector struggles to finish.

"Cause we were fall-in', I'm sah-ree, ah bay-bay," Zerina continues with a smile.

Wincing, Hector replies, "Cause we were fall-in', I'm sah-ree, ah bay-bay."

Smiling at her one last time, he removes the chip and places it in his pocket; Zerina transforms back into Otto.

"Fine woman you got there, Cap," Otto acknowledges with a wink and nod.

"I know."

Hector hops out from the exposed side of the cockpit and onto the desert ground. He looks down as blood pours from his stomach, then falls down. Grimacing, he opens the first-aid kit, slowly sits up, and pulls out his small tube of Nanorem. He unloads the entire tubeful on his wound, and the microscopic nanodes frantically go to work. Breathing heavily, Hector takes in the blinding sunlight one last time when a large shadow shields him as he passes out.

In the cockpit, Otto looks up at the *enormous silhouette* towering through the SkyHawk's exposed windshield; he whistles.

"Now that there fella's wider than my sister's cooch," Otto blurts out as a gigantic tarp covers the SkyHawk.

Balance

Three hours later, Union dicks, SkyHawks, and a MedHawk converge on Hector's motionless body. Sev, Angel, and Maj. Hickson exit a DC and rush over to Hector lying beside a blanket, bucket of water, and large tray of cooked meat. Sev holds Hector in his arms while Angel kneels beside them.

"Pop," Sev cries out as he cradles his semiconscious father.

"Son…"

"Yo, Hec," Maj. Hickson calls out.

Hector, Sev, and Angel look up as Maj. Hickson points at Ree, wearing limited protective gear, walking back toward the demarcation line. She stops and turns back to see an army of Terrans staring at her from a distance.

"Fuckin' Xeno gonna pay for dis, Pop," Angel says.

Sev looks over at the blanket, tray of cooked meat, and bucket of water.

"Angel, stand down," Sev orders. "Hold Pop for a sec."

Sev and Angel trade places.

"Sev?" Hector exhales.

"It's okay, Pop," Sev says. "Be right back."

"I got you, Pop," Angel replies.

"If anytin'—anytin'—happens to me—"

"Yeah, boss," Angel answers.

Maj. Hickson stares down the large Xeno.

"On my signal," Maj. Hickson says into his comchat.

Union forces aim everything they have at Ree, waiting for the order to fire.

"Hick," Sev yells as he runs over to Maj. Hickson and grabs his weapon.

"What de fuck you doin'?" Maj. Hickson asks.

"I got dis," Sev says.

"For real?" Maj. Hickson asks.

"Trust me," Sev replies. "I go down, he's all yours, yeah?"

Sev nods at Maj. Hickson, who nods back.

"Nudda day, bro," Maj. Hickson sarcastically concedes.

Maj. Hickson steps aside. Sev cautiously walks toward Ree while Union soldiers anxiously watch. Sev stops a few yards from the alien, who silently stares back with her finger on the trigger. A few seconds pass in total silence when Sev lowers his weapon, raises his free hand in the air, and waves.

"Tanks," Sev yells. "Tanks for savin' my father!"

Ree can barely hear the sounds from Sev's mouth. However, his gesture convinces her to lower her weapon, slowly raise one of her free limbs, and wave back.

"I wish only balance with your species," Ree growls. "Do you understand?"

Although Sev cannot understand Ree's growls, a mildly pleasant sensation from her low pitch courses through his body.

"Ho-lee shit," Sev mumbles to himself.

"Boss," Angel yells.

Sev lowers his hand and turns to see Angel helping medics slide a floating gurney underneath a dying Hector. Sev turns back to Ree as she lowers her limb, turns, and proceeds back through the demarcation line, disappearing into the fog.

Sev turns back and runs toward his father.

"Stand down," Sev orders the men while waving.

"Stand down," Maj. Hickson repeats to his men.

The Union soldiers all lower their weapons. Sev takes Angel's place beside Hector. Angel shuffles over to Maj. Hickson.

"See dat shit?" Angel asks.

"I'll see it in my sleep," Maj. Hickson replies.

"Uh-huh," Angel concurs.

Hector dips into his pocket and pulls out Zerina's chip. He hands it to Sev as he coughs up blood. Sev sticks it in his pocket. Angel hands Sev a sanipad to wipe the blood from Hector's face.

"Finally…got your…wish," Hector coughs out.

"Hey, old man," Sev says. "You gonna be—"

"Proud of you…son," Hector interjects. "Always."

Looking up at the sun, Hector's vision fades as he floats toward the MedHawk.

"Pop? Stay wit' me now."

"Congrats…to Oach…" Hector trails off as he passes out.

"Pop?" Sev cries out. "Pop?"

Medics load an unconscious Hector onto the waiting MedHawk with Sev joining them. The MedHawk takes off and heads west while the rest of the Union contingent follows.

السادس عشر

The Fallen

Hector rests peacefully in a pressurized deadtube. Tears trickle from Toi's face onto the deadtube glass then drip onto the floor. Sev, wearing his new Defense Club *Subgeneral* skins, tries in vain to comfort her while fighting back his own tears.

"Nudda day, my love, yeah," Toi whimpers.

"Rest well, old man," Sev chimes in.

The mediroom door opens; Manny enters holding an e-tab. Sev walks over to him.

"Subgen," Manny says.

"Director," Sev replies.

Manny hugs Sev then turns his attention to Toi.

"Ms. Madagascar?" Manny greets. "I'm—"

"I know you," Toi replies.

Toi hugs Manny and kisses him on the cheek while Sev uses the opportunity to wipe away his tears. Teary, Manny's studies Hector's expressionless face. He takes a deep breath then places his left palm on Hector's deadtube.

Sev and Manny glance at each other. Manny nods; Sev nods back.

"Hil's on her way up," Sev says. "Toi, you need anytin'?"

"No tanks," Toi mumbles.

Sev exits the room and shuts the door. Manny remains beside Hector.

"Heard you openin' up de new Sec, yeah?" Toi asks.

Manny nods and replies, "Have a promise to keep first."

Manny places his e-tab on the deadtube and activates a virtual rendering of Hector taken in Manny's office prior to the assault on Sugar Bunker.

"Hey, roomie," Hector says. "If you're watching this, I am so, so sorry for missing breakfast. And most importantly, big sorries for being such a stubborn asshole. I wasted too much time feelin' sorry for myself and not enough on the things that truly mattered. Old habits die hard, I guess."

The e-tab lights up and displays a finsig pad.

"Better late than never, yeah?" Hector continues. "Consider this restitution for time served—plus interest. And don't worry, I added a second-chance clause so you can opt out when you find someone worthy enough to seal the deal with for real. Everyone deserves a second chance, right? So you'll have no excuse to make the same mistake I did. Live, my love. Pinky swear. Forever's a long time to regret... but never enough to love. And I do love you, Talinda Madagascar. Always."

Breaking down in tears, Toi pounds on the deadtube before draping herself on it. Manny comforts and gently escorts her to the e-tab.

"The record shows that Hector Elias Contreras VI has having positively affirmed all lease declarations, riders, and applicable clauses in this document, which shall expire thirty days from today, if left unexecuted," Manny explains. "Therefore, Talinda Harmony Madagascar, do you wish—"

"Yes, yes, yes!" Toi interjects as she cries over the e-tab.

She places her index finger on the wet e-tab, which turns red.

"Your tears," Manny says.

"Yeah," Toi replies, offering Manny a watery grin as she dries the screen.

Hand trembling, Toi again provides her finsig; the e-tab turns green.

"As registered...officiant, I now...pronounce this contract commenced," Manny exhales as he chokes up. "You may now...seal...the deal!"

Toi walks over to the deadtube window opposite Hector's face and kisses the glass.

Outside in the hall, Sev sits with newly promoted Subgeneral Mayweather Hickson.

"Congrats on liddle Oach makin' YOP, yeah?" Sb. Hickson says.

"Turd yungess cadet officer evah," Sev boastfully replies.

Gen. Lawson walks up carrying a small box. Sev and Sb. Hickson stand at attention.

"He'll make a great general someday…just like his old man," Gen. Lawson says. "At ease."

The subordinates exhale. Gen. Lawson hands the small box to Sev, who opens it. Sev pulls out a star similar to Gen. Lawson's, with the exception of a small green gem on one of the points to signify a retired/inactive status.

Nodding, Sev replies, "Tank you, sir."

"For those of us who recall darker times, he was a father to us all," Gen. Lawson says.

"All dis time…did Pop know?" Sev asks.

Gen. Lawson shakes his head.

"Derek was my recruit," Manny interjects. "After too many most of his spies we compromised, your father thought it best not to know."

"Besides, someone had to keep an eye on your old man," Gen. Lawson replies. "And his family."

"Gentlemen, I gotta train to catch," Manny says.

Gen. Lawson and Manny embrace.

"Try to stay outta trouble, yeah?" Gen. Lawson asks.

"Hell, after this job, consider my old ass retired," Manny replies.

Gen. Lawson turns to Sb. Hickson who waits for Manny.

"*Thor* when you get back, Unk?" Sev calls out.

"Wouldn't miss it for the world, Éxi," Manny replies.

Sev and Manny nod at each other.

Sb. Hickson escorts Manny out of the building. Gen. Lawson walks over to Sev.

"Sir, you tink Jax was right?" Sev asks.

Gen. Lawson sighs. "Don't get it twisted, son. She was never about saving the Union—or humanity. She was always about ego and power. We just never seem to learn."

Sev nods. "Men say before de Sugar Bunker went boom, Tegashito's men went cray-cray killin' everyone."

"Side effect of those VImplants," Gen. Lawson replies. "We found what was left of Shima. But so far, no remote…or any uncorrupted files pertaining to Vanguard."

"And if someone tries again, sir?" Sev asks.

Gen. Lawson taps Sev on the shoulder.

"Big day tomorrow. Try to get some rest before the ceremony."

"Pard?"

"On New Year's Eve, your father will be awarded the Union's highest honor," Gen. Lawson answers. "You'll accept it in his stead."

"*De Wayne Newton?*" Sev asks.

Smiling, Gen. Lawson shakes his head. "Chillax, Subgen. You'll have our top speechers at your disposal."

"Speechers?"

"Can't let you broadcast across the entire planet cold pidge. Who do you think we are?" Gen. Lawson replies with a salute.

Sev silently salutes as Hilga and Ocho approach. Ocho stops and salutes; Gen. Lawson reciprocates. Gen. Lawson then nods to Hilga before leaving as Ocho runs over to Sev. Sev picks up his son; Hilga enters the mediroom to console Toi.

One for the Road

Both wearing new Defense Club skins, Gwenda and Henn share another round of SinWater with Angel at Bygone's, a popular cantina across the street from Hector's Sin Vegas Medi. In addition, Bygone's also accommodates *sovirts*, who virtually socialize with consenting patrons via implants.

"De fallen," Henn says.

Bandaged and bruised, the three slowly lift their cups, toast and drink.

"So what's our two new reps plannin'?" Angel asks.

"Don't know. Tinkin' bout a visit to NorPac—*Pac-Sec*," Gwenda replies. "Hoard enough socreds for de long trip home."

"Long trip?" Henn responds. "Bitch, you from P-Bloc."

"My fore-fah-dahs home," Gwenda responds. "My namesake."

"*Newzeeland?*" Angel chuckles. "You tink dem stories for real?"

"Girl is cray-cray," Henn chimes in.

"I am," Gwenda answers. "But my fah-dah say it chroo. He say his G-Paw tell him so."

Angel laughs. "Foh-get de Xenos, de strays, de pirates, and de man-ee-tahs. Even if you get dare—and de island for real—what you tink doze Benedicts gonna do?"

Gwenda chugs the rest of her SinWater and slams down the cup.

"Dey gonna pay," Gwenda replies. "Like we do."

Both Angel and Henn stare at Gwenda in awe. Henn downs her drink and slams her cup down.

"Anywho, I gonna book de biggest pad in de tallest building wit' de hottest roomie," Henn counters.

Angels chugs, then slams his cup down.

"Wit' luck, I gonna go to bed soon," Angel replies.

Gwenda and Henn trade glances. They shrug and turn back to see Angel staring at the main bar. They look toward the main bar to see a cybernetic male smiling back at Angel. The man silently invites Angel to join him. Angel uses his retinal display to both pay their tab and upload the man's profile via facial recog.

"Clean," Henn says as she reviews the man through her retinal display.

"Hope we won't be later," Angel replies as he rises. "Nudda day, bitches."

Angel heads for the main bar.

"Nudda day, bitch," both women reply.

Gwenda and Henn finish their drinks and exit the bar. Outside, Henn spots a hint of sadness in Gwenda's demeanor as they walk.

"Bitch, we help save de Union," Henn says. "We *reppin'* now! Gotta celebrate. Old times, yeah?"

"Don't know—"

"I get first round?"

"And last?" Gwenda asks.

Henn laughs then sings, "We know each udda for so looong."

Gwenda sings back, "Your heart is achin', but you too shy to say it."

Locking arms, the two women sing as they weave their way through a very crowded street.

"So I call you Gweny now?" Henn playfully asks.

"Only if you pay wit' dis arm," Gwenda jokingly replies.

The women laugh and sing in unison, "Neva gonna give you up. Neva gonna let you down. Neva gonna run a-round and de-sert you!"

Noose

Ree and Hyfor finish setting up an enormous antenna array in the middle of a large room. Blinking lights and holographic images of the solar system—and beyond—project from this array.

"Coordinates set?" Ree asks.

"Coordinates set," Hyfor replies. "Do not fear failure."

"We have sacrificed much," Ree says.

"Friend Ree, our faith remains," Hyfor counters.

The entry door beeps, then opens.

"The array's full power should be enough to counter the anticipated solar disruptions," Ree says as the two turn to the door.

Bandaged, Nooz enters; the door shuts behind him. As he walks toward them, he notices the front half of Hector's partially covered SkyHawk. A virtually frozen image of Otto looks up at him from the cockpit, vanishes then reappears again, startling Nooz.

"Shit," Nooz shouts as he steps back.

"There is no threat," Ree chuckles. "Ha!"

"I do not wish for the medics again," Nooz replies as he reviews their work on the array. "First they make false clones. Then they kill us with our own tech!"

"Not this cycle," Hyfor adds.

"Elaborate," Nooz replies.

"Ree rescued a wounded Terran outside the demarcation," Hyfor explains. "She returned it to the preserve when a Terran swarm arrived. They did not attack."

"No?" Nooz asks.

Hyfor turns to Nooz and says, "My mate, you repeat my inquiry."

"Their scout leader approached, stopped, and lifted its limb in a nonthreatening display," Ree replies, lifting one grappler. "I reciprocated."

"What transpired after?" Nooz asks.

"It turned and rejoined the wounded Terran," Ree replies.

"And the swarm?" Nooz asks.

"They did nothing. So I left."

"You...left?"

"I brought caution," Ree answers. "Besides, they were more interested in their wounded friend."

"Perhaps a caste leader?" Nooz asks as he turns his attention back to the SkyHawk cockpit.

Every few seconds, Otto's image appears and disappears. Moments later, Otto vanishes for good...or perhaps until the SkyHawk's remaining solfils taste sunlight again.

Nooz grabs a Lorian tool to adjust a piece of equipment Hyfor had been using.

"Maybe one day we will achieve balance with them," Hyfor says.

"We are Lorian," Ree replies. "We achieve what we believe."

A Greater Union

On December 31, 2189, a Union Service Transmission, or *UST*, broadcasts its signal up to one of the few functioning satellites in orbit. The satellite then relays the UST across the entire planet for anyone willing—or able—to intercept. Within the Sin Vegas Union, including the newly christened NorPac Sector Six, or *Pac-Sec*, the U-Stream broadcasts the same signal on every channel and active display.

At a heavily guarded, secluded compound located somewhere on the former British Columbia Coast, Archon enjoys a glass of NorPac Red and a blowjob while watching the UST of new Sector Six Director Alexi Goatee and his staff applauding from their executive box in the Vancouver Coliseum. A scantily clad female waitress enters the room with four shot cups of SinWater. She downs one of the shots while Archon grabs two and holds one toward the display.

"Arrivederci, my fallen friends," Archon toasts. "Helluva ride it's been!"

Laughing, Archon downs the first shot and tosses the empty cup across the room. He downs the other shot then begins choking. Grabbing his throat, he collapses on the floor. The woman on her knees confirms Archon's death then downs the remaining shot. The waitress opens an encrypted comchat from her implant.

"Jackass has been neutralized," the waitress says.

Custodians enter the room.

"Union stronger," Manny replies via comchat.

The waitress nods to the custodians; the custodians reciprocate and carry Archon's body away.

"Union stronger," the waitress parrots with a smile.

Meanwhile, new Sector Five Director Rotney Qinerin broadcasts from the Sanjose Veterans Arena. He waits for the applause to subside before commencing his speech with help from a holographic teleprompter.

"Nudda day," Dir. Qinerin says to all.

"Nudda day," citizens shout back in near unison.

"And a day it is! Dare's an old saying: what doesn't kill you makes you stronga, yeah? We survive wars. Pollution. Hunger. Genocide. Flood. Invasion. And Unrests!" Dir. Qinerin pauses for applause. "We fall, we get up. We learn, we adapt. And dis will continue chroo de new cen-tree!"

"Union strong," citizens chant.

Qinerin waits for the chants to subside before be continuing, "And as we recall our sacrifices, we have very special words to share not only for de citizens, but for all de bros and sistas of Earth—and off-world." He points upward, then finishes with "And now, I send you live to de Hive and our newly elected board-certified president, Fray-mah… Toe-pazzzz Titssss!"

"Titts! Titts! Titts," citizens chant.

Fireworks and drones blanket the Union skies. An accepting populace cheer on their cybernetic and robotic Defense Club members as they peacefully march through the center of each sector in a spectacular display strength and order.

Wearing his namesake's Distinguished Service Medal with the faded red stain, Sev waits backstage with Toi, Hilga, and Ocho. He nods to trooper Kaleb Akintola—also backstage—bandaged and sitting in a *hoverchair* pushed by Berkly, Kaleb's female roomie. Smiling, Kaleb nods to Sev, who tries to psyche himself up when Toi approaches.

"You gonna be great," Toi says.

"Never like him," Sev replies.

"No. Like you," Toi counters. "Yeah?"

"Okie-dokie," Sev says with a smile.

Toi checks out Sev's DSM on his chest. "What dis?"

"Pop gave to me long ago. Sometin' to show de world what's possible," Sev answers.

Above the Hive, an enormous hologram of President Topaz Titts waves to hundreds of thousands of citizens cheering outside the Capitol Zone.

"Union strong!" Topaz shouts three times.

"Union strong!" citizens thrice reply in near unison.

Within the Great Hall, Topaz stands at the podium as he reads from his holographic teleprompter.

"Nudda day, citizens. Given all we been chroo deez past few weeks, I pinky promise to be short," Topaz replies as the crowd laughs. "I too was a child of Man Fall. I recall when de *Last Nations* fell. I recall deez global tribes, wit' great differences, fightin' togedder—as one. Wit' all dare might, de Xenos try to destroy us. But we still here. And as long as we live...dare's hope. As we grow, dat hope grows. Den one time, dat hope becomes real. And for real, *we will take our planet back!*"

Amped crowds across the Union erupt in cheers.

"But till dat time, we must have each udder's backs. We must work for de common good. Recall, no madder who we are, no madder where we begin, we are all members of de same club. De human club. Dis is President Topaz Titts. And may we build a greater Union!"

"Union strong!" citizens reply with excitement.

Aerial drones engage in a synchronized performance. Roars of exuberance travel above and belowground, releasing hundreds of millions of pent-up emotions.

Topaz waits for the cheers to die down before continuing.

"Now before we all get fucked up on Sin liquors and Packy wines, I must present our newest, highest honor, awarded for extraordinary service to our Union. Our first winner was not just a defender of dis Union. He was a defender of humanity. Pretty please, a moment of silence for de winner of our first *Gen. Hector Elias Contreras the Fifth Award* goes to...his son, Framer General Hector Elias Contreras VI," Topaz announces to silence. "Takin' dis honor in his stead, his son, Outer Subgeneral Sev Contreras."

Sev makes his way to the podium as Topaz wipes away a few of his tears. The entire Union remains silent out of respect for a fallen hero. Sev and Topaz fist-bump each other and embrace.

"Tanks," Sev says.

Topaz notices Sev's family medal.

"Nice pin," Topaz whispers.

Topaz places Hector's Contreras Medal, emblazoned with a holographic image of Gen. Contreras's face over the new Union Republic logo, around Sev's neck then concedes the stage. Alone, Sev looks around at the enormous crowd gathered and places both hands on the podium as media drones capture his every angle. Through the bright lights, Sev seemingly catches a brief glimpse of Hector and Zerina proudly smiling at him from the crowd before vanishing.

"Another day!" Sev properly shouts.

"Nudda day," citizens reciprocate.

"Pop's stories you all know by now," Sev says. "If not...you belong in Needles."

"Needles!" citizens joyously scream.

"When I was a pup, Pop used to say, 'Doze who forget history shall recall it,'" Sev continues. "I taught it was some Old Nation bullshit. But I was wrong. We all were wrong. We not here cause of de Xenos. We here 'cause we didn't come togedder until it was too late. But yet we still here, yeah? We been given anudda chance. A chance we must use—"

Suddenly, the sunrays momentarily pierce the thick, hazy skies to the astonishment of many. A *strange electrical interference* momentarily affects every Terran and Xeno device on the planet. Once the sun retreats back behind its hazy curtain and devices return to normal, Sev continues.

"No one sees de fyoo-cha. But we can see what happens when deeds of de evil overshadow inaction from de good. Wedda above or below, inny or outy, we must stay alert. And when needed, we... must...fight," Sev says as media drones capture him *bang on the podium with both fists*. "I am Subgeneral Hector Elias Contreras VII. And to you all, I wish anudda year," he concludes with a roar.

Sev glances at the countdown clock approaching the New Year.

"Nu-dda year," citizens repeatedly chant as Sev walks off the stage waving. "Nu-dda year!"

Sev returns backstage. He first hugs and kisses Toi on the cheek. He then hugs and passionately kisses Hilga before picking up Ocho. Toi's attention turns to the countdown clock when Sev, Hilga, and Ocho absorb her into their group hug. Confetti falls while media drones capture every moment.

"Anyone else hungry?" Sev asks.

"Hec, yeah!" Ocho yells.

"Liddle smart-ass," Sev says.

"Just like his old man," Hilga replies.

"And his too, yeah?" Toi sarcastically asks.

"Yeah," Sev says and chuckles with a nod. "Yeah."

Framers Annex

One week into the new year, Sev walks through the Framers Annex when he spots the Native man wearing uncommon skins and accompanied by his tall cybernetic bodyguard sporting the wolf tattoo securing the Stormblood mausoleum a few doors down. They approach Sev on their way out.

"Subgen," Zevrin greets him with a nod. "Congrats to you. And your boy."

Sev studies the two men, including their intriguing tattoos.

"Tanks," Sev replies. "And tanks for your help up dare!"

Zevrin glances at the Contreras mausoleum.

"Small price to pay for peace," Zevrin interrupts. "Our sympathies for your father," Zevrin adds. "He was an honorable man."

"We meet before?" Sev asks.

Zevrin extends his fist. Sev fist-bumps him.

"Depends on your point of view," Zevrin cryptically answers. "Zevrin Stormblood, counsel for the chief minister of the Can-Chee Nations. This is Beta Joe Destiny, my friend...and *Ma'iingan*."

Sev studies Beta Joe's wolf tattoo.

"Sounds like badass mudderfuckah, yeah?" Sev playfully asks, extending his fist to Beta Joe. "Nudda day, sir."

Though Beta Joe continues to scan the area for potential danger, he nonchalantly fist-bumps Sev.

Briefly turning to Beta Joe, Zevrin raises an eyebrow then turns back to Sev.

"Hmmm..." Zevrin laments.

"Good sign, yeah?" Sev asks.

"For you? Very," Zevrin answers.

Sev nods toward the Stormblood mausoleum behind them.

"Your fallen…" Sev trails off.

"My father's mother. Seems the stories I've been told were true. For the most part, anyway."

"Yeah, we do love our creative licenses," Sev replies. "Stormblood? Why dat name ring bells?"

"She was among the last to serve the Old Nation," Zevrin replies. "And the first to give your father a hand after Man Fall."

Sev pauses.

"Tink she and Pop…" Sev asks.

"Now *that* would be T-M-I for me," Zevrin replies. "Apologies, but we are running late. And you have a visitor. Next time, Subgen."

Zevrin nods; Sev nods in return.

"Call me Hec. Another day, Counsel," Sev replies. "Do I call you…" Sev trials off as Zevrin and Beta Joe head for the exit. "Later?"

Sev continues to the Contreras mausoleum and finds it unlocked. He opens the door and enters to find Manny facing the holograms of Gen. Contreras, Karla, Hector, and Zerina as if he were having a real conversation with them. Zerina's the first to see Sev.

"Hi, baby," Zerina greets lovingly. "Always good to see my little boy."

"Long time no see, Mom," Sev sarcastically responds.

"Now, you're fucking with me." Zerina says.

"And you're late," Manny sarcastically adds.

Manny turns to face Sev; they hug.

"My bad. Got a liddle distracted," Sev replies. "So only a week on de job and you quit, huh?"

"Politics was never my thing," Manny replies. "Just wanted to ensure a smooth transition."

"So what now?" Sev asks.

"Who knows what the future holds?" Manny answers.

"Or de past."

"Huh?" Manny asks.

"Walk wit' me," Sev says.

Puzzled, Manny shrugs as he follows Sev two doors down.

"See dat shit de udda day?" Sev asks.

"Who didn't? Everything shut down for about ten secs," Manny answers.

"Course it happens during my epic speech!"

"Easy on the SinWater," Manny jokes.

Sev and Manny enter an unmarked mausoleum. Inside, soft lights activate. They stand in the middle of the room surrounded by construction debris.

"Sorry for de mess. Tings kinda cray-cray here. You tink a sub-gen can get tings done faster, yeah?"

"Who's here?" Manny asks.

"Family," Sev answers. "Duh."

Sev remotely activates the room.

Two holograms appear: Manny's wife, Desiree, and their toddler daughter, Pacifica.

Tears form around Manny's eyes.

"How the fuck?" Manny asks.

Sev uses his retinal display, which commands the mausoleum to project a digital image of Manny with Desiree and Pacifica."

"Pop found dis in your possessions aftah you…went undah-ground," Sev explains.

"Just before I shipped out to Pearl Harbor," Manny states.

Sev opens and reaches in one of his concealed pockets. He pulls out a tiny chip similar to the one carrying his mother's virtual essence.

"Now, you see them anytime," Sev adds.

Manny's eyes swell with tears. He then bear-hugs Sev.

"Mahal kita, Éxi," Manny says.

The two men silently embrace while the Desiree and Pacifica holograms hold hands and smile at them.

"Back to you, Unk," Sev exhales through Manny's tight embrace. "But maybe save some love for *dem* too, yeah?"

About the Author

Born and raised in Boston, Massachusetts, Ron graduated from the University of Southern California and currently works in commercial real estate while writing in Las Vegas, Nevada.

EPILOGUE: Transmissions

No Inhumane!

With Hyfor and Nooz's assistance, Ree transmits a powerful Lorian Activist Transmission, or LAT, into space where a large Lorian satellite orbiting the moon picks it up. The much-larger and more-advanced alien satellite inadvertently kidnaps part of the UST broadcast, taking it along for an intergalactic ride.

Concurrently, a powerful solar flare irritates the Earth's atmosphere, causing a momentary global disruption of all terrestrial and extraterrestrial electronic equipment.

Traveling at a speed incomprehensible to Terrans prior to man's fall, Ree's LAT uploads to the Lorian Interplanetary Broadcast (LIB) Network for her entire species to stream. Lorians who access the broadcast see the following video montage of clips from events on Earth secretly recorded by Ree and her team over the past two centuries:

Horrifying shrieks pierce the darkness. Every few seconds fuzzy images flash across the screen like an old television set searching for a stronger signal.

Symbols for:

WE PLAY

...appear as the screen flickers. Unidentified humans scream in pain and desperation. Shadowy figures tease the camera. Strange sounds are followed by weird blinking symbols on the screen.

Symbols for:

WE TREAT

...appear below a grainy montage of video clips from a series of historical global conflicts between various nations. Atrocities are followed with joyous celebrations from the human victors of these conflicts.

Symbols for:

WE KILL

…appear below hazy footage of Lorians abducting unsuspecting humans in the dead of night. It cuts to unidentified Lorians conducting gruesome medical experiments on their human captives.

Symbols for:

FOR MEAT

…appear below footage of Lorian silhouettes as they taste test living and deceased humans beside a wall with faded Japanese characters in the background. Blood splatters across the screen to the sounds of crunching bones.

Symbols for:

THAT NOISE… IT'S PAIN!

…appear below the screen as painful human squeals echo. The screen flickers, making it hard to distinguish what appears to be a warehouse full of naked, human captives.

Symbols for:

NO INHUMANE!

…appear across the screen as blurry images—which never come fully into focus—appear in the background. The images focus, revealing naked women of all variations wearing metal helmets while confined to Lorian gestation recliners. The women moan helplessly—some scream, though none put up any meaningful resistance. Lorian maintenance drones quickly remove blood from the floor while the wails of newborn humans riding on conveyor belts penetrate the soul.

A pregnant young woman cries out, "Me…lin…da! Mel…ind…a!"

In the background, a Lorian silhouette holds up a human male wearing a metallic halo attached to his head. The Lorian appears amused at the male's predicament.

As the broadcast fades to black, the Lorian symbol for *NO* vanishes while the symbols for *INHUMANE* slide to the center of the screen. After a few moments, those remaining symbols vanish as well.

On the black screen, symbols for:

ENDORSED BY THE TERRAN PROTECTION
ADVOCATES FOR SPECIES EMPATHY

...appear for a few seconds then disappear, ending the transmission.

SAD

African American NASA scientist Dr. Erik Sherman and his armed Marine escort wearing a special purple badge wait for passengers to empty one of six elevators. They enter it, and the Marine escort promptly rebuffs the few personnel attempting to board with them. Erik stares at the elevator panel that shows only the first, second, and third floors. He looks up as the front elevator door closes; the Marine escort waves a special badge over the sensor beside the panel.

To Erik's surprise, a plate below the panel of buttons extends out and slides downward, revealing an additional *thirteen underground levels*.

The guard presses the button for Level U13.

"So much for superstition," Erik sarcastically laments to a joyless audience.

From the corner of an eye, the Marine escort spies the male toddler backpack and female teen laptop case Erik carries.

Sensing eyes on him, yet still looking forward, Erik simply replies, "Long story."

"Well, my kids really enjoy your short ones, sir."

"Thanks," Erik says. "How many?"

"Two, sir. Three-year-old son and four-year-old daughter."

"Enjoy it while it lasts, soldier."

"Every breath, sir,"

Erik pulls out a business card from his shirt pocket and hands it to the Marine who tucks it away.

"Leave your contact info, their first names, and a brief message," Erik says.

"Thank you, sir," the Marine replies with a smile.

"No, thank you," Erik counters.

Suddenly, Erik hears a few unidentifiable sounds from outside the elevator, ignored by the again emotionless Marine.

"For your service," Erik deadpans.

The elevator stops at Level U13 and the doors open. Erik and his Marine escort exit the elevator and make their way down a long corridor as personnel walk around them. They walk between a series of electronically locked rooms on each side that come with a small window, an armed Marine, and a security camera. As Erik passes each pair of doors, he sees captives wearing various degrees of bandages around their heads and necks. All have dried bloodstains from wounds to the backs of their necks.

Erik follows the Marine escort to the end of the hallway where it splits in two opposite corridors. They take the right corridor and continue to the end where Marine guards post on opposite sides of a large sliding door. The Marine escort directs Erik to the sliding door's retinal scanner while a security camera peers down on them. The retinal scanner confirms both Erik's and the Marine escort's identities while the guards remain stiff and silent. The sliding door opens just enough for Erik and his Marine escort to enter before closing behind them. Erik looks around in awe.

"Holy—" Erik begins.

"Up here, Erik!" NSA Deputy Director Kyrin Talbot screams from two levels up.

Erik looks up at Kyrin, a Vietnamese woman whose gentle smile and build temporarily conceals the intelligence and ambition that now places her above him.

"Someone's been holdin' out on me!" Erik says.

Erik looks around from what appears to be ground zero of a three-level control room. Five yards in front of him on the main wall are two gigantic displays covering the entire three levels.

Momentarily distracted by the number of NSA personnel tending to various tasks and control panels, Erik turns to discover that his Marine escort has vanished.

"Play your cards right, and this can all be yours!" Kyrin says, pointing to the glass elevator.

Erik walks into a lift. The lift floor lights up as it rises two levels. As he ascends, he watches the two gigantic main displays:

The first displays a digital reenactment of a solar flare disruption that has apparently—and negatively—impacted the entire planet in some way.

The second tracks the current trajectory of NASA's New Horizons Probe, floating out into the stellar abyss many light-years away.

The lift doors open. Erik turns to see Kyrin waiting for him.

"Figured you'd dig the scenic route," Kyrin says.

"Figured right," Erik replies. "Always good to see you, Kye."

"Mostly good to see you, Erik," Kyrin replies. "For a minute there I thought we were all toast."

"Ten seconds to be precise," Erik says. "Some scary shit, huh?"

"All scary shit to be precise."

After a moment of uncomfortable silence, Erik follows Kyrin to her office, which overlooks the entire control room.

"*So?*" Erik asks.

"Have a seat. Chillax," Kyrin says. "Love the accessories, by the way."

"Long story."

"There's always one with you," Kyrin replies. "Sorry for the travel accommodations. You know how it is."

Erik throws his stuff on the couch and sits down beside it. Kyrin walks over to the bar. She opens the fridge and pulls out a small bottle of water.

"For all I know I've been flying and driving in circles," Erik replies.

"Definitely not in Austin anymore," Kyrin says. "But the food here is excellent—as are the drinks!"

"Count on you to wrap silver lining on a box packed with shit," Erik replies.

Kyrin hands him the water bottle.

"First things first," Kyrin begins.

Erik opens the water bottle, takes a few sips, then smacks his parched lips. Kyrin retrieves a book and pen from her desk. She hands them both to Erik; he looks up with a smile.

"I thought children's books weren't your thing," Erik says as he inscribes an inside cover page.

"Let's just say the last few weeks forced me to be a bit more... open-minded," Kyrin replies.

Kyrin walks over to her desk console and presses a button; doors and windows close, blinds shut, and the lights dim slightly.

"Armageddons have a habit of doing that, I guess," Erik deadpans.

To Erik's right, a large display screen drops from the ceiling and displays an old black-and-white video of a historical space-rocket launch.

"Explorer One. Our first response to the Sputniks," Kyrin replies.

"You remember we met at Caltech, right?"

Kyrin walks back over to Erik.

"Don't make me slap you," Kyrin snaps. "So you do recall the JPL analyst who went missing after—"

"Spence Fitzgerald," Erik interrupts. "Claimed aliens were trying to communicate with us. And whose urban legend partly inspired—"

Erik holds up the book *Little Marco's Space Adventures* by E. D. Sherman

"Thanks," Kyrin says. "Ollie's been bugging me."

Kyrin grabs the book and pen and carries them back to her desk and places the autographed book inside a drawer.

"This ought to be good," Erik deadpans.

The digital display switches to a profile of NASA Dr. Spencer Fitzgerald.

Erik takes another sip of water.

"What would you say if I had in my possession a highly classified audio recording of NASA's oldest urban legend discussing a faint signal embedded in Explorer One's logs and recorded just before a radiation surge temporarily disrupted its communication link to

Houston?" Kyrin asks. "A radiation surge caused by an unusually strong solar flare back in 1958."

Erik takes a third sip of water.

"As Dad would say to Mom, drop it like it's hot," Erik answers.

The digital display switches to Explorer One's trajectory through space.

"Unfortunately, you don't have the clearance—yet. But I can tell you, it appears the signal that Explorer One intercepted shares a similar pattern to the one discovered within the light pulse that New Horizons picked up during the solar flare nightmare the entire planet witnessed eight weeks ago."

Erik drinks the remaining water and places the empty bottle on the table.

"You think it's a message," Erik deduces.

Kyrin nods.

"And I also believe Prof. Urban Legend here may have unwittingly discovered the key," Kyrin says. "Which is why I convinced the Veep to let you spearhead our newly created Special Access Division."

"Thanks, but I'm happy where I'm at," Erik replies. "For real."

"Your team. Your budget," Kyrin responds.

Erik grabs the empty water bottle and holds it out to Kyrin, gently shaking it.

"Come to think of it, I have been a little depressed lately," Erik deadpans. "Perhaps something a little stronger?"

Smiling, Kyrin snatches the empty bottle and heads for the bar. She tosses the bottle into her mini recycler next to it and grabs two cold glasses and some ice from her mini fridge. She places them on the bar and fills them with dark rum. Kyrin delivers one to Erik.

"Where were we?" Kyrin asks.

"Therapy session," Erik replies.

They toast glasses and sip. Erik sits while Kyrin heads back to the console.

The digital display switches back to the New Horizons' current trajectory.

"As you know, we determined that the unidentified light pulse the New Horizons intercepted must've originated hundreds—if not thousands—of light-years away," Kyrin says.

"But every attempt to locate a point of origin lead nowhere," Erik replies.

"Not quite," Kyrin says. "And we have 'Lil Marco to thank."

Kyrin finishes her drink. Erik chuckles then wets his beak with liquor, pretending to ignore Kyrin return to the bottle of dark rum for a refill. She then walks back toward Erik with the rum bottle in hand.

"And how the fuck does a children's space adventure I wrote eleven years ago as a birthday present factor into this equation?"

"Not *how?*" Kyrin answers. "*When?*"

Kyrin tries to top off Erik's glass, but he rebuffs her. She recaps the bottle and places it on the table.

"You want NASA to prep a teenaged astronaut?" Erik sarcastically asks.

Kyrin rolls her eyes.

"Wormholes allow Marco to travel between solar systems instantaneously," Kyrin says. "Keepin' Li'l Marco well…little. Right?"

"Not exactly rocket science, but go on," Erik replies.

"What if you flipped the distance and time variables?" Kyrin asks.

"Then I'd probably still be a science professor hypothesizing in my basement," Erik scoffs. "Because Li'l Marco would be long dead before he even—"

Erik's eyes widen.

"Got anywhere?" Kyrin sarcastically finishes. "Wheels now turnin', wiseass?"

The digital display switches to a real-time feed of the Earth's solar system where a blinking red dot shows the unknown light pulse's calculated point of origin, an area of empty space within Earth's project orbit over time.

"Your point of origin?" Erik rhetorically asks.

"As you can see, there's nothing there but space," Kyrin replies.

Erik studies the display. His jaw drops while Kyrin refills his glass.

"Nothing there...*yet*," Erik responds. "You're not tellin' me the signal came from Earth. You're tellin' me it...*will come?*"

"Based on our recalculations, we've narrowed the pool to somewhere in the Southwestern United States, approximately one hundred years from now. Give or take," Kyrin answers. "Cray-cray, huh?"

Eyes glued to the display, Erik sighs as he grabs his glass and gently raises it.

"Asante," Erik thanks her in Swahili.

Eyes still glued to the digital display, Erik chugs his entire drink, puts down the empty glass, and then slumps back with his hands rubbing his head. He takes a deep breath while Kyrin chugs her drink, grabs the bottle of rum, and raises and gently shakes it.

"So are we depressed? Or are we *sad?*" Kyrin asks.

Erik lowers his head. He grabs and raises his empty glass for another pour; Kyrin obliges.

10.28.2084

Seven months later, major renovations take place around the secret underground military facility where Erik met Kyrin over bottled water and dark rum. Surrounded by Halloween decor, Erik and Kyrin stare intensely at the two gigantic digital displays. Kyrin looks around and hisses at the mesmerized NSA and NASA personnel to get them back to work.

"Mr. Vice President's on the line, ma'am," a female NSA specialist confirms.

"On two," Kyrin orders.

The NSA specialist complies.

"My bad, Kye. Pretty crazy around here," Veep responds via transmission. "Take it things aren't much better down there?"

"Actually, there's been a very interesting…development."

"Really?" Veep asks. "What does it say?"

"Unfortunately, audio only picks up what's best described as… grunting."

"Okay. So you called me here for…*grunting?*"

Kyrin turns to Erik, who slides closer to Kyrin to ensure the Veep can see him.

"No, sir. Actually, we discovered that the light pulse contains a second independent signal apparently sharing the same frequency."

"Second?" Veep asks. "Two messages?"

"It would seem so. And although the primary signal's origin still remains unknown, this one appears to be human, sir."

"Go on," Veep responds.

Erik turns to Kyrin.

"This is where things get a little more…interesting," Erik says.

"Doc, do I look like a man who's got all the time in the world to dick around?" Veep asks.

"What he means is that we need you to be the judge," Kyrin interjects.

Kyrin nods to the NSA specialist who switches one of the main displays as everyone in the room again stops what they're doing to look up at the display.

"This your idea of a Halloween prank?" Veep asks.

"Hec, on my mother's spirit, this ain't no prank!" Kyrin replies.

"Sir, as…unbelievable as this looks, we can tell you with 100 percent certainty that what you're seeing…is totally real," Erik says.

Kyrin and Erik stare up at the main displays where the left display shows Vice President Hector Elias Contreras III, *the spitting image of his great-great-grandson Sev.* The right display features a black-and-white frozen frame of Sev wearing his grandfather's namesake medal around his neck. Sev's arms are frozen at the moment he bangs the podium with both fists during his speech.

Veep squints at the Distinguished Service Medal on his doppelganger's chest and orders, "Zoom in on his chest—that pin!"

To his surprise, Veep's able to make out the tiny, faded dark stain on Sev's DSM.

"Hec?" Kyrin asks.

"A little rough around the edges but not a bad-lookin' dude," Veep sarcastically answers. "But if that's real, I'd like to know how the fuck do they know about my grandfather's medal when it's been sitting in my son's safe-deposit box for the past eight years?"

Erik and Kyrin turn to each other then back to Veep; they both shrug.

CPSIA information can be obtained
at www.ICGtesting.com
Printed in the USA
LVHW032208221221
706957LV00002B/196